About the Author

I am Paul Tuley. Having done nine years in the army, I have travelled and enjoyed it immensely.

I have been a security officer on the Thames Flood Barrier. Followed by about thirty years in warehousing.

I enjoy the written word as well as the spoken word. I am now retired, living in north-west Kent.

I do have a story or two to tell, if anyone has the time to read me.

Awon Iya Orisha

Paul Tuley

Awon Iya Orisha

Olympia Publishers

London

www.olympiapublishers.com
OLYMPIA PAPERBACK EDITION

A CIP catalogue record for this title is
available from the British Library.

ISBN: 978-1-78830-134-3

This is a work of fiction.
Names, characters, places and incidents originate from the writer 's
imagination. Any resemblance to actual persons, living or dead, is purely
coincidental.

First Published in 2019

Olympia Publishers
60 Cannon Street
London
EC4N 6NP

Printed in Great Britain

Dedication

Victoria Daniel Ngozi, the Igbo firstborn of the Awon Iya Orisha.

The unique Faridah Ado, who takes her sisters and leads them into the light.

INTRODUCTION

O Na-Eto (IGBO)
Ndi di nro na-adoro mmasi
okpueze ogwu
mubara,
Nye ndi maara ihe
o na-eto.
Okoko osisi ahu lere ya anya
na-enweghi obi uto iju iju ajuju-
"M ga-enwe nchebe mgbe m no
na oge ntoju?"
Onye ahu bu osisi nke ndu,
o hulatara jide ya nwayo,
chere ru oge.
Wee gwa ya n 'olu.
"Chekwaa okooko osisi gi rue mgbe
na-eto eto karia.
Too ogwu gi
ike siri ike-
n 'ebe ahu maka nchekwa gi.
Mgbe ogwu ahu no

ha kacha ike,
mgbe ahu okooko!
Na-eche nnwere onwe ahu,
nnwere onwe gi bu nke gi
nweta ya toro nime ya.
Mgbe ahu o buru na onye nwere mmasi choro
iji mee ka I daa juu-
m ga-agwa ya,
o bu m nwe okooko a.
M ga-ekpebi ihe m ga-enye
mma ifuru m.
Biko hapu m."

SHE TREE
The soft tender bejewelled
Crown of Thorns
grew close,
to the wise wizened
She Tree.
The sprig looked up to her
unashamed, unabashed asking-
"Will I be safe once I am
in full bloom?"
She who was the tree of life,
bent down held her gently,
thought for a while.
The told her in a whisper.
"Save your blossom until
you are older wiser stronger.

Grow your thorns
hard strong vicious-
there for your own protection.
When those thorns are at
their most aggressive,
then blossom!
Feel the freedom,
your liberty is then your own
acquire it grown into it.
Then if an admirer wants
to deflower you-
my precious you will tell him,
this blossom is mine.
I will decide who I give
my flower to.
Now begone from me."

CHAPTER ONE

First there was nothing. Then one almighty bang! The fabric of everything, split wide open. The fibres ripped from its very heart. The tectonic plates sliding for a moment; Helios was shining so hot, as the fibrous, interwoven network of the universe, stretched for an eternity. The blinding light, the enormous flash, distorted the fusion, the connectivity of the complete galaxy; knocking it sideways. The enormous rocks, metals, gasses and other diverse material, flung far out into the dark abyss of known existence. Helios dulled a while, but soon regained his brilliance. We his bright, scalding tongues, flashed even more brilliantly; after the solar explosion. Not far from us, was a small planet, reeling from this major disturbance. All molten, savage, spitting fire, along with big licks of lava in every direction. I was that imminent starburst. I was that violent, beautiful impacting supernova! I was the imploding sun, emitting the rays of ultraviolet light. The unassailable course of violent energy from a far-off galaxy, milky way.

I stood all that distance away, watching it dissipate, cool, slowly turn from black, humid intensity, to a calm, green planet, even with all that turmoil, the heat generated, two thirds of its 'surface', still covered in seas and oceans. The solar flares dancing around Helios, not wandering too far from our father. But curiosity got the better of me. I broke away, ventured too close. Finding I could not return to the great Helios. I was on my own, venturing closer and closer, to this forbidden planet. As I coasted between the debris of the aftermath of this interplanetary disturbance, I could feel myself change. My abilities had grown.

I noticed I had the ability to shape-shift as well as being a changeling. I cruised the outer limits of the endless pit of space, as a rock, a beam of light, a cloud of finite dust. I was part of two starbursts, I was intermingled within a cloud of poisonous, toxic radioactive rain. Revelling as the tail end of a comet. I felt the exhilaration, the energy, the inexhaustibility of perpetual motion, as I played for a while as a shooting star.

I was an asteroid, careering all over the inexhaustible expanse. In complete control of myself. Enjoying my limitless energy. High octane action, with no one to tell me to what to do. Destruction prevalent, at no extra cost. Not a sound to be heard, in this dim lit world, time is of no consequence, it is my friend and will always be. On my arrival here, I had to learn to be calmer; with more self-restraint. Act with more composure, to share my resources. To revitalise myself, when and whenever I had the chance, with whatever was left of the old existence. Then to cherish the new, as a means of a different order. A fresh beginning!

***

Trying to control myself, to muster my thoughts; to express myself as who or what I want to be, during all this flux, upheaval, within the cosmos. I journeyed to a dark, distant corner, away from all the panic destruction. There I hid for a time, developing my powers, my seemingly inexhaustible energy, the power to dim myself, change myself at a whim; change my shape right before my eyes. So as far as I could see, there was no rush to do anything. My time was limitless, to hide; to reveal was all at my pleasure, my discretion. So, within me, was the power to do almost anything, with just a thought, a wave of my hand. It was this that needed my attention, so that my anger did not upset, disrupt or destroy anything, other than that within my focus.

I feel the need to be recognized, so I must assume an identity at some point in my existence. My name will be, I will be remembered as "A AHON INA".

Some will think a strange name, but it links me to my past; to my time with Helios. Before I was alone, drifting, surviving. Now I am finding my way, controlling my thoughts, remembering my experiences. I feel as though I am the only creature out here with a mind to think, to be able to gather my thoughts in some semblance of order.

I attach myself to the back end of a comet, in amongst the heat, sparks and dust of the tail. I enjoy the free ride, the joy of existing as part of something, instead of just a lone entity. A mass of black ensues as we travel in amongst the debris, fallout and unsettled planetoids in our path.

A small object attracts my attention. Oval shaped, as we get closer, I see it is far larger than I first thought. I detach myself from the flaying comet. Ponder for a moment, inhaling, smelling nothing that I had not already come across, during my lengthy excursion across the vast void.

Darting down through the exosphere, the thermosphere, hardly stopping for breath, I challenge myself to fight through the mesosphere, stratosphere. Then finally the troposphere. Then, there I am, sat on top of a high, robust volcano. Alive, kicking out the lava, ash and magma. Here I felt at home, embracing the fire, bonding with a subject that distributes its own heat source.

I slid down the side of the volcano, the harsh thermal conditions not affecting me in the slightest. It was a joy to play, without a worry in the world. To feel not overwhelmed by anything, just the happiness of not being a part of Helios any longer. All that is long forgotten, all I can do now is move forward. Make a plan for my new life, here on this planet, in this environment. It will be lonely, desolate for a while! Perhaps it is within me to change this world, in the same way I am able to change myself. Perhaps other life would have a chance, if it was a little cooler, if there was forestation, a coolant of some sort.

I think.

I wait.

Then I calm myself, transfix my eyes inwardly. Taking deep breaths, I regulating my being. Slowly, I absorb the heat from the planet's surface. I feel like a furnace, but nothing overpowers me. I take the strain as I slowly push some of the fires deep below the surface, out of harm's way. Granted the fibre and body of this place looks a little alien, but then so does everywhere else at this moment in time. Now the surface is hardened. It no longer looks like a molten lake, carrying everything off in its path. Stationary is good. I can hear the land masses settle, fight for space. As it does, I slowly revert to my old self, a life form feeling his way into a brand new world, existence; but uncertain of where it is going to take me!

CHAPTER TWO

I am sitting alone, a little solitude, still in silence desolate as I look out across the landscape, it is barren, perhaps a little foreboding. I see, feel underfoot, as much as I can feel beneath my feet. That the land is scorched, parched, a mixture of rock lifeless dirt, nothing with any form, or sign of life whatsoever. Shingle, gravel and inert atoms, ions, fumes, nauseous gases, quagmires, surround everything. If anything was alive, it would be dead now.

Anything I can see that is ineffectual, that will not destroy, or interfere, with other sentient beings, or life forms, will be left here. But anything else, whether it be gas, solid, whatever stage it is at, in its development will have to be dispatched one way or another. With a lightness of touch, I dispel the fumes, all the rogue charged particles, as well as the ceaseless obnoxious gases. They are consumed by my rage and infernal heat, slowly removing the haze, fog, mist, from the very air, it has infiltrated for such a long time now. Even if I do say so myself, it feels a little cooler, the atmosphere is not so repressive. No inhaling of so many toxic fumes, or gases. Back at my retreat, still alone, not repressed, but wishing I could work faster, to mould this place, into a sanctuary, for myself. But still the plates of the planet are unsettled, still moving around and causing disturbances.

After what seems an eternity the internal unrest finally begins to settle. The planet at last, resolves all its subtle movements. I render myself into the shape of a spiral—white hot. Penetrating the robust organic material on the surface. Piloting myself towards the centre of the earth, the material gets more compact. I have to make myself more defined, slender, harder to penetrate all the stone, magma and residual cosmic rock deep in the bowels. But after all my determination, I make it to the core. I stand off, expand, making myself hot, extremely. I self-combust, confining myself as a small ball at first. Then expanding out slowly, waiting for the temperature, to catch up with me. I reach the glorious temperature of 12000 degrees Kelvin. I wrap myself around the core, absorbing the heat, cooling it down. So I can feel, hear, everything around me, cool too. Having neutralized some of the heat, I return to the surface, the same way I arrived.

The undercurrent of unrest seems to have subsided. No more strange noises, I stand and listen around me! For the first time, complete silence. Total rest, the final submission, as even the volcanoes are silent, the echoes from the rift valleys are quelled, finally peace. To be enjoyed; satisfaction at a job well done. But still it looks dark, foreboding. Nothing moves, because there is nothing here to move.

I actually feel quite secluded. So I feel it is time to amuse myself. I turn myself into a fireball, smacking myself as hard as I can against, the nearest upheaved mountain. I split myself in half, turning myself into a pair of creatures, fighting each other. But after a while that gets monotonous. I cojoin once again, pondering the future, what it might mean, if I am to be alone; for the rest of this existence. Once again, I become a hermit, hidden away deep in the black hard soil of this place. I notice something quite magical, especially amongst the hardened magma, and loose gritty soil.

Green shoots, so miniscule, they could get damaged, destroyed, killed, with the slightest movement. But with the tenderest of care and attention they may well survive. Likened to moss, lichen and the fleetest of growth and life expectancy, they will eventually, no doubt, stretch into the farthest reaches of this subtropical stench of a place. I flit unobtrusively around all the surrounding area. I find other growths so delicate, so fine that it will take an iron will to spread the seeds of determination, and a will to live, like nothing I have ever seen before. But if I am able, I will tend to my plant life, ensuring their survival, as well as the spread, of their like as far as I possibly can take them. They bring the only colour to a desperate, dark relief; which seems to be maintaining its power and drudgery, over everything I can sense.

As my search encompasses vast swathes of this scorched land, I come across other forms of life. Microcosmic stems, green shoots, fungi, all entrenched along the forest floor, with no desire to move. All finding rather remote, sheltered spots to do their growing, alone, unhindered, in the unspoilt wild terrain, which covers just about everywhere, at this moment in time. As I pass, I see them bask in my warmth. So if they feel they need my attention, then I will parade along all the lines of greenness, sending out my heat, radiation, to supplement their survival and long-term lifespan. Now I feel as though I have some purpose here after all. Not just an endless pursuit of wasting endless time. A thought, memory, the formation of an idea, ensues my small ability to reason! Amongst all this parched wasteland, there seems nothing that is in a liquid form. We had, still have some gases, we have solids in the form of rocks, stone, gravel, sand and such fine particles, you would never see, no matter how hard you tried. But something to stop the torment, of the arid land, dryness, the scope of movement, aiding abetting life, growth; combating the durability of everything around us. So, making myself lighter, transforming into a light fluffy ball, inhaling these strange molecules, hydrogen along with oxygen. Getting them to mix, adhere to each other. Then releasing them, entwined, formed into a new identity. Watching it fall to the ground, around, across, over my little green friends. It was a joy to see the dampness seep into the ground. Also, I noticed it cooled the surrounding air a notch. So this was the magic ingredient, that was required to instil sustainability into this zone. To make it a paradise of some sort.

Having said that, I do not know what makes a paradise, or even what a paradise is. Then if I say nothing, then the thread of the story is lost, I realize I am just the remnants of a solar flare, a tongue of Helios. In truth I am telling you the story, in retrospect, as best as I can remember. So please forgive me, if the story seems long. As I am an old forgotten remnant of somebody's memory, faded with age and very little remorse, but the adventure needs to be told, to be added to the myth, legends and fables of Nigeria and its many and varied peoples.

As time passed various grasses, ferns and wild creeping ivy took over the forest floor. Sharing spaces with the over-wild lichen, mosses and various fungi. All sharing the space equably. There was so much space to be had; there was giant calliergon, split leaf, star moss, faring well. Alongside was fruticose, crustose lichens, spreading over the dormant rocks. The grasses billowed with pearl millet, Bermuda grass, weeping cover grass giving a fine covering where ever it spread. The aquatic ferns, spreading their colour and vibrancy too, Sessile joyweed, African mosquito fern, water primrose and lady's thumb, add some gentle features to the once barren landscape. I was enjoying the show, just sitting back and watching, learning and absorbing all that I could see.

I also noticed the small pools of water: where there was no movement, they had been encroached upon by other life forms. Stagnating, allowing something known as algae to sully the clear, bright water. All forms alighted upon the surface. Black brush, phacus, zygena. Just their spores emanating from the surrounding air, as if at will. Then knowing exactly where to land. How to be a spoiler, at the first possible chance.

Time seems to be erased, because it passes so quickly. Other growths take root. From where they have come, I have no idea! They grow tightly grouped, tall, awe-inspiring, trying to block out the sun. Capture all his energy for themselves. These large upwardly mobile enchanters are known as trees. Impressive, bewildering, overpowering. So many, in such a short space of time. All with such enchanting names such as kwakwar, alawefow, oha ojii, mangoro, ahun, ayan, akoko, uturu, ukutu, with so many more filling the landscape with such beauty and awe. They amaze me, because of their growth; they seem to add so much to the barren, desolate landscape before me. Stillness, the solitude, quiet, just makes everything else seem so small.

From the small pools of water, it would seem life was just taking hold. I notice small eggs, lingering actually in the water and at the side. So a cycle would seem to be taking place, without my knowledge, without my intervention. Time is my friend as I take to the heavens, admiring the essence, the perfection of all that surrounds me.

I fling myself through the various layers of this world, wanting to see if anything has changed since I left. It seems such a short time ago. But I have no way of knowing, if it has been a short period of absence, a long one, a lifetime. As I have no way of measuring or calculating, the period that has passed. But I see already flying life forms, so small, beautifully coloured, the flash of metallic blue, deep reds, purples and yellows. Could they be mayflies, or perhaps dragonflies? I cloak myself within the confines of a small body. I feel the wind pushing, pulling my fragile body as I fly from one end of the rock pool to the other. A timely existence! With no thought, just the need to survive. Small ugly-looking things, slowly roam the undergrowth. Some new plant life. Fungi! Honey fungus, amethyst deceiver, along with angels bonnet. They do look very appetising, but beware, not everything is as it seems. Cockroaches, encapsulated within their hard black body, slowly moving across the carpeted floor. Oblivious to everything else, except just my own world, how to live my full cycle, without ending it too soon! Cockroaches, cumbersome, hard, resilient, so senseless to everything. I hear a multitude of sound coming from just about everywhere. I venture out onto the plains, there I see them. Large, slow and cumbersome.

CHAPTER THREE

Prehistoric, primeval, so many smothering the grasslands and plains, here before me. The savannas ring with their growls, snarls and unending scraps. I sense violence, fear, animosity. Large beasts are unsettling each other. Afrovenator, the African hunter. Astrodon, the star tooth. Jobaria, Nigerosaurus, the Niger Lizard. Ouranosaurus, the brave monitor lizard. Rebbachisaurus, rebback lizard. Lurdusaurus, the heavy lizard. Rugops, wrinkle face. Valdosaurus, the weald lizard. Suchomimus, crocodile mimic. This at last brings life to these deserted scopes of infinity. As a shape-shifter, I extend myself. Imitating the Suchomimus waiting in the undergrowth. Quietly, hardly daring to breathe. Then a Valdosaurus crosses my path, unsuspecting as I lunge out, taking his leg from beneath him. I clamp my snout over his throat. The thrill of a kill, the warm blood running across my face as his life force slowly leaves him. I eat the raw heavy flesh, feeling it fill me energize me. But with the smell of death comes other inquisitive beasts. So I change back to myself, vacating the scene for the incoming interlopers. The trees have changed, having grown into vast stretches of jungle. The undergrowth is strewn with mosses, lichen and bushes.

I feel the land is too dry, not accommodating all the needs of the various life forms. So with a strike of my solar wing, I force my searing heat between the rocks. Feeling for the cool liquid that everything desires. A spout of water—my first spring perhaps?— slowly dribbles to the surface. The source of a river, perhaps? The rivulets run away from the source. I will leave them to their own devices, where they will lead I do not know. They will form brooks, streams and rivers, in some future age no doubt!

Now is the time to converse with the trees. To train them, fill them with goodness. To enhance their power, geometry. To bind this land together, as a cover to protect all that dwells here. I change into the Sapo, feeling the warmth, strength, the connectivity with the earth. As I start to grow, filling myself with carbon dioxide, my growth genes do not feel inhibited. My roots stretch long and deep into the chasms of this land. I cast myself deep within the wood, aligning myself with the rings of the tree. Feeling every inch of me being taken over by the spirit of the tree. I feel its love, compassion, its need to fulfil a purpose. I transfer my energy to the roots, causing a slight change in the tree. Here it will help in the future, as a painkiller, assists with childbirth, antidotes for venomous stings and bites. Also, the root along with the bark will aid with rashes, eczema and diabetes, as well as abdominal pains. Be a laxative, preventing fevers.

While I am here, I traverse beneath the ground; via the roots of the many trees. I casting my sensitive touch to the many and varied forms of fungus. Making some edible, I destroying the toxins within. Harbouring them with a pleasant aroma, with such delicate colouring. I slip and slide along the long tangled roots of the Alawefon; encapsulating the minute molecules. Redesigning the elements, so that this tree is enhanced, should it ever need to be used. The bark can be used for the sufferers of dropsy, gout and swellings of the limbs. The leaf, if made into a balm or salve, can help relieve paralysis, epilepsy and convulsions.

The life forms it seems change so quickly. The big old lizards still fight, tormenting each other. Now a new beast has appeared on two legs, crouched—a toolmaker. Covered in thick matted hair, grunting and sits idly looking. Trying to contemplate, his being here, what it means. Then most importantly, how she is to survive, she being so small in this still barren wilderness. She is Neanderthal woman!

CHAPTER FOUR

Now that the animal known as Homo sapien has entered the conundrum of this small blue planet, the creator comes down to equip her with survival tactics. Not wanting woman to elude, give up or just fade and die. A Ahon Ina relishes the thought of helping in the advancement, of this kind of thought-provoking animal. He comes down in the form of Homo erectus, just a little more advanced than the species he hopes to help, with all his prior knowledge. He plans to assist him in looking after himself. Using all the flora and fauna, the diversity of the trees. Showing her what she can eat. How to prepare it. What can be eaten raw, which is most of his food as he has not been introduced to the spark, flame or fire yet. How to extol the benefits, by removing the toxins. What can be used for medicinal purposes. How the remedy is concocted, which part of the tree or plant to use. Where to apply it, how to apply it. How to hunt, lay the trap, kinds of traps. Weapons to be made, constructed from the most basic of materials. Then having made the kill, how to prepare the meat, use the skin to clothe herself. Protect herself from the elements. How to eat the meat, the fish, berries, either alone or as a mix, to enhance the flavour of each item when served together.

Then the process of making a spark, converting that to fire. Catching the open spark on a delicate tinder. Thus, creating fire. Heat, protection to ward off other animals, predators. A means of seeing in the gloom of the night. Then as the world, or at least this part of the planet populates, how to communicate with each other? With grunts, gesticulations, cave drawings, use of the hands, fingers. The use of the larynx, to give them speech. How happy they were, talking to one another.

Then having felt he could give no more, she gave them the freedom of expression, thought, voice, ideas, the translation of all this into their own medium of thought and forward thinking. It was up to the male and female of the species to interpret all the information, for their own good and advancement.

Then having felt he could give them no more, that their fate was now within their own destiny, their own fortitude. It was up to man and his mate, woman to expand their combined knowledge. To learn from what he had spent time teaching them. He eventually shape-shifted back to being the creator, teacher that he had become. So he could watch their advancement, guide them, if they needed it. Or just leave them to their own ends, to see what they would make of it all. Either be part of it, take it forward, or seize with power, overwhelm it, all the beauty, the life held within, then eventually destroy it, with his own greed. Then to add insult to injury, claim someone else is responsible for the destruction. When in fact it is man himself who will eventually destroy the earth, with all his preconceived ideas of wealth, fame, infamy, greed and dictatorship keeping the poverty stricken down at heel, giving them nothing. But leading the world by extortion, lies, his own self-importance, the sanctity of being in a safe place until it finally falls apart at his own undoing.

Perhaps they would need his gentle touch once again, but he would decide if he would help, or just let them go under, after the mistreatment of his blithesome, colourful blue planet. It might some require harsh abstersion, and the will to start again.

But for the time being they had formed into their own individual communities, tribes peoples. They managed the art of speech, talking to one another. Communicating by shouting, making the art of signs understood. Each forming their own dialect, or completely different language. So that they were able qualified to communicate very freely, unless they were confronted with someone from a different tribe or area, where the speech was different. But in turn, they taught their offspring how to chat, just like their other cherished experiences; cooking, foraging, hunting, medicine, tracking and trapping. All passed down from mother to daughter, father to son. Through all this beliefs were sewn into their societies. This turned into religions, of all sorts of varieties. Having their own juju, spiritual leader or shaman, this led to their own customs then to gods. Some believed, some did not, some wanted to, but could not understand the need. For some, their faith just not strong enough.

He alone on the Mambilla Plateau felt a touch of remorse as he thought about companionship for himself, if he really needed it! He was a little wistful, longing for someone or something to share his time with. He toyed with the idea of creating his own goddess whose charms would be irresistible, especially to him. So he sat pondering on what would attract him in another being. What would besot him, arouse him, amuse him, converse with him? Yet also communicate her motherly intentions, to the race below.

The race of bipods with their air of sense and sensibility, would in one way or another always need guidance, spiritual leading and healing. Therefore the goddess would in the fullness of time, be for mankind, not for him. He would need to construct something so overwhelming, that the mortals below would believe in her magic, mystique and eternal enchantment. Or they would end up self-destructing, not only themselves but every other living thing on this tiny, little island planet, in the middle of this vast solar system, whether they realised it or not. He spent time beyond eons, beyond the physical imagination. Resolute that a single goddess would not fulfil his need, or that of his people below. To start it all off he sculpted, from the cool waters of the river, Oba, a river goddess, a deity. Along with Amirini, who he directed towards the Yoruba. To see how they would take to having their own goddess who would be there for them. All went well. But then some of the other tribes tried to steal them for their own. So in finality, A Ahon Ina, saw the need for all his goddess to be friendly towards all the tribes, not to pick and choose. To be there for one and all, not discriminating but to hold all life precious, regardless of the tribe, the language or the culture.

CHAPTER FIVE

He would need four, or perhaps five goddesses to cover everything. The mortals below the heights of Mambilla Plateau would seek their advice, perhaps pay homage to one or all of the deities. Once they started this deliberation and finding that the goddesses were willing to spend time with them, equip them with new ideas. In return the tribal elders paid reverence by having special feasts for one or all of the deities they held in high regard. That in return, the goddesses would bestow their love upon each and every one. Their beliefs, fantasies extending beyond all hope, expectation and wildest dreams. Now the creator not at his merest whim, but with all his experience within him, he investigates, smiles, contemplates the outcome. When he chooses what to make his feminine deities from, he has all the items right at his very feet that he plans to use for the formation of these glorious, grandiose, illustrious goddesses. Also the form, guise, substance, knowledge and particular speciality, art or craft, they will all indulge in.

Absorbed in his creativity and his abiogenesis[1], he is drawn to featuring a collection of deities that form a circle of sisterhood. Each having their own abilities, but who are so much stronger when they are unified as a single element. Collectively they will be known as Awon Iya Orisha. Then he thinks out loud to himself.

"First, I will have a great Goddess, the first vibrant, female orisha. A preceptress, resplendent figure of power, greatness in this part of the wilderness. The orisha of the ocean and motherhood. The mother of the waters. A Ahon Ina took a handful of the purest waters from the ocean, thus mixing it with the flow of the Niger. Softly creating the subtle curves, childbearing hips of a wonderous mother. He then cast her down, upon the earth. As she walked, the earth parted whereupon fountains, springs came forth. The goddess of fishes, her own insignia is of alternating blue and white beads. She is the great witch, the ultimate manifestation of female power. Long may she look over and protect us, Yemayah."

A Ahon Ina in his continuing wisdom once again dipped both of his hands into the fast-flowing waters of the mighty Oshun River. There he found the beauty of the blue lyretail, very much to his liking. With just as much care and gentle application, he turned the smooth, lined adorable fish, into a soft, feminine, attentive woman, worthy of adulation. Her name was Oshun. The orisa of love along with sensuality, a tall beloved woman, patroness of the rivers and the bloodstream. Wearing seven brass bracelets and a mirror at her belt, to admire herself. Always companioned with a peacock,

---

[1] Production of life from inert matter.

as well as a cricket. The goddess of all the arts, especially dance. Beauty belongs to Oshun, she herself is the eternal beauty. The sunset, the smile, the eyes of a woman.

Ochumare came to me, the idea that physically she would be part of me. Made not only by the creator, but from the creator as well. He stands before Yemayah and Oshun, reaches high up to the moisture-laden clouds, gently folding one into his hand. Squeezing the water into his molten palm as the sunlight given off by A Ahon Ina combines with rainwater, he waits. Then slowly as if by magic, the colours of the sun separate as they enter the myriad of raindrops. There before them a rainbow, but more importantly Ochumare! A sensational orisha, sensitive, she opens her arms, kisses he who is now part of her, she acknowledging she is now part of him.

She links all the other orishas to the earth. She is nude, unashamedly so. Elysian, quixotic, enamoured, redolent and sonorous. Wearing a winged mask in the colours of her rainbow; red, orange, yellow, green, blue, indigo and violet. Her mask is a sign of strength, compatibility and power within her mystery. She sits in the lotus position, the ever-present rainbow, balances between her two outstretched arms. She resides in the beauty of self-awareness, bliss and serenity. Her nudity symbolises her purity and pride of self.

Then to the forest, the glades hiding all its natural beauty, magnificence. But A Ahon Ina using his delicate vision, finds the most wonderful flower, "the Bird of Paradise". When it is in full bloom to bears a striking resemblance to the most exotic bird itself. He removes the soft, gentle blooms and the erotic leaves one by one. There underneath all the foliage, in her naked form, the most resilient, stunning properties of a young woman. Here he happily introduces Aja. Young, nimble, gracious. The forest orisha, who instructs her followers in the use of medicinal herbs and flowers. The world is, will be a better place, now Aja has arrived.

The creator casts his hands deep into the bowels of the earth. Seeking treasures he has hidden away for so long. They sparkle, glint, glisten in the sun as they sit in his open hand. There sits manganese, fine topaz, rubies and emeralds. Closing his hands, he squeezes all the coarseness until it disappears. Then with a touch of abiogenesis, as only a creator can, without dropping or spilling any part of the component pieces of this delicate operation. With his warm breath he blew into his cupped hands. Then as he parted his hands she stepped from his right palm, growing all the while into the most resplendent, charming orisha, Aje, the deity of wealth. Fortunate are those blessed by her wisdom. They all sit with him atop the Mambilla Plateau.

Then two birds, one a Sunbird lands on his right hand. At the same time a Firefinch chirping quite happily alights on his open left palm. A loving undaunted smile, the creator sings a song to both birds, courting them both with a love song. As he sings his charismatic tune, his warm breath ensnares the two birds. As his song comes to a finish, the true nature of the Sunbird and the Firefinch is revealed.

First the Firefinch turns, transforms into Odudua, the creator and earth orisha. The Sunbird in all its splendour does not fade or die. Keeping all its dynamic colour and its soft, warm voice, it turns into the most gentle, attractive, virile young woman. Oya! The warrior goddess of the wind. Mother of chaos. Her power is associated with tornadoes, lightning, earthquakes along with other storms, hers is the power of the cemetery and death. Her motherly strength is to embrace change. Using her sword of truth to cut through stagnation, she is adept with horses. This orisha is tall, stately and fierce in battle. She is the goddess of creative power and action. Every breath we take is the special gift of Oya.

Standing aloft on the acme of the plateau, softly caressing the sky, imposing blue; a pinch cast into the palm of his hand. Scooping his hand into the fresh sparkling water of the Niger. Then with a single bound, he hits the ground. Taking fine grains of Nigerian soil, once again he puts the earth into his palm, along with the other two elements. Then transmorphing into the part of Helios he once was. Baking all three constituents, his ability to use abiogenesis all come together in that millisecond. Reclaiming his seat on Mambilla, he has with him yet another woman, so full of splendour, elegance and charm. He introduces Ala to all the assembled goddesses. She is the orisha of the earth and fertility; the underworld. She would be the mother of all things. In the beginning she gives birth. In finality, at the end she welcomes the dead back to her womb.

He sings to his very attentive female audience. Again he jumps towards the earth, seemingly disappearing into its depths. They all look, watching, waiting, a little impatient; with bated breath, hardly daring to look away! He laughs aloud, as he reappears behind them.

"Look my stupendous, enchanted orishas—vegetables, fruits of the earth. Two yams, two sweet potatoes, a selection of love apples. Please all of you, blow on them for me, altogether. Your warm breath will be so magical, for me, for all of us."

So they blew all at the same time. A warm breeze, casting a will, a solid shape, a thought. But this time, cast by all the gathered goddesses surrounding A Ahon Ina.

There she stood alone, proud, a little coy. A wonder, an amazement to all the others around her. Shapely, curvy, a hint of the colour of the yam, sweet potato in the delectable tone of her fine skin.

"My dear, what is your name, pray tell?"

"I am Aha Njoku, goddess of the yam."

"Please tell us more, if you would."

"I am the orisha of the yam. The growing, the tending, the harvesting, the replanting of the seeds. The following season, that will be most precious, the central ingredient to another successful year. This will be the main staple of their diet. I will be looking after, nurturing the women, who care for and tend the yams. If they are unsure, feel something is wrong, just call for me. I will be at your side."

A Ahon Ina leaves all the orishas alone. They rejoice as one, holding hands, sing, shout out each other's name, loud and clear, so it reverbates across the whole of the Mambilla Plateau; out across the whole of Nigeria. It sounds like a choir of angels, a heavenly burst of love and enthusiasm. All so happy to be the newest part of this existence. A Ahon Ina moves his seat to the rear, well out of sight. A seat for each goddess, made from the tree of life, the Moringa, appears. Then bowing in reverence to the sisterhood, that is the Awon Iya Orisha. He lets them all be seated high above on Mambilla, so that each and every deity can look and inhale the panorama before them. Seeing, claiming their diocese that stretches forever in front of them. Just allowing all the female counterparts, the glory, the frontage, the spectacle, enthroned orishas give to any party, or serious gathering.

They give the aura of being there for the people. They go in amongst their people, as phantasms, as a thought, an idea. They physically appear for them, for the shaman. Allowing their followers to pray to them, to be able to use their name or names, if referring to more than one of them, at the same time. The want of having them in their midst, to guide, assist, aid, give instruction, in all that they do; either alone, together, or as a whole community.

CHAPTER SIX

The people mix, mingle, split and go many ways. Traversing the rivers, hunting and travelling to far-off places. Settling all over this, vast stretch of land families follow different elders, forming their own tribes. Occupying different parts of this country. Happy to settle where it is not so crowded, least congested. Giving themselves different names, binding various groups to certain areas, certain elders, statesmen. Names influencing, keeping communities together; the Yoruba, Igbo, Hausa, Ijaw, Anaguta, Fulani, Dupe, Idoma, are but a few of the many and glorious tribes as they form over this vast area. Slowly life changes; man begins to walk upright, shoulders his responsibility. The idea of thinking, forming ideas, using his natural ability to make decisions, whether right or wrong; gradually learning from his mistakes. Taking all his kindred spirit forward; the striking of flint together. To start fires for heat, cooking, improving their security by keeping the nightly prowlers away. A visitation from the mother goddess showing us how to perform these wonderful, astounding miracles. She also showed us how to catch insects. To eat the raw creature. They would catch flying termites, caterpillars, giant silkworm, dragonflies, crickets and grasshoppers. Then if they were really hungry, they would root out the massive rhinoceros beetle, the palm weevil. Everyone would enjoy them in various ways, with different cooking techniques. Roasting or drying them in the white sand. Boiling or sun-dried, or skewered then fried roasted over the open fire. Eaten with such relish, with bread and foni yan.

We believe in the sublime orishas. But we know the day we stop believing in them, they will no longer be there to help us in our daily life. So we must believe, talk to them constantly, praise them, hold them in high regard. Then in return, they make themselves available to us, avail themselves in all their serenity, their regard to us. As we give ourselves to them totally, with no restrictions bounding our healthy respect for each other. So all we have is due to them. We need to look after all that we have to keep it safe. We must treat it as we treat ourselves, with lots of respect so that others after us can enjoy it, after we have gone. Their food is given by the grace of the orishas, as well as the creator.

CHAPTER SEVEN

Yemayah with a wealth of allure and charm, goes to the creator. Then sitting herself comfortably on his lap, nibbles his ears.

"Wise one, why do you sit here all alone? You created us then leave us to our own devices. Are you afraid of being in our company?"

"No, my glorious orisha. You and all your sisters are now your own person. It is not my place to interfere with the great Awon Iya Orisha."

"But do you not feel alone, sat here outside of the circle you created?"

"Yes, Yemayah, have you come to me because you are lonely too? But you have all your sisters that surround you."

"Of course, I know they are there for me always. But I feel there is more to be had. I am a woman, I always seek attention. I need attending to. I need to be gratified, satisfied. My hunger sated. As you are the only man here, I come to you for my satisfaction!"

"Then come to me, my glorious young orisha, Yemayah. Into my arms so I can coddle you, feel you, touch you, smell your innocence; your womanly fragrances. To caress your silky softness for the first time ever."

A Ahon Ina takes her svelte, supple body into his welcoming arms. Thoroughly enjoying the feeling, the closeness as she sits into him. He takes her to his chamber, within the plateau. He disrobes then the young orisha too. Unable to wait, the two bodies rubbed, chaffed against each other. Their lips glide across one another's, as the attraction grows expands. The fire, intensity, extreme physical verve. His eyes a roasting cobalt, hers enflamed rubies, bodies white hot! Nothing hidden, as he kissed her full ripe bosom. Her hands jerking on his erect, outstanding weapon. Sucking her intense, inflated nipples. Laying her back softly on the bed, his rod held tightly between her closed hands. As he knelt over her, her gilded lips opened. Filled with his opulent, swollen crown. His fingers preying on her virginal venus mound, parting her over developed labia, feeling her wetness with his fingers. Striving to control himself long enough penetrate the goddess. She tastes his saltiness, happily releasing him, as he now guides himself, the thickness, rigidity, into her glorious recess. With all his embodiment, power, in a delightful, downward thrust. Through her maidenhead. He penetrated deep, infuriating her red clitoris with an almighty languid hump. He excels at giving Yemayah, as well as himself complete unadulterated pleasure, joy. Making both feel so complete in their ecstasy. Two bodies colliding, expressing their love in no uncertain terms. Laying exhausted at each other's side. Laughing aloud, for all to hear. The enjoyment the pleasure of a goddess along with the creator, at ease with each other, in tune.

New birds flew across the skies. Adapting, adopting new colours, dramatic size, new songs. The yellow casqued hornbill, Bateleur, black kite, little bee-eater, lizard buzzard, Bioko batis, red-eyed dove, the white throated bee-eater. The trees came alive as they settle high above the canopy. Trilling, singing all their own wonderful songs. The landscape changed as mountains appear. As the land started to settle, to sit comfortably amongst all the old upheaval.

The heights of Nigeria changed drastically as mountain ranges were scattered far and wide. These geographical explosions adding a gloss, a depth, a panoramic centrepiece to the country. There were the Gotel Mountains, whose peaks ranged from five thousand two hundred, to seven thousand nine hundred feet, in the south-east corner.

There was the Shebshi Mountains in the north-east corner in Adamawa State, near the Cameroon border. With its highest peak, Mount Dimlang at six thousand six hundred and ninety-nine feet. Finally, Nigeria's highest mountain Gangirwal, at seven thousand nine hundred and sixty-three feet, in a remote corner of the Gashaka-Gumti National Park. All a perfect haven of grandeur.

Then the flowers, looking amazing, giving off their overwhelming all-powerful scent. The Bird of Paradise flower, in all probability looking too delicate to touch.

The large mammals that competed with man for food, habitat and for room to survive. The Cross River gorilla, elephant, chimpanzee, lions, pygmy hippopotamus. Some obscure creatures scuttling around, such as Sclaters guenon and the crested chameleon.

Then the little critters that make you stop in your tracks. A bead of sweat leads to another as you cross paths with the Hercules babbon spider, cello spider, dark option spider, six-eyed sand spider. Beware my very dear people, a warning this spider jumps. A perilous critter, the jumping spider, be careful, be cautious.

Upon the plateau we watch, we smile, as the world beneath us changes. The tribes communities all grow. The festivals, the homage paid to the orishas is appreciated, accepted with the dignity it is offered unto them. Now speech is used, people can communicate, indicate, speculate coherently without grunting, pointing or shrugging. Words make all the difference. The many and varied peoples flourish and live happy lives. The heavens lighten, Helios is strong, bringing forth a good harvest, once again. The glorious goddesses introduce other fruits, new vegetables and various trees to revitalise diets, along with interests in new foods and medicines. The soursop, plump, delectable, flavoursome white pulpy flesh. Introducing its other attributes; its juice is good for liver ailments, the flesh used for poultices on wounds. The root and bark is an antidote for poisoning, the flowers for alleviating catarrh.

The orishas reach far and wide, giving their wealth of experience to everyone and anyone. Being amongst their people, giving, explaining, being there talking and walking they all enjoying the varied jaunts, events and experiences they have all been pleasured by. Not compromised or pressured. Just loved, adored and idolized beyond any measure.

The joys, hidden wealth of the Bush Grape. Endearing the treatments of jaundice, dysentery and anaemia. Introducing these happy, joyous people to taste the fruits, the oils, the pulp, flesh and skin. All so good, nutritious, for the physical outlook as well as the mental aspirations. The melegueta pepper, the fruit used in bredies. The leaves to treat leprosy, the root to control and aid lactation — mothers would be so pleased. The Neem Tree, with its oils to repel insects, the hallowed bark, leaves and fruit to ease rheumatism.

It has been so quiet upon Mambilla Plateau. But he can hear their return; all peace and quiet shattered, all girls together, sharing their experiences, laughing enjoying the thoughts, love and closeness of their adoring believers.

CHAPTER EIGHT

Just relaxing on his own, he shouts to anyone that is willing to listen to him.

"Is everything OK? Did it all go well?"

"Yes A Ahon Ina. It was overwhelming, even more so when we showed them the delights of the new fruits and tree. It is always the case, when we spend time with and amongst our beloved people, believers."

"Did everyone enjoy their time?"

"Yes, so much so, two of us stayed down below. They were not ready to come back with the rest of us."

"Which two?"

"Aha Njoku along with Odudua, said they would return later."

"OK."

So with those replies and a short conversation, he rises from his very comfortable seat and smiles to himself, then, as he goes to move away, two of the goddesses approach, each taking an arm.

"Pele O Aje, Aja. This feels very special, being attended to by two glorious, extravagant beauties. An enchantment to be sure. Please join me."

"We would love to. Lead the way, oh joyous Creator."

So the three of them happily link their arms, with A Ahon Ina in the middle. Walking together, they enter Ajas' boudoir. Throwing the creator on his back, they run their fingers through his hirsute body, as thick as a carpet. His hands cupping their well-defined, tender buttocks; so curvaceous, sensitive, magic. One pair of lips is biting, sucking on his mighty, short plump nipples. Another pair of responsive lips and hands, fingers too, hold onto his staff while she squeezes, pulls to get him erect. As he grows with all her ministrations, she sucks, licks with sheer delight. The other straddles his heaving chest. He licks and laps at her sweet, tender loins with his very eager tongue. With both of his hands free, he massages and soothes her fabulous breasts, caressing softly. Tracing his fingers around and around her darkened aureoles. Her tantalizing nipples spring forward, wanting, needing instant attention to. He gently scores those beauties, with such control, he can feel them grow as he caresses those cherries, each in turn. Now gripping her thighs, concentrating on, eclipsing, her needs, wants, desires. His oral muscle penetrating her frantic loins making her moist. He is hard, upright, as he tells her,

"Sit on me most glorious orisha. Push down, I will push up into you. Slide, twist, lunge, screw down onto me."

The goddess grinds down as he pressures with upward strokes. He feels her hymen split as she takes him all the way into herself. The minor obstruction clear, he feels her warmth, her moist welcoming body. She cascades, her sticky cream forthcoming for the very first time. A virgin no longer! Ushering in her pure delight as her first man makes her cry out as she orgasms, thrilled as she flows, her mound white with her own juices. The two orishas change places. The wet sticky loins mask his face as he performs cunnilingus upon her awakened torso. So he licks at her quim, all delight and pleasure. The other goddess climbs upon him straight away. Ramming down, not needing to be told what to do as she had watched her sister perform on him. Her maidenhead split relenting as she grinds down to his hilt. Feeling the first lunge, followed by his overexcited throbbing organ, headed by his swollen, sensitive dome. Culminating in his thickness gyrating against her vaginal wall. She inhales, jiggles, wanting so much more. He gives her all he has, exposing, relenting; ejaculating filling her with his stickiness, wetness, his milk gushing into her as she herself cums all over him. As this happens, the other maiden flows oh, so gently over his open mouth. So much, that he dribbles down his chin.

"My dear, stunning young ladies! That was sensational. You are amazing, so much love to give. I could not love you more."

"Creator, you showed us the way to another new experience. We love this too, sharing all with you was special."

Aha Njoku along with Odudua stayed far down below. Dressed as young unaccompanied women, they felt free and unbridled. A little unsettled, but wanting to discover how lives were lived, here amongst their peoples. The children run free, playing with one another. The women are treated like chattles, cattle, worse than dogs; which they feel is extremely unfair. But do not get involved. Aha Njoku and Odudua accost two young men as they pass by, asking them why this happens. The young men slap them, telling them not to speak to them in that manner. The two women, completely unafraid at this moment in time, strike both men back harshly. The two males do not believe what has just happened. That the two ladies dared to strike them back, to retaliate. So taking hold of the two orishas, marching them both to a darkened alley and then with complete disregard for their sex, they take both women up against the wall. Forcing themselves onto them, they take them against their will. Tears, shouts of anguish, pain and squeals of discomfort, but no help came. The two men finished, leaving them where they lie, crying,

"We are sorry. We should have left with the others. Can you hear us? Help us please."

A Ahon Ina hears their pleas, very distinctly, so he knows he has to go to them straight away.

"Aje, Aja, would you excuse me. There are two of your sisters, that need our help. Would you come with me?"

"Of course Creator, you lead the way, we will follow."

As he shape-shifts, he incorporates the two young goddesses into his change of the high flying kite. Soaring high, searching for his wards, he spots them, a tangled mess down below. Shooting directly to the scene he is unsure of what really happened. Speeding down to their assistance from the great height. Once again shape-shifting, he allows all three personages to gain their individual personalities.

"My dear deities, what has happened to you?"

They were so tearful, there was no immediate response. So the creator, without any hesitation, invokes his power of empathy. Then within a blink of an eye, Aha Njoku, Odudua, Aje and Aja are all transported back to the confines, warmth, the security and safety of Mambilla Plateau. There the other goddesses gather round to assist their humbled, and mistreated sisters. Who are somewhat confused and confounded by what has happened to them.

Still a little tormented, hating themselves for what happened, they are rested and put at their ease. The sisters all make sure that they are not left alone, at any time. They make sure their recovery is as swift as it can be.

Sitting at the foot of Aha Njoku and Odudua's platforms, willing them both to recover as quickly as possible. The collection of orishas, that is The Mother Goddess, sit quietly in the serenity that surrounds them. All contemplating the treatment of their two younger sisters. They decide between them that if this is to be the way of the mortal males, there would be a hefty penance to pay.

If their patronage was to be defiled in this way, then these wayward thugs would in turn pay for this unwarranted attack and debasement of the youngest orishas. If this was the regard they held any female in, then the male of the species should be subdued as a sign of recompense. Just to show he was not the master of all he surveyed.

So forming a circle around their two sisters, envisaging the two culprits. Holding hands including those of Aha Njoku and Odudua. With a single thought they cast the pestilence of leprosy and insomnia upon the two heathens. Upon which no one ever touched the two men again.

The peoples are spreading across the whole land mass. Cultivating, farming, building homes. Finally making use of all the finer things, their goddesses have provided for them. They now use them to share the secrets, the knowledge with their children and their children's children. So all this knowledge will be kept and known. Gleaned for everyone's future. So that the whole community, the tribe will be kept safe. But equality must become more apparent, a part of the tribal way, to survive. Everyone must be included, in a fair and civil way. Or this violence will grow, become uncontrollable and ingrained. The vision is tolerance, love, appreciation of one another. But it will only take one or two of our believers to violate this creed. Then this will break down, be destroyed for some obscure, incomprehensible reason. An odious ritual, that man is superior to woman. This is not the case.

So with this in mind, he of the Mabilla Plateau will come from above to share his wisdom, enlightenment and knowledge with all that will listen down below. He says all his goodbyes to all his orishas, telling them if he is needed, just to call his name. Or to send his friend Aeolus, the Wind, to come and find him.

Off he goes on his travels, as a herbalist, physician and medic, to help all his clans, tribes and communities. To advise the elders and kings. Help them to understand that the belief of belonging is everyone looking after one another. Regardless of sex, age or orientation. He descended to the fragile vaults below. A scheme, an idyll, set up by the human race; so it would never be perfect, fair, especially if it is dominated by the male of the species.

But would people listen to an idea from a complete, supposed stranger? He shape-shifts into the guise of an older man. With age comes knowledge, wisdom, experience and wit. As he walks, he uses a walking stick as a support. He stops at a stream to quench his thirst. Then carries on forward, to the square he can see of a village so very close by. He sits as humbly as possible. Then to a cooing nearby, he replies. The Creator holds out his arm very still, until the red-eyed dove comes to sit on his hand, talking, enthralled with each other. Telling of our experiences, our friends. Then before we know of anything else, some of the local children gather, enchanted by what they see. All gather round as the dove and the physician tell the tale of a young lady who was mistreated by the older man, who was her guardian. He treated her as his personal thegn. Anything she did wrong or without his direct instruction. He would chastise her, he would denigrate the young girl with loud derision being the odious old man himself. He would afflict grievous pain on her young body, causing heavy contusions and lacerations across her whole torso. He abused the girl causing her to become very skittish, afraid of her every move. After spilling a cup of water over him, purely by accident, he gave her such a violent whang and flaying, he nearly took her life from her. She lay there in a supine position unable to move, not able to protect herself from the scathing advances of the old man. As women were only chattels, not considered to be of any worth, he just left her there in agony, lots of physical pain. The old man was mephitic; she profligate. He called her in virulent tones; but still she just lay there, unable to respond.

Then a radiant light lit her corner of the room. There before her was Amirini with her bag of cures, the bag she always carried with her. The old man is odious, chiding her as he came back with nothing but trammels, for the young woman.

"Who are you? What do you do here?"

"I am Amirini, here to care for she. That you old man have inflicted wounds upon. Not cared for, even though she is worth two, no three of you. She is a woman not a cow, or ewe, or your pet dog. She needs care, food, love, attention, just the same as you. Even more so, given the way you look after her. I am here to attend her. Not to worry about you, old man. So begone, before I cast you away."

Shocked he approaches, but with a wave of her hand he is banished, vanquished, from the orishas presence. She spends time creating the correct unguent from the cabbage-tree roots to calm the rashes on her damaged broken skin. Then from the kwakwar tree, a mulch from its leaf, laid gently on her bruised stomach. Other ointments she applies generously, as she cradles her gently in her loving arms, singing softly. Giving her all the attention she desires, requires.

"But why all this care for one, single woman, oh wise one?"

All the children cry out together.

"Ah, my dear children, you miss the whole point of the story. She should not have been beaten at all. She worked hard for the old man but he did not feed her properly. The young girl was tired and she did not get any proper rest. What you should ask is, why did the nasty old man beat the young girl so viciously? The answer is because he could.

51

Because she has not been treated properly, without any love or tenderness. She needs this just like all women. Just as much love, care sweetness tenderness as any man. You must learn that women and men, alike both need the same amount attention, respect and care. You must all remember that, promise me you will."

"We will, thank you for the story."

"It has been my pleasure. You all keep safe. Remember to love your mother just as much as your father. Perhaps a little bit more, just to show your appreciation for all that she does for you."

As he leaves the village, he taps his walking cane. Springing up over the whole village are new crops of pawpaw, African pear, garri, mangoes, yams, corn and utazi. Just to brighten up their lives.

He wends his way along the highway of life enlightening all that would listen to him. Next he was off to the Jibu, in the Kwarfa kingdom and in the Mountains of Gashaka. To spread some light, hopefully a little of his knowledge and idealism within their mountain culture.

On arriving at the Jibu kingdom he was given a very warm welcome. They tell him they did not see very many strangers come this way. They asked who he was. He told them a herbalist, physician. They asked if he was willing to share his expertise, wisdom, with their elder and young medic?

"Surely, surely. What is your pleasure, to take me to them, or bring them to me?"

"We will take you to them. Please follow."

So he followed the members of the tribe to their meeting place. They ushered him into the middle, as the rest of the tribe formed a circle around him. All stand as the tribal elder and physician makes an appearance. The aged physician stood upright before them both, bowing as a mark of respect and of their seniority within this tribe. Then the elder and her physician came forward together, both clasping one of his hands as a sign of acceptance, greeting and a welcome to the tribe. The three of them sat down first within the circle. As they did so the rest of the congregation followed suit. First Adesuwa addresses the gathering.

"We have among us a wise ancient elder who is willing to share his knowledge with us. The gathering is now yours physician."

A Ahon Ina holds his arms aloft, raising his voice to ensure he is heard by all.

"Pele O and I thank you for the warm welcome. Can I say what a pleasure it is, to see your elder and physician are both women. So rare, normally it is the men."

"Do you complain oh, wise one?"

"No, just to say that it makes me happy to see women, involved in the tribal affairs."

"We thank you for your courteous introduction. We are pleased that you accept us so readily."

"I have during my travels been explaining to others the virtues of including women in everything they do. So I quite happily accept the wisdom, knowledge and female instinct that comes from the female overall. No matter what their age, belief, trade and status."

"Now that is good to hear. Even though you are just a mere man, would you share what you know with us?"

"Of course I will."

So he went on to explain, how various trees along with different constituents could make medicines, poultices, salves and balms to contain a problem, or ease a problem. It all depending on what you wanted to use it for.

"I hope this would not be conceived as contrite, or rude of me. But would you tell me your names?"

"Of course, I am Adesuwa, the Elder of the tribe."

"I am Kauna, the physician. May we ask your name, honourable physician?"

"Yes I will tell you, when I have disclosed my knowledge to you both."

So he started slowly, giving his wisdom, knowledge and expertise. Gently, so it could be absorbed and understood, so it could collated by everyone, here at the communion.

The angoro tree, the leaf could used in assisting breathing difficulties. The bark with astringent properties, helping the relief of dysentery and diarrhoea. The oruwo tree was used in treating leprosy, tumours and as a sedative with the leaf. The akoko tree, the cleverest of all, the biggest aid in his satchel, the most potent. The bark, root and leaves used for the treatment of roundworm, dysentery, elephantitis, malaria, convulsions, migraine, yellow fever, hernias, infertility and earache.

"So shall we instead of just talking, see if we can find these wonderful, magic trees? Then I will show you how to make the medicine, how to apply it and where to apply it."

"We would love that. If you will lead the way, we will follow you Master."

"Then be at my side, Adesuwa, Kauna, as we look."

They walked outside the village, the three leading the rest of the community; women, men children alike, all stopping their daily chores to follow the Pied Piper in their journey to discover these new medicines.

"There is the akoko."

"Children then gather some bark, root and leaves for us, if you would be so kind." There in the sunny little groves they came across the mangoro from which everyone set about gathering the leaves, whilst also attempting to harvest some bark.

"It would seem there is no oruwo tree," Kauna voiced.

But he would not let it be so. Tapping his cane thrice, he pointed out into the distance, his finger indicating,

"Kauna look at those beautiful trees. Children go, look for me. Return with the fallen leaves."

He puts his hand on Kaunas' shoulder,

"Do not despair, young woman. You will know all before I leave, I promise you."

She smiles at him, now taking his arm, as does Adesuwa.

"I will tell you now, I am A Ahon Ina. But I am here purely as an old medicine man. First let us do our job. Then I will reveal all to your happy, contented people. Let us eat and sleep, we will then prepare the medications tomorrow."

On the return to the village; there came a a wonderous surprise. A meal had been prepared. But everybody had been out with the medicine man and elder. So they all looked at one another, confused and in awe.

"Do more than just look, my people. Eat, enjoy! A gift from the goddesses, the orishas from on high."

Adesuwa waved them all to sit and eat. Dance, make music, to enjoy the feast, each other's company. When he tapped his walking stick, he also introduced avocado, limes, African apple, peppers, uziza leaves, bitter leaf, cassava, to the mountains. Along with fit, firm kwakwar, ayan as well as guafa. All to assist this charming mountain tribe.

The festivities were monumental. They went on, on and on. Everyone was in the mood. Even the medicine man joined in, dancing with both his charming hostesses, as well as a myriad of countless children, boys, girls, ladies and men. All thoroughly enjoyed each other's company.

As the sun said goodnight to one and all, smiling as he disappeared, everyone else went along that self-same route, to their beds. The Elder and physician showed their new friend to his quarters. Closing the door, the two women were in no rush to leave. They disrobed, even helped A Ahon Ina with his robes as well. They both lay next to him, feeling very comfortable in his presence, as well as against his hairy body. They felt it change, from an older gentleman to a young man— proud and gallant and in the company of two gracious, desirable, gorgeous young women. With both hands cupping, caressing both breasts. Both of her tantalising bosoms, firm, full, round perfection. Adesuwa climbs on top, in her favoured sixty-nine position. Taking hold of his erect manhood, she licked the swollen crown. Sucking his plinth of gratitude, her mouth wide open to accommodate his rampant staff. She gorges herself on his upright, throbbing pole. Taking him against her warm, succulent lips, she nibbles him with her teeth. He kisses her sweet durable loins. Then he caresses her plump venus mound with his coarse oral muscle. Making her tiny love lips swell, he inserts his virulent tongue, eager to taste her. Kauna gets in very close on top the young man, taking his hand and getting him to rub her eager quim. Placing his long middle finger inside her heaving, longing body. Wanting, needing that penetration, she had not had for so long. Adesuwa wanted his rod deep, so she climbed above, astride his groin. Watching herself as she feeds him into her hungry, wanton loins. Now feeling his pulsing, hardness inside her.

Kauna jumped on his chest, rubbing her soft, gentle bush up against his mouth; he was just as hungry for her. She holding her pussy apart, he darts his tongue in and out of her very tasty morsel. Then pushing, sinking his oral muscle as deep as she would allow him. She wanted him as deep as possible, so she got in as close to him as she possibly could. The queen was riding his raging, rampant tool, pumping, grinding, she cumming thick and sticky. Grunting and sighing, she wants and needs him to join with her in all ways. Finally he relents, exploding, making her feel complete, satisfied. He responds by keeping himself deep, his milk rushing up against her vaginal walls—a crescendo of joy for her. She then dismounts, kissing him full on the lips. Kauna removes herself from his chest.

He gets her to kneel on all fours, gently taking her from behind. Thrusting his exposed hardness into her loins, he splits her sweet, tight, delicate labia; she grunts as he pushes entering her, filling her tight with his staff of pleasure; her eager, anticipating quim allows his pulsing erectness to fill her completely. He has grown very comfortable inside this young maiden. He pumps slowly as he does so, he twirls and twists her large, long nipples as he grinds and pummels her juicy tight muff. It delights him that she is so tight as she hugs his pole. She loves it as she can feel every ridge and contour of his pronounced manhood. He is very hairy too. He runs his fingers through her long, lush auburn hair. They excite, thrill each other to the very climax. Cupping her dangling breasts, he massages and caresses as she is milked. Then he unburdens his milk into her very receptive body. She orgasms, her body shaking involuntarily as he pulls her back onto him. Splendid, both gratified; he falls forward kissing her neck. Pushing in as deep as Kauna will allow. She reversing, eager to feel. engage all his enraged, pulsating manhood, for as long as possible.

"My queen, my exceptional Kauna, can I say you both exceeded my expectations? It was an honour and truly a pleasure to have been with you both."

"I thoroughly enjoyed you, master. It has been such a long time since I have been with such a man." Adesuwa tells him, as she lays back looking at him.

"I just want more of you, but you have tired me so, but you are so generous."

Kauna relaxing against him, tells him she is content and satisfied.

All three of them content, eventually they fall asleep, in each other's arms. All huddled, cuddled up tight together, *aro ko*. But a touch of wandering hands, the physical closeness of a man, which has not been the case for a very long time; this all leads to a sexual awakening of everyone's desires and fantasies. Nipples plucked, pulled, twisted. Venus mounds caressed, rubbed; partially penetrated. A manhood massaged, jerked, aroused to an uncommon level, erect, very pronounced. Pink, velvet, exposed, sticky; love lips gently soothed. Kauna smiles as she licks his red, swollen dome. Then she mounts his tactile, robust penis. Soaking up his volatility, loving his blue vein as it gently throbs, his shaft pulses. She rides him. After her first time with the creator, she wanted to have at least one more time. Now she has her chance, unable to help or control herself. She dwells on his thickness, his sensitive, bevelled, hot crown. Leaning forward touching his eager lips with hers; both biting each other's lips. Again she pumps hard, forcing his hardness up against her needy clitoris. Wanting so badly to climax. He drives himself up to his hilt, making her cry out. He feels her juice trickle at first, then gush across his thighs.

"My love free yourself, give it all to me. Give your very heart, so that I may quake beneath your storm."

She relaxes her hands, squeezing his gonads, teasing. He jerks, losing his self-control. As she squirms, she grits her teeth. He sits bolt upright! as they are both engulfed with their liquid love, the sticky white milk oozes out across both heated bodies. Their attempts to hide their satisfaction was impossible. Kuana kissed the creator, gently climbs off her mount—not wanting to but making way for Adesuwa while he was still erect, hard.

The queen straddles her throne, luxuriating in the thickness, heat, the rampant upright flesh flashing before her. It all slowly penetrates her very willing and able loins. The pleasure immeasurable, as she slowly slides then slips down his welcoming pole. She slams down, wanting to feel him immediately. Fully inserted into her tight, starving quim. Feeling his thick, coarse pubic hair.

"My queen, are you safely on me? Are you where you want to be?"

"Yes I am. I love your manhood, so thick and hard. It is good to be here, it has been so long, like I told you before."

She jiggles and wriggles, hands reaching to caress her large firm bosom. Fingers tracing around her uneven, very dark aureoles. Kauna sucking, chewing Adesuwas' amazing nipples. Nibbling tormenting them hard, feeling them grow within her moist mouth. Her hands gently rubbing his swollen balls. All three enjoying each other, thoroughly. He pushes, longing to fill the queen with his opulent, heavy, milk-laden shaft. Kauna squeezing, Adesuwa grinding, he rises stiffening, feeding further and deeper into her very receptive womanhood. Willing her, making her gush. Both heavily climaxing; she leaning forward enjoying, sensing, thrilling, at taking the full force, torrent of thick white cream, winding its way through her empowered body. Finally tired again, all three find sleep and rest once more. The fondness, allows them to be in each other's arms, so gratified and fulfilled. But unbeknown to both Adesuwa the elder and, Kauna the medic; they had been disposed and exposed to the creator's seed of knowledge. So having enjoyed all his advances, they were also able to recollect, recall and remember all the advice and information, he had given to the both of them.

On the return of the rising sun, having washed one another, refreshed. Kissed, fondled each other in the process; wishing each other another good day. They all three go outside to the clamour of the tribe. They all sit partaking of a communal breakfast. Then Kauna goes to the middle of the gathered peoples. Thanking him for all the gifts and knowledge he had shared with them all. She then sits telling the tribe of the of all the benefits of the trees and how to make the salves, potions and other medications. Once again she introduces the physician, telling them there is something that he wished to tell them, to share with their permission before his departure.

He stands before them all, shedding his old man image. Showing his changeling, shape-shifter ability. As he resumes his true persona, A Ahon Ina, they all stand.

"No, no, I do not want you to bow before me. I am a father to you all. Just as the orishas are your mothers. I just want you to feel our presence, be affiliated to us. That we are here for you, to help, assist, in any way we can. To look after you, keep you all safe, protected. We just want all of you to be treated the same. To excel, to propagate, to succeed. No matter whether you are a man or woman. That you are doing your job very well. So I should be bowing to all of you. Paying you my homage, admiration."

They all cheer, clap, smile as he bows in front of them all. He goes back to be part of the large circle. Kauna whispers to him.

"I am amazed, I remembered all that you taught and showed me Creator."

"Ahh, I told you that you would remember. Perhaps last night helped you absorb all the knowledge that you needed, my young pretty one."

"I feel such a flood of detail, since last night. I do not know how to thank you enough. It has been a privilege to have been taught by you in person."

"The pleasure has been all mine. You two ladies have been very contrite and ameniable. I will always be with you, I promise."

They all kiss, hug, not wanting to let go. But they eventually let him go as he waves, then wends his way down the mountainside. Enjoying his walks, he decides to try the mountains again. Heading towards the Adamawa range, He climbs Gangirwal, seeing as far as he could, being on top of Africa, or N'jer at least. Taking in all the fresh air, his lungs are empowered by the experience. Joyful with the fact, that he is spreading the word, ideology that women are very good, on par with the men, if not better, in any society. Which is of course the whole idea of his trek and wanderings.

On his many and varied travels he has met and been involved with a considerable number of tribes including ,the Zaranda, the Gwom and the Yagba.

His journey was now going to take him past the Ikogosi warm spring, the Arinta Waterfalls, Chappal Waddi. Finally to Hamman Kankadu, to visit the Ngizim tribe. To speak, enlighten and assist, so that all regardless of sex get the same treatment, the same regard, the same education and the same chances in life. He stops for water, sating his thirst. He passes the Kainji Lake, stopping to cast a line or two. Patiently he sits in the sun, relaxing, enjoying his own company while he has the chance. Pulling in his lines, he resets them in a different part of the lake. Then almost immediately he gets a bite. Catching a tilapia, croaker, Nigerian killi, and a vundu. Packing them away, already as a gift for the Ngizim. Then paying allegiance and homage to Oba, the river goddess. Telling her to come to the plateau, any time she wishes. Finally he gets to the tribe he wished to see.

"I come to you, with peace in my heart, with gifts as an offering."

"Come enter, as we welcome you to our village wise man. We thank you for your offerings. Come, eat with us."

"I accept your thanks and the offer, of a place to rest."

The tribal leader smiles, sits him down at the fire where people are already eating. His offering goes straight to the fire to be cooked. The smell of fresh fish wafts across the village. All being enjoyed, loud chatter, the inquisitive people ask him who or what he was. His purpose for being here. He duly explained he was just a wandering herbalist, a medicine man just collecting leaves, bark, roots and sap for his concoctions. Also he is spreading his knowledge, wisdom to all those that would learn, or increase their vision and learning. That he would explain more in the morning. He goes to the shelter of a nearby Ahun tree, lays his satchel down and then slowly goes to sleep.

He feels his shoulder being shaken, a soft little whisper.

"Wise man, do not sleep out here in the open. Come with me."

As he awakes and stirs, he says, "I am grateful, but I do not wish to disturb anyone."

"But I am here, to show you to my home. I am Fiddausi. I hope you will feel safe in my home, with me."

"Fiddausi, I am sure I will."

He follows the woman to her home, thanking her for taking the trouble to find him, to make him feel very welcome. She shows him the room, "Is this your only bed?"

"Yes, it is all I have."

"Then I will sleep on the floor. You go back and enjoy your meal."

"I have had my fill, thank you ancient one. But now we are alone, I wanted to talk to you, about being a medicine woman."

"In that case let me put my satchel down. Let us make ourselves comfortable together. Then you can ask me whatever you like, young lady."

"Thank you. I will get a little ogogoro."

They sit across from each other, sipping from two mugs filled by a bottle that is poured by his generous hostess.

"Wise man, can you tell me, could I become a physician?"

"Of course, why do you ask?"

"I have been told, it is a man's job, not for a woman."

"Any job, any position, any craft, any skill can be attained by a woman, as well as a man. If you excel at something, then everyone should enjoy the success that you achieve, for yourself, as well as that of the tribe. Also, everyone can learn from it. Never let your traits or sex restrict your advancement, in any way at all. I hope to get the chance to explain tomorrow."

"I do hope you can."

"Perhaps because you are a lewa woman, they think that distracts you, or the tribe from your vocation. But that should make no difference at all. Would you like to help me, in my quest, in the morning?"

"Of course. What would I need to do?"

"When I ask if anyone would like to learn the craft of being a herbalist, physician, I would like you to stand up, to declare your interest. Would that be possible?"

"Of course it is possible, I would love to declare my interest."

"Do you know anything that would help your case at the moment?"

"Yes, I know of the Ahun tree."

"Please Fadussia, tell me what you know of the Ahun tree."

"Wise man, the bark is used for malaria, the bite of the mosquito. The root, bark and leaves are used together for treating worms, yellow fever, as well as for breast development."

"That is superb, young lady. Is there anything else you can tell me?"

"Yes, I know a little of how you catch different diseases."

"Extraordinary, you are gifted Fadussia. Then tell me what you can."

"First, you get diarrhoea from food. From dirty water you can develop typhoid, hepatitis."

"Go on my dear."

"From the air, or insects we have malaria, yellow fever, dengue fever. Then from contact with dirty, stagnant or infested water, there is leptospirosis, schistosomiasis. Any contact or bites from wild dogs, will give you something called rabies."

"You are brilliant Paradise. Very perceptive, a genius. So much knowledge, for one so young. You would make an outstanding physician for the tribe. This would do you no harm at all, gaining more knowledge and wisdom."

"Do you really think I could be a medicine woman?"

"I think, young lady, you could be whatever you wanted to be, without really trying. You have a gift for absorbing information, then being able to use it. You would be a world beater, in any community."

"I thank you for your opinion, wise one. But that does not help me with the tribal leaders. Anyway, join me in my bed. Be comfortable for the night with me."

"Thank you for the offer of comfort. But I will not crowd your room, your space or your life. The floor will do just as well."

"I insist that I share all I have with you. You will upset me, if you do not accept my hospitality."

"In that case my beautiful hostess, I will share with you. If it is that important to you."

"It is, it will mean a lot to me, as you are my mentor, my benefactor."

"In that case I am in your very capable hands. Please guide me."

"Just join me in my bed. Make me happy, please."

Fadussia takes his hand together they stand, he starts to disrobe. But she smiles. Then, standing in front of him, she undresses him. Kissing both his hands, he obliges her. Her svelt, young body naked, glorious in its perfection. He looks directly into her smouldering, brown eyes. Proffering both of her hands to his lips, she kisses the hands of the soon to be herbalist, medicine woman. Once again taking his hand, she shows him to her bed. He lays upon it, as she follows and lays beside him.

She feels for his hands, he offers it as they interlock fingers. Then they pass off into sleep. She draws close to him, nestling tight in and up against his warm, hairy body. Feeling his hardness against her. Parting her legs, letting him rest up against her thighs as they slumber, so very close to each other. Clenching her thighs, feeling, absorbing his swelling manhood increase in size, She enjoys the feeling, unsure about the urgency she feels. Awoken totally by the surge of heat between her loins. Reaching down, finding his throbbing organ, softly rubbing, gently caressing, feeling it grow as it lay between her eager, nimble fingers. Going beneath the covers, she encompasses the swollen glowing head between her moist, eager lips.

Running her vibrant soft lips down his entire length, while she massages his full sac. The saltiness she enjoys, as she sucks his erection. She softly rubs him, to increase her enjoyment; hopefully expounding on his pleasure as well. Now she wants a little more, now she has a man with her, in her bed. An accomplished male at that. She throws back the covers, unable to contain herself. Her quim itches like never before. The more she rubs the more excited she gets.

"Paradise let me do that for you. After all you have aroused me along the way, with your ministrations."

"I am sorry wise one, I just could not help myself."

"Fadussia, it is not a problem. I welcome all your attentions. Now let me at least end some of your frustrations. Come to me if you will."

He sits up, as she sits on his lap facing him; he kisses are long and intense. Gently running his fingers through her long, thick, auburn hair that shimmers, as dark as midnight. Then slowly licking, chewing on both of her long, thick, nipples. His hands cup both of her small, desirable breasts. She pushes herself towards him as she starts to rub his fine, turbulent organ. She cannot help herself, rubbing, massaging her loins up against his thick, hard, growing erection.

"Wise man, when will you enter me?"

"Young lady, do you want me to penetrate you?"

"Yes, of course I desire you now."

"Will this be your time, are you a virgin?"

"Yes master, treat me gently please."

"I will. I have some salve, that will make it more pleasant for you, young Paradise. Wait a moment."

From his satchel he finds a small amount of balsam, made from the otago tree. As he walks back to the bed, he reaches out his hand:

"Fadussia, add a little of your spittle, to the salve if you would."

She dribbles some into his open hand. "I want some of yours in the salve as well please."

So he adds some of his saliva into the mix as well. Then when it is mixed, gently he applies it to her warm mound, pushing it into her. Tight up against her tight maidenhead, his sharp finger piercing the hymen.

"Are you ready young lady, to mount me? So I can impregnate you. So you can feel me deep within your scintillating body."

"Yes old man. Please now, so I can remove this infernal itching sensation."

She climbs over him, as he lays on his back for her. She mounts his upright, erect pole and slithers down, not stopping until she has all of him inside her. Which is what she desired from the beginning. Very tight, welcoming, soothing away that itch, she smiled finally at the sensation.

She can feel him rub and gyrate tight against her walls. His thickness overfilling, delighting, fulfilling the irritation she had, knowing that it is subsiding. Because she now has the cure, she wanted to finally have a man make love to her. To feel him throb between her warm thighs deeper than she had imagined. Then she can rub her clitoris, with his excited, well-endowed manhood. Feeling his blue vein pulsate as he held her thighs, driving himself into her pubic covered quim. Feeling his thick, coarse hair writhe against her sweet loin as he twisted.

She now drove down his turgid, rotund erection. Her juices are flowing, lubricating his long, round rod. She riding at a gallop now, unable to control her body as it contorts, wanting, needing and desiring every inch of him. Pleasuring in every little ridge, burrow, fold, embossing she can grind against and along his hungry tool. She rode ever faster. Having climaxed more than once, she still wanted more from him.

He gives the beautiful, bountiful Fadussia all she craved, with more. The itch now gone, only pure pleasure, joy now in its place. Giving her the satisfaction, the orgasm, she willed. Her cream thick, substantial, cascading across her thighs. Paradise loved being on top. She rode his unexploded cannon, while he obsessed with her tiny bosom.

He twisted and twirled her lavish, elongated, ripe nipples. He caressed softly and stroked her very firm pert breasts. Plucking and pulling her divine, virulent nipples, he just loved her nipples, along with those very dark aureoles of hers. The shape-shifter beneath her changed into a youthful young man, his manhood all stout and throbbing with the excitement of fulfilling Fadussia's dream. Paradise now even more eager to ride her mentor, to finally make him succumb to her feminine wiles, to make him ejaculate. Then filling her with his sticky milk. Now she could go no faster. An uncontrollable fixation, with his round, erect muscle, inside her. She sweating, wet, sticky, flowing white from her eager swollen labia and loins.

"My gorgeous young woman, why do you fret so?

"Oh wondrous one, I want to feel your liquid love cascade into me. But I do not feel anything from you."

"My gorgeous young maid, would you like me to give you my thick milk? I know you deserve it, how much you do want it."

"Ooohhh yes please master. I want all of you inside me. Then I am going to squeeze my thighs, holding you in place, until I am satisfied, pleasured."

"Then you shall have me, my dear charming Fadussia."

She plunged right down to his pelvic girdle, his groin. His hot, raging shaft burrows deep into her most secret void. There he stayed to shoot his cannon. Filling, nay more than filling, overflowing a warm, white torrent engulfed her needy desires.

She could feel; every drop as it excited her, fulfilled her wanton desires as she drowned in his love. Elated, she orgasms yet again. Gripping his turgid thick steeple of manhood with her eager, ravaging thighs. Refusing to let him go. Not until he had finished his salvo. Then waiting for his cannon to soften, hoping it would take a time. She wanted to feel him, keep him, for as long as she was able, planted in between her nubile, virginal loins.

"Paradise, your first time of making love! That was astounding, magical, sublime, enthralling. you were perfection, if I may say so."

"You master, were a genius. I never knew quite how much I wanted you. Not until you were inside of me. I could not stop riding you, no matter how I tried."

After his very successful and turbulent carnal session with the young woman Fadussia, A Ahon Ina was now more than satisfied that he had planted the seed of knowledge within her. Now all she needed to know was within her before he had actually taught her anything. Just like all the other female mortals he had instructed, not only did they have his knowledge but also the desire and practicability to teach and instruct other females in their fold.

"Come let us sleep now."

"OK old man, but I want to be in your arms."

Off to a deep slumber they went, both very close. Fadussia lies in the arms of A Ahon Ina. He draws her in tight, wrapping his arms around her; just so that she knows he is very close to her. Not going to leave her anytime soon.

They wake, with her nestled in against his body. She feels warm against him. His physical presence nudges her tight buttocks. She parts her thighs, welcoming him in. As he slides in between her loins, she squeezes her thighs around his not so mild staff.

"Wise one, would you like me again? I want you ever so much."

"Yes, I would like you Paradise, very much."

"Then take me. I am yours, my very own wise man."

Then he nudges her cute, curvaceous behind. She smiles as she raises her rump. Putting his swollen crown tight against her cheeks, he eases himself in. Softly he pushes himself into her receptive secret place. She wriggles, submitting herself to his whim. He slips in, satisfying her as well as himself.

"Naughty old man, I can feel every inch of you. I like that too. You are very special, I will remember this day."

Then with a few slow lunges, gently and tenderly he makes his blood flow as well as the young maid's. He withdraws, then penetrates her more than willing quim, slipping straight into her already wet haven.

"This is doggy, a favourite of mine. I hope you enjoy this as much as me."

As he pushes deep, he twists her enormous nipples, she cries, sighs, all wet and sticky. She laps up all his attention. She grinds, pushes up tight against his raging manhood. He twists, pushes his organ into her. She squeals, enjoying the pleasuring he is giving her.

"I cannot wait anymore, are you ready for me young Paradise?"

"Yes master, please now, all of you. Do not hold anything back from me."

Exploding into her very receptive body, his jizz overpowers her. She just sits absorbed, in all his loving, his giving. Feeling his kisses on her back. then turning her over, licking her very dark aureoles, then smiling he sucks her small delicate nipples. She writhes beneath him as the pleasure becomes very intense, almost unbearable, her nipples very close to exploding. Along with his incessant pulling, twirling and rubbing. Just really too much loving from him, for her. But she enjoyed every stroke, he gave her.

"Fadussia, while we sit here together, in this splendid duplicity, in this aura of love. I have to tell you that, I am A Ahon Ina."

"GRACIOUS, then you are more than my master, wiser than a wise one."

"I am just one of you. Here for you, at your disposal. Promise me that you will still do as I asked."

"I promise. I am on your side, in all and everything you do."

CHAPTER NINE

They both wash and get dressed. He is reintroduced to everyone. He stands up alone smiling to the gathered throng. Telling everyone the reason for his travels is to increase everyone's knowledge, men and women alike, and to spread his wisdom and practical abilities as a physician. The gathering, resourcing protection of regeneration, replacing of all the natural supplies, medicines, foods and meat at our command. All that we find in the woods, forests, hedgerows and in and of the trees. We use them all for a variety of reasons and purposes. Therefore as we pick, gather and cut from them, so we sow, re-grow and nurture new growth—plant our seeds, to make sure we do not expunge or obliterate any one variety, colour or type of foodstuff or medicine. Otherwise all will be lost to the mortals. Also while he is here, training herbalists, physicians, medicines, to anyone that is interested. To insure that women are treated as equals, in that we do, say, achieve. The women of our gatherings, tribes, have generic rights. To be involved in everything we do, especially as they form, make up half of the population of any community. So they must be treated as equals always, by everyone.

"So now I am going to ask, if anyone would like to learn to be a physician, herbalist?"

"I would love to learn, wise one," cries out the glorious young Fadussia, as she stands up to be recognized.

"We would like to learn as well," a chorus of three, willing young women stand up alongside Fadussia. The tribal leader stands, holding his hands aloft, for quiet.

"It shall be. The four young women shall learn all that they can. From now on my wife shall be, will share with me, the duties of the tribal chief, leader. I shall value her knowledge, experience, in all that we do."

A Ahon Ina stands once again and he informs the congregation of who he is. He welcomes the chiefs' change of heart, in allowing his wife to be at his side, properly. Also, that he will stay to train the young women in the art of herbalism, and in being good physicians too.

"We can start now, if you are all ready. Please, come with me. We will start this journey together."

So the three young women and Fadussia, follow the wise one. Paradise takes his arm, all ready to start school all over again. All committed to a life they never expected. The days pass, all working, practicing. Getting valuable experience with the tribe, curing the sick and infirm. Fadussia takes the lead, insuring the other three are enjoying, loving their work and new-found status within the village as the newly appointed physicians.

"A Ahon Ina, A Ahon Ina, it is I Ala. Can you feel me, hear me?"

"Yes, dear Ala. I can sense you and the trepidation in your voice. I feel your words."

"Then you must know that Yemayah is about to give birth. Then I must return Ala, I am on my way."

A Ahon Ina pays a last visit to his new physician Fadussia.

"Paradise, I know I can leave all this in your very capable hands. I have to leave, but if you ever need guidance, or me, just call my name."

They kiss softly and tenderly as swains, having known each other intimately, just for a single night. The creator is assured that Fadussia has all the knowledge she requires for her people and the ability to teach other women in the role of physician. Then in front of her,

"Ochumare, divine lady, orisha of the rainbow, can you bridge me, to the plateau, on one of your exquisite arcs?"

"Of course A Ahon Ina."

"Remember, you are always welcome at the plateau, my very dear goddess."

The colourful arc appeared, he saluted Fadussia, and the tribe, as he walked, then disappeared amongst the seven colours. Back to Mambilla. Back to the excitement, confusion of the birth of a new baby, she the daughter of an orisha and the Creator.

CHAPTER TEN

A Ahon Ina was the accougheur[2], the only midwife available. He prepared by washing and having all his medications ready at his side. He had root of the sapo, used as a numbing agent, a painkiller. The kernel oil of the kwakwar for any infections, another medication of the ahun; induced from its root, bark and leaves. To help breasts with their lactation process. Finally the otago tree, made from its twigs, to enhance, to make the pregnancy easier, especially for the mother.

He steadies her, using his already prepared remedies and salves along with his other preparations. Slowly and gently releasing the new life held within. He gives the baby girl to her mother, Yamayah. Then he goes the other two orishas, Aje and Oduduwa he treats them just as gently, with just as much love. Assisting them both, in the birth process. Both providing two healthy looking boys. Both know they will both be brought up down amongst the mortals below.

All three goddesses feel well, fine, all coddling and nursing their newborns.

---

[2] Male midwife

"I will stay to keep watch over the mothers as well as their infants. If you all want to stay, that is not a problem."

So the night passes by without any problems. Everything is deemed very good. No setbacks, all loving smiling, well into the morning.

"Yamayah, have you decided on a name for our amazing young daughter?"

"Yes my great father. I like Victoria. How about you?"

"I think that is a perfect name. Victoria, victorious, victory, vanquished."

He takes the child, putting his mark on the inside of her tiny toes. His mark is a single letter on each of her tiny digits. N G O Z I: blessedness.

"I name you Victoria, the daughter of Yamayah and A Ahon Ina. The first daughter of the plateau. Destined to be great."

Then going to the sides of Oduduwa and Aje, he smiles down at the two young mothers:

"Do you have names for your sons?"

"Yes we do," they both replied in unison.

"Oduduwa, what will you name your son?"

"I will name my son, Ikaki."

"Aje, what will your son's name be?"

"I will name him Eshu."

"You know this is only so that you will both recognize them, at a later date. Then as from tomorrow, Oshun will take them both below. Ikaki will be taken to the delta, then left with the Kalabri people there. Eshu will be left with the Yoruba."

Oshun stands up.

"It will be done first thing, Creator."

He then goes back to Yamayah, where he holds his daughter, looking deep into her eyes. Drawn into her subtle, defining beauty. Seeing her mother there in all her magnificence, prowess and charm. So beauty bestowed upon her, along with wisdom and sensitivity. A sense of endearment for all her aunts. Then at some later date, she shares herself with her subjects below.

But that is some time off, as yet. So now he kisses the young Victoria then plants a loving, sensitive kiss upon the lips of Yamayah. Making his way to his chamber, to rest and sleep. Slipping out of his robes, so much more comfortable. As he lays his tired body down, Ala follows just keeping an eye on him. Seated opposite him, eyes wide open, she commits herself to a vigil, making sure he is at his best, always. He opens his eyes:

"Pele O, Ala, what ails you my mistress?"

"Nothing master. Just your health. I just want to make sure you are well, always."

"Ala, come here, lay with me. Keep me warm. I will keep you safe. I am fine, just tired. I will be even better tomorrow."

Ala disrobes and smiles as she gets in beside him. His arms around her, as she feels his latent body heat. Feeling so secure with A Ahon Ina, slumber comes to them both rather quickly. Snug, happy asleep.

Awoken early in the morning, a surge of blood, to his loins. Giving him an instant erection. It nudged the Orisha, sound asleep at his side. But he felt her hand come across, feeling for the problem. Finding it, then wrapping her hand around his swollen hard organ. Caressing, rubbing so softly, she found he was enjoying her massage. While she was enjoying his excitement as well!

His shaft grows with her intense ministrations. He caresses her ample, sensitive breasts. Feeling for, finding her countersunk nipples. Gently he rubs to bring them out of hiding, plucking her delicate young buds, softly he caresses the tips with the warm, sensitive pads of his fingers. Making them both shine.

"Orisha, rub me just a little bit harder, if you will."

Ala grips a little tighter, feeling him grow in her very willing hands, massaging him along the full length.

"Ala my ravenous beauty, please lay on your back."

She releases him, lying on her back for his pleasure. Looking up at him he sits across her midriff, his rod in his hands. He lays it gently along the valley of her oversized bosom.

"Ala, would you roll your mighty breasts over my erect, throbbing staff? Then feel for me."

As she wraps her generous orbs over his swelling manhood. He rides her heaving breasts, his flesh rubbing, grinding against her warm, delicate mounds.

"Master, I can feel you massaging up against me. I feel you throb so hard. You still grow as well. Is there anything else you can show me?"

"Yes my glorious goddess, turn over then kneel up for me."

Ala faces down, sticking her soft, nubile rump up into the air. He gets behind her, then taking her doggy style. He penetrates her with one clean lunge. Swift, clean breaking her hymen. Entering her as far as his hot, molten sac. Ala sighed, yelped, then relaxed as she felt his long, thick organ poleaxe her. She accepted it, as if it were a gift to her. She wanted more straight away. She reached behind her, holding him, keeping him inside her, luxuriating in the comfort, heat, power, electricity, she now felt between her thighs. Stuck deep within her very needy quivering loins. This was her first time, hoping it would not be her last. She would want it again soon, with A Ahon Ina. Now she bucked, humping against his rod. She wanted her whole venus mound aroused by his thick, hot shaft.

Now he drove into her like a hammer. She could feel herself get all worked up, wet, sticky and flowing very freely. He pulls, jerks, twists on her round, stubby nipples. He cups her massive breasts as he bangs into her virginal quim. He makes her climax, she overflows, her cream spread across both their heaving bodies. She is now obsessive! He makes her orgasm, she cannot stop herself as she keeps up with all his stroke work. The heat between the goddess and her creator makes them adhere to each other. He now ejaculates, his white sauce entering her divine being. It flows freely into her, his power surging through her. Burning, arousing, searing; her appetite is sated. His manhood shares all his knowledge, wisdom and aura with her.

CHAPTER ELEVEN

Holding Ala by her hand, they transmuted into a pair of kites. Then they swoop down from the Mambilla. Taking the mighty, empowered fertility goddess, the Mother of All Things, to see her people. To touch the Ibo, integrate with her definitive daughters. To be part of them, they to be part of her. Soaring high, then diving to the very feet of Adesuwa. Then reclaiming their more traditional form, as man and woman. Here Adesuwa as well as Kauna both smile, running up to him, kneeling before him, the wise one. He shakes his head, proffering them both to stand.

"Rise my beauties, my lovers do not need to kneel before me, come greet me in our proper fashion."

They both come close, hugging and kissing him long, lovingly, as though they had missed him for an aeon.

"This my maidens is the noble Ala, the Mother of All Things. Here at her own bequest. She wants to know all her people. She wants to know you all, so that you feel comfortable with her. So that you know you can call her anytime you need her."

"Greetings, salutations mighty Ala."

Both maidens acknowledge her with their sweetest, most glorious smiles.

"My blessings to you both, Adeswua, Kauna. Would you show me around your village?"

"We would love to, mighty, stupendous Ala. Would you allow us to take your arms?"

Ala extends both her arms to the young maidens. Adesuwa and Kauna take an arm each getting in close to her magnificence. Then the three of them walk, together. Talking, discussing, how far their ventures had taken them.

Adesuwa, the ingenious chief tribal elder, had gained her bravura over the past few seasons, since the creator's first visit. Her temerity along with Kauna's was now doubly bolstered now with his return. Their empowerment and respect now shone like a star in the heavens, as Ala the fertility orisha arrived with him.. Also seen by everyone else, she feels entitled to see that all women are given the chance to succeed in all that they do, achieve. Even to the point, that extra education, training in any craft, trade, profession is given freely, openly, so that they can reach the top at any given time, just alongside the men.

She has created a special relationship with Kauna, her very own herbalist and physician. The two of them are bringing all their women to the fore so that not one of them is ignored. Fidaussi has excelled, as he knew she would. The three women under her wing have extended their sphere of power and expertise. Fidaussi is now on the Council of Elders. Chasing, ensuing, encouraging the chance of increasing the number of women on the council, even allowing more women to give their opinions within the council. Her influence spreading as her number of physicians has increased.

She also has a school for girls. A place of learning, for them alone, away from the distractions of everything else. So many advances, her study forums open to other tribes and communities. Other tribal women take advantage, coming to her, expressing a wish to get involved, to learn anything, to make their lives more valuable.

So it continues, the sudden awareness that women, girls of whatever age and experience, are able, so willing, are more than capable of showing men the way forward. How things should be done. Leaving a legacy through love, patience, tolerance, sincerity and freedom. Not war, strife, slavery or death. The power of the Woman unites, as nothing else can.

***

Ala so impressed with the work, kisses the hands of Adesuwa, Fidaussi, along with Kauna. Then kisses them all on the lips.

"You have astounding work, my ladies. Please keep it up. I have to go now, but you know this, Ala is your goddess, call me anytime. I will be here for you."

"You are so gracious Ala, we are yours to command. The honour was ours, always will be."

So the Creator, with Ala at his side, once more flew back to the Mambilla Plateau.

CHAPTER TWELVE

A Ahon Ina delights in welcoming the three goddesses to the Plateau. Ochumare, the Rainbow Orisa. Oba the Orisha of the Santeria River. Amirini, a Yoruba goddess, to visit the new born daughter.

Yemeyah as happy as can be, as a very proud mother. She breast feeds the eager Victoria. Watching her grow, unable to hide the joy, exhilaration and pride of her daughter metamorphing from an insignificant, dull little moth, into the most splendid, alluring and stunning butterfly. Her absolute pleasure in sharing, with all the other orishas—Victoria's very attentive aunts. None of them wanting to miss a moment of their new niece's life.

The circle of sisters feeling somewhat aggrieved, subdued and remorseful, whilst enjoying and engaging with the new life that is Victoria. In their midst is Aje and Oduduwa who had just a short time ago given up their semi-mortal sons to survive an upbringing with mortal families. The Creator has been down to the Kalabri, in the Niger Delta, to check on the growth of Ikaki. Then to the Yoruba, to check on his cousin Eshu. They are both doing well. Both families assisted with their welfare, without any contact from the orishas. He also wants to get back to Mambilla Plateau, so he can console Aje, alongside Oduduwa. Mainly so he can play, enjoy time with his very own young, delicious daughter, Victoria.

He relishes time, all time with Yemeyah. If the truth be known, he enjoys all his time here, on the Plateau with all his associated orishas.

***

The people down below, the followers, the believers, the ones that hold their goddesses close, now sing praise, pay homage and offer small sacrifices, to the orishas, to show their thanks, in the belief that the deities can see all so that the offerings they bestow in whichever goddesses name they choose, will give them the guidance and assistance they seek to improve their lives. Even if it is only in a small, insignificant way.

In the distance they hear, as they all stand high on Mambilla, a single udu, playing alone, unaccompanied, unattended. Then a second udu joins along with a quartet of calabash, fills the air. A quintet of bata softly and gently blending into the background. Then slowly overpowered by retinue of gangan. A choir of dundun, invoked into the melee of music along with the calabash and udu. An orchestra of ikoko, igbin, ipesi and ilu not competing, but joining in; to create a crescendo of audacious, magnificent sound.

Voudou is all about the creator, the great spirit. Allegiance to the One. Relating your spirit, affirming yourself to the practice of endearment. Encouraging the understanding of all natural practices, processes of life. As well as the spiritual natures that surround them. Praising them for being alive, being allowed to be part of their existence. Being part of the Creator's creation.

So all through the jungle, the drums sounded, reverberating, singing their song of approval. So it could be heard, way on top of the plateau as it was intended. The people danced and sang to the hypnotic beat, to the pace of the myriad of drums, in praise and humble obeyance, of their ownership of life. But also, in the Creator's ownership of them.

A Ahon Ina along with the mighty goddesses listened, enjoyed and danced together, to the beat, rhythm and life of the drum. They smile down in admiration, on their folk enjoying their life to the fullest extent.

Then the Creator attends his chamber, unaware that Aje along with Oduduwa were following behind him.

"A Ahon Ina," they both call, as they kneel before him.

"Yes, my beautiful, outstanding orishas. There is no need to kneel before me, at any time at all. You are all my equals, please remember that always."

"We were not sure how low we were deemed, after our affliction that happened down below, when we were out of your sight."

"My dears, that was not your fault. An accident to be sure. But we learn from our mistakes. That is what makes us wiser, more knowledgeable. That was due to the animal lust still prevalent in some men. You must both consider yourselves still on an equal footing with all the other orishas, now and at all times."

"Thank you for your understanding," they say as an inspired couple.

"In fact, come with me now."

He has a goddess on each of his arms as they enter his chamber, all together. But not one of them notices Oshun close behind them, following in their wake. Eager to learn, by whatever means possible.

The Creator removes his robe, along with the rainment of the two orishas, with him.

"Now lie on the bed for me. I will show and instruct you how young, beautiful and stunning women should be attended to, delighted and sexually satisfied. Above all adored at all times, not dismissed as a third-class being, or as a pet!"

First with Aje, he gently ruffles her long, divine locks of thick auburn hair. Putting his tongue into both of her ears, he nibbles on her ear lobes. Kissing both of her eyes, then going down her, he touches her hot, delicious lips with his. Kissing her long and hard, with all his passion Then he does exactly the same with the enchanting Oduduwa. Then kneeling over her sublime supple body, he trails his moist tongue all the way down from her magic lips, down her long neck, along the valley between her firm breasts. He caresses her small, refined bosom with his eager fingertips. At the same time sucking on her extravagant, plump, juicy nipples. Masticating so hard, drawing milk from her, he enjoys the accompanying sweetness as he attends both of her orbs, along with her nipples. He then travels down with his oral muscle, to her pubic-covered venus mound. There he licks and nibbles both of her labia, enraging and despoiling. Then pushing his tongue past both Oduduwa's plump love lips, pleasuring her the deeper he penetrated the deity. Thus revealing her pink sensitive flesh, which was eager for attention. In whichever way he felt would excite her most.

"Oduduwa please turn over for me, while I show Aje."

The Creator imposes himself on Aje, treating her to all the soft caresses and gentle strokes he performed upon Oduduwa. Getting her to turn over as well, He massages her back, softly rubbing, paying special attention to her perfectly rounded buttocks. He parts those, pushing his oral muscle deep, to her tight little hole. The tip of his tongue reaching, as it darts in, out, in and out and teasing her immensely. He then performs all the sensual, erotic moves upon Oduduwa.

"Now my glorious, elegant orishas, you can turn back over again. You may find this enjoyable, so I will teach you. The spiralled shaft."

Taking Oduduwa's hand, he gets her to hold his manhood at the base. Then softly to run her hands up his length, twisting gently as she does so. She smiles openly as she watches him grow, expand. Then Aje has a go. Both enjoy the contact. He gets the two of them to take it in turns to arouse him with their mouths. Both fervently enjoy this escapade, with the taste and the pleasure of making him aroused. As well as being overexcited themselves, they now between them have one enraged, hard rotund organ.

"If you will both kneel on all fours for me, I am going to take you from behind. You can tell me if you like, or dislike the satisfaction you get from this position."

Slowly sinking into the delights of Aje, he slips all the way. Tight, hugging his length superbly. He pumps with his slightly lubricated weapon, withdrawing. He slides so much easier into her wet, sticky quim. Straight all the way in, holding onto her breasts. His shaft glides in, out. Taking full advantage, making sure she is fully accommodated.

Then kneeling over Oduduwa, clutching her large, round, amazing orbs, he enters both her glorious holes as well. Giving her all of himself, too. Having made both damsels climax.

"Orishas, tell me, how was that for you?"

Together they replied:

"Our enjoyment was overpowering, immense. We loved both entries. So sweet, loving and very generous of you."

"Then next, one at a time, I want you to sit on my thick hardness, ride me, until you have had enough. Do you understand?"

"Yes, great one."

He lies on his back, his erection dominating his body, thick, languid and yet towering. Oduduwa gently caresses his red, sensitive, swollen crown. Then she straddles him, sitting atop, slowly sliding down his throbbing muscle. She feels every inch of him inside her wanton body. Once she is on, she starts slowly. Long deep strokes, feeling her way as she goes. Once she gets her rhythm, she loves the flesh inside her loins. As she gets wetter, she takes shorter strokes, lunging down. Climaxing again and again. Ferocious in her action, not wanting to admit defeat, nor get off, until he had given her his all. But she has to relent, as her loins, sticky and white bathed in her juices, alights from his jutting organ.

Aje gets on, straddling him and holding him, she feeds him into her raging, greedy body. Again he cups her soft, warm impressive breasts. She starts to pump his throbbing, heaving staff. Mystified by the want she feels with him deep, buried inside her. His body heat arousing her, making her like an animal. But again she climaxes multiple times, enjoying the pleasure he gives to her. But she has to rise off his raging muscle, with only her own satisfaction partially completed. Not completely pleasured, as she would have liked.

"My beauties, you still have more to learn. But with more knowledge, you will excel, you will both conquer me."

As they start to dress, they hear a noise. The two orishas approach the sound, only to find Oshun in the corner, naked and toying with her large nipples, trying to copy some of what she had just seen. He lifts her up, so they look eye to eye:

"So, Oshun, how much of us did you see?"

"I saw all of you, and my two sisters, what you done and how you all enjoyed it, thoroughly. But it is all so new to me."

As they talked, he still naked, her hand gently grazing his swollen, unburdened, thickness, roundness.

"Then it would seem we will have to teach you as well, young Orisha. Where would you like to start?"

Oshun goes down in front of him. Taking his brash, round erection into her mouth. She takes all of him into her oral cavity, sucking, engaging her tongue with the very tip of his fiery penis. Pushing the tip into the eye of his sensitive, red crown. Working into the dome, she tastes a little of his saltiness.

"Creator, I would like to start from there!"

"In that case come with us. I can show you the rest, at another lesson."

He carries Oshun across to his bed.

"Now Mighty Orisa, if you would allow me. But first would you get comfortable, on all fours."

Oshun, young energetic, jumps out of his arms and onto his massive bed, in the doggy position. All ready for her initiation, she is very eager to learn all she can, putting her complete faith and trust in her creator.

Kneeling behind the exuberant, excited young goddess he rubs his swollen crown against her buttocks. Pushing so softly, watching as he slips in an inch. A little wiggle, a twist, she widens as his overbearing dome gets sucked in. with a tender push he slips the rest of his emblazoned manhood deep into Oshun's dimpled bottom. The young, provocative deity temptingly wriggles and jiggles her tight round cheeks.. Pushing back onto him, she makes sure she has all of him, gently pulsating.

She does not want to miss anything. To feel the pleasure he can give her. The comfort she can attain, from her ancient one; if she listens, indulges, acquiring some of his knowledge, she learns through him.

He rubs Oshun's pert young breasts, twisting her vibrant taut nipples to indulge them both. She can feel his hands go to her loins; gently, softly he rubs her bush. Sliding his middle finger along her crease, she parts her thighs. Her love lips respond as they swell. His fingers in between her labia reveal her tight, virginal quim.

"Did you enjoy that, mighty Orisha?"

"Yes, wise man, I did. Are you going to put him in me again? But somewhere different this time?"

"Oshun, so you were watching, very intently if I may say so. Yes, I am going to put him where you had your fingers, when we found you."

He withdrew very deftly. Yet just as quickly he re-enters her tight, pubic-covered mound. She gives way to instantly to his rapt, precise, cut through her maidenhead. Sliding, slowly, tightly against her delicate walls he fills her so full, so completely, she felt she was going to burst with his powerful, pulsating thick manhood now within her. Sitting, nestling, as she writhed on his muscle. Loving the feeling it gave her of being so fully consummated by a man. She could feel him, kissing her back. His hands cup her small, refined bosom. Caressing and twirling her even smaller nipples. Now lunging, diving into her with slow, long strokes. He makes sure she can feel all of him on every downward as well as the upward stroke. Thrilled, Oshun senses her wetness trickle across her thighs. Burning, the plunging shaft adds to her the pain, pleasure, thrill, more joy, than she knew possible; more than she could handle.

He retracts, lying on his back, seeing if she knows what to do next!

She turns, gently holding his shaft. Running her hand up its length she twists gently as she goes up. Feeling him enlarge, get more turbulent each time she does it. Then sitting astride him, she pushes her hot, receptive torso down onto his erect, rotund, organ taking all of him in one almighty go. She loved the thrill, the pleasure of him being in her once again. Her wetness, cream saturating his thighs and loins. She smiled and kissed his hands, put them on her desirable orbs, then she just rode him. Fast, furious, unable to control herself. Just wanting him there, below her, for as long as she could keep him there. She climaxed, orgasmed. Her cream along with his milk flowed thick across both of their bodies. Enticing his sexual muscle to gyrate, smack and strike her needy g-spot. To arouse this perfect, provocative orisha to her full potential. With his wit guile and sexual craft. Oshun even though she was chaste and virginal up to this point in her very short life, wanted to satisfy his desires and carnal satisfaction, so she could feel the force of the explosion of his seed into her nubile, fanciful body. Wanting his man-milk all to herself.

Gripping her thighs tightly together, his and her love juice combining, sanctifying their joining. Both covered in a thick, white mess, love complete, satisfaction gained.

Yemeyah enlightened, by the love, adoration, given to her by the young Victoria. The mother of Victoria discovers true compassion in her motherhood role. She bonds so easily with her daughter. Returning all the adoration, attention and love with carefree abundance. To pick her up, talk to her, play; share all her time teaching her; just being a mother to her very dear, irresistible, perfect daughter.

A Ahon Ina still reclined, still with a hard, overpowering weapon. Aje goes beside him, astride him and mounting him. She wants him very badly, after having watched the young Oshun perform and get her way. Crying out, as she took him into her. Short sharp bursts of her wonderous body, grinding against his stiff, engaging organ. Feeling him surge, as she is wet all over again. With slow deliberate pressure, she finally overwhelms him. He loving all the attention, her vibrant quim gouges him relentlessly. She is engorged by his power and energy, she feels him rub up against both her labia. Her whole being loved by his indomitable, heaving purple dome. She having now been baptized with all the sex she wanted, all in one sensual trip. Still not satisfied, she wants him in his entirety. One powerful, slow, pressured lunge, by the mighty orisha finally made him spill all his seed. So hot, thick, into her wilful, tantalizing, desirous body. She got her own way finally. Was very thankful as she kissed his lips, then kisses

Oshun. Before she got missed, left out in the cold, Ododuwa uses the spiralled shaft technique on A Ahon Ina—she keeps him hard, erect and upright. His blue vein throbs gently as she climbs over him. Kissing his sticky, salty shaft. Licking him, giving him fellatio, filling her mouth with his beguiling weapon. Sucking gloriously, his saltiness not overwhelming her. The taste of his fiery flesh, so moorish.

She now on all fours, before her creator, wanting him to take her immediately, impatient for him again.

"My dearest A Ahon Ina, take me please. I want you, all of you to satisfy me completely this time."

He kneels behind her and sinks himself deep satisfying her hungry body. She is very comfortable as she sits back onto him. He fills his hands with her plump, full, round bosom. Squeezing her thick, juicy nipples. Then gets into his stride, pumping into her with slow, loving strokes. She squeals as she feels him grow inside her. His tool grows more rotund the longer the crown expands, making her cream flow, her nipples burn, even thicker. His hot, thick stream of white milk fills her, mixing with her fluids. She stays fixed on his mighty erection. Her itch more than satisfied, she now feels the complete goddess.

His swelling fades as he kisses her back, rubbing his finger between her very wet loins. Licking his finger, he applies his fingers to their loins once again, he then smears the stickiness all over her breasts, nipples and aureoles. Withdrawing, the Orisa turns on him, sucking his semi-rigid tool and kissing his dome. Then she joins Aje, Oshun in jubilation to have been taken by the Great Spirit that created them. Going to the three orishas, he kisses each one, hard on their lips.

"It has been torrid, raging, like a fire out of control. Tormenting my loins; you three are exceptional. I thank you for your time, my exquisite young maidens."

"Great Spirit, it has been our honour to grace you with our presence."

Having shown another three deities the art of sex and its various forms, refreshed, dressed, all four of them, make their way to Yemayah. Upon entering into her presence, he goes over to greet her with a kiss. Whereupon Yemeyah gives Victoria up to her father, who quite happily takes her, partaking in the required baby talk, both understanding each other equally well.

"She is becoming even more lovable as she grows. A real tease this one," he says, as he holds Yemeyah, kissing her, as well as their very young daughter. Proud of both of them, he knows they will both be very special in his life. His little charm gurgles, chuckles and dribbles, as he holds her very close, feeling her little heart beat, so full of life. Looking deep into her vibrant, dark brown eyes, sensing, knowing that he will have to keep tracks on her, sometime in her future, to keep her safe and away from meddling hands and outside influences. But all the time she is here, at the side of her mother and father, she will ever be protected safeguarded from any form evil, or adverse influences.

CHAPTER THIRTEEN

Far up in the northern part of the country, a new following is occurring. They are building walled cities, as protection from other tribes, invaders, on the Jos plateau. The Nok culture, west of Bornu; the Hausa live in walled cities. Islam pays a visit to West Africa, Nijeria. By way of the merchants from North Africa. The Nijerian-based Sokoto calphate, led by Usman Dan Fodio, exerts considerable effort in spreading Islam with its new ideas, theories and idealisms. It was well established in the Kanem-Bornu Empire during the reign of Umme-Jilmi with its five pillars of faith—Shahada, Salat, Zakat, Sawn and Hajj. So it spread across the Bornu Empire to be adopted by leading figures, during the reign of Mai Idris Alooma.

A Ahon Ina along with the mighty, influential Orishas, still feeling enlightened, surrounded by the love, belief, adoration from below. Their believers not forsaken them, offering their voudou; the playing of the many drums, still stirs them, in their belief, and sacred origins. All the folk holding sway, with the old religions, still being satisfied by the Goddesses.

The Yoruba tribes establish themselves in Ife, between forest and the savanna. Filling all their creative modes, hidden and out of the way; away, alone, happy, secluded, peaceful. Awash with big, bold blue skies. With the birds as neighbours, the Yoruba thank all their Orishas. Tonight the drums are extra loud. As all the names are adored, glorified, sanctified. Repeated over and over. A single udu, for Yemeyah along with Victoria. A single calabash for Oshun. A single bata for Aje. A single gangan for Oduduwa. A single dundun for Ala. A single Ikoko for Oya. A single igbin for Njoku. Then a single ipesi and ilu to celebrate Ochumare of the Rainbow, Oba of the River, alongside the age-old favourite Amirini.

Then once each goddess has been cherished, praised in all her glory. Then the drums play in concert, together; louder, louder, louder still so the air is filled with their combined force and music. Until the creator and all the accompanying orishas, show their combined appreciation, casting good fortune on all their people.

Up at the plateau, the creator, orishas and Victoria look down from above, all dressed in their finery. Then in a blink of an eye they all appear at the celebration in Ife. Dancing with their people, touching them, inspiring them, talking and calming them all. Their lands are fertile, they only had to praise them and never give them up, never betray them. Their orishas protect and safeguard them; in return they praise their womanly deities. Hallejuiah!

On their return to Mambilla, life is good, very good. Their souls are full of grace, love and admiration for all their peoples.

He goes to his chamber, as all the women talk congenially. One breaks away to follow him. Oya the Warrior Goddess follows, she thinks without him knowing. But he knows, she was there behind him, wanting his attention. He paused and turned.

"Eloquent one, forgive me for following you. But I want the learning that you have given to the others."

"Come walk with me, to my chamber."

"I would much rather that you came to mine. Would that be too much to ask?"

"No Oya, wherever you feel most at ease. Wherever you are most comfortable."

So they walk together to Oya's boudoir, where she invites him in. He closes the door. Oya's back to him; he comes from behind her, cupping her fine, firm, superb buttocks.

"You are a magnificent, young woman. I can tell you ride horses. Your firm bottom, such powerful thighs."

He kisses the back of her neck. She feels his hands remove her robe, dropping it on the floor. Gently rubs her soft, bushy mound. Then disrobing himself his shaft, hard and erect slips in between the goddess's very firm, flexed, nubile thighs. Making him feel very good, she squeezes his manhood, without too much trouble.

"Oya, that is amazing. Please do it some more. You are arousing me, giving me so much pleasure," he whispers in her ear.

"Is it that good, master?"

"It is very good, I love all the pressure you apply."

He moves his hands up to her majestic, very prominent bosom. He cups and caresses those overdeveloped breasts.

Then rubbing and jerking her thick, long, pliable nipples. Her body is supple, warm and so very pleasing. He releases her, turns her around and looks into her simmering brown eyes. Taking her hand, opening her long nimble fingers, she puts them on his unrelenting, throbbing manhood. Still guiding her, he shows her how to arouse a man if he is soft and limp, from the base stroking, rubbing, massaging upwards. To help a man enjoy her, as well as gain his fulfilment. Gripping his manhood with both hands, with either a tight or loose hold, depending on his personal delight.

He picks Oya up, taking her to her bed. Laying her down he kisses her softly on her closed lips. Now her hand takes hold of his pulsing, rampant rod; pulling him, long slow strokes as he kneels over her fragrant torso and sucking her long, open neck. Taking a nibble then taking a small fold of Oya's skin, clenching his teeth and biting, producing a small discoloured patch of skin, leaving a small love bite on the bottom of her soft, silky neck. Then he lowers his mouth onto her voluminous ripe nipples. Sucking, he loves Oya's soft, yielding flesh. Her treats so sweet, juicy and plump, swelling so very sensitive to his gentle touch. Kissing her heavy, heaving, luscious orbs; sliding up placing his protruding proud organ between her bosom. Rubbing hard up against Oya's magnificent, powerful swellings. Pressing both down against his own flesh. Slow, easy motions, as he loses his self-control. His thick milk jettisons all over her upper body. Yet he is still hard, wanting more of her.

"Great orisha, would you like to eat him?"

"Yes, give him here to me."

She takes him in her eager hands, gently caressing and cajoling. Placing all of him in her mouth, she sucks and nibbles on his rotund, succulent, shiny dome. Tasting his saltiness, she sucks on him, as she squeezes on his sac. Playing with his straining genitals, teasing. Then rather audaciously she puts her mouth around the base of his surging manhood and closing her eyes, bites into the base of his organ, leaving a generous imprint of her teeth, like a tattoo around the bottom of his column. Then Oya kneading and buffing, forcing his pole to explode. Closing her mouth, drawing on him. Oya catches all of him, drying him up completely.

"I loved every single drop of you. But still you are hard. You want more of me, my creator!"

"Yes, my mighty goddess. I still want to taste your delectable, tight honeypot."

"Lord, it is all yours. Please show me. Pleasure me, take me, just like you have done with the rest of me."

Oya lays on her back with her legs raised in the air. The creator rolls her back so her legs are either side of her head. Then A Ahon Ina perches above her, facing down on her, licking her velvet and watching her divine jewel reveal itself. Then his hot searing lance pierces her. Sinking in deep to her eager loins, he pummels her virgin flesh with short, sharp strokes. Then with slow and deep, gentle lunges. His flesh connects with all her erogenous zones, all at once. Also he inserts his longest finger, just to make sure she gets the whole sensation. Curling it up, stretching and reaching, she rocks with his momentum. Sighing and grunting she forces herself upon him as she takes the brunt of all his physical force. She climaxes, her cream spilling from her tight little quim. She lubricates his manhood at the same time. His pumping action and speed causes mayhem and convulsive jerks through her own chaste body. His staff thickening, his shiny crown swelling. She can tell he is almost ready, even though she is a virgin, this is her first time with a man.

"Can you feel me? Are you ready for me, my young orisha?"

"I can feel you. I know you are very near to exploding within me. I am ready, I want you now Creator, all of you."

The creator pulls his body up and away from Oya's, watching closely so as to leave just the head of his vibrant purple organ within very close proximity to her labia and vulva. Then thrusting downwards with one deep uninterrupted surge, he strikes at the core of her tantalizing, magnificent torso. Her loins taste his heat as he erupts uncontrollably. His flow of milk fills her to overflowing. Oya orgasms, but not for the first time, along with her lord, her guide. Their juices mingle, coupled to become one in a glorious union of male and female. A great joy for both creator and the enchanting orisha. The pleasure, sensual excitement makes Oya's body burn with carnal rapture. The ecstasy of both is fulfilled, both Goddess and creator sensationally enjoyed each other. Both are completely at ease with each other. Sexually aroused, the coupling astounding, both beyond, far beyond the point of self-control.

Both are now on the bed, tired, worn out, sexually complete. He left Oya asleep and enjoying, perhaps even dreaming of her sexual awakening.

As he got to his chamber, he heard his name being called.

"I am here, I am here, do you need me?"

"Lord, Ala is ready. She needs you now, please."

"I will get my satchel Njoku, I will be right behind you."

A Ahon Ina lays out all his prepared balms, salves and other medication, vowing to all the assembled orishas to teach all the goddesses the art of midwifery. Everything was ready. Ala laid before him. Everyone hushed as the creator performed his well-practised art of midwifery. Ala was without pain, her husband ensured that. Then finally he brought forth another bright-eyed, glorious and healthy daughter with big, healthy lungs, just as gracious as her mother.

"Do you have a name for our amazing daughter?"

"No lord, would you like to suggest one?"

"There is Halimut, Murna, or even Nafisa. Which appeals to you, mighty mother?"

"What do the names mean?"

"Halimat is gentle, generous. Murna is joy. Nafisa is precious. So which would best suit our little gem, darling?"

"I love the name Nafisa. So precious she is."

"Then we name her Nafisa. I mark her so. I mark her as her father: N G O Z I on her tiny digits. So she will be blessed always."

All the other deities gathered round, adoring the young Nafisa; the new addition their growing family. The now cousin to the elder Victoria. As they gather around, kissing the recovering mother, They all want to hold their new niece.

He makes his way to his chamber, slipping away from the fuss, noise and the overpowering love involved there. But he is accosted by Njoku. He turns to meet her, smiling warmly at her big brown eyes, full of wonder, along with sensual fraility.

"Excuse me lord, I do not mean to delay you, or stop you from your work."

"Njoku you do not delay me, or stop me from my work. You have as much right as anyone else to talk to me. To take up my time, question me, whenever you want. Come find me at any time that suits you. My time is yours, will be yours. Ask whatever you want, whenever you want. I will be here to answer for you, to discuss, to hold you close."

"Can I ask you why you have never taken me to your chamber, or mine, then spent time with me?"

"You have never asked me, Njoku."

"I thought I had to wait my turn. Because I was the youngest Orisa. Just the junior goddess."

"Njoku, there is no junior goddess. Can you recall how you came into being, how you were created?"

"Yes Ahon, I was crafted from the fruits of the earth, mainly the yam and the sweet potato. Then you cast your breath onto me, to give me life,now here I am."

"But Njoku, that is only partially correct. Let me tell you the proper story. I disappeared into the bowels of the earth, to recover two yams, two sweet potatoes and, a selection of love apples. Then I asked all your sisters, to blow on them altogether, because their warm breath was so magical. As they blew upon the fruits, what transpired was what all the other orishas, your sisters, wished and hoped for as they blew into my hand. You emerged like a breath of fresh air. You Njoku are in part your own sentient being, your own orisha. But you are also made of various parts of your sisters. They all know this, now you do as well. So you enjoy your sisters, feel equal with them and towards them. Because you are the only one that is all of them."

"Now I understand why they all look at me, and I can hear what they think all at once. Then what they want to say to me, then I give them the answer they want, before they ask me."

"Now Njoku do you understand that there are no juniors, only clever intelligent sisters, who all look out for each other. It is that you are so demure, shy. You need to spend more time with all the others. Become as one."

"But will you take me soon? I do not want to miss out on your very special attentions and instruction my dear one."

"Go spend time with the others. Mix with them, I will show you all that I know, very soon."

He smiles, kisses her lavishly and with such intensity, full on her quavering, warm lips. She blushes heavily as she returns his kiss with the same passion. She turns, going back to Ala's chamber. Joining in the celebrations there She feels the warmth, sistership and the camaraderie between all the gathered sisters. Njoku enters Ala's chamber, finding all her sisters together. Not one of them fighting or squabbling over the newly born Nafisa. As she gets closer the circle of sisterhood opens, happily taking the coy orisha into their fold. On seeing her Ala asks,

"Would you like to cuddle Nafisa?"

"My dearest sister, I would love to hold and cherish the young Nafisa. To get to know, attached to my newest niece."

"Then come here. Make way sisters, for our youngest, most blessed orisha. Take her."

Njoku holds out her arms, taking the weight of this beautiful young infant to her bosom, cooing and hushing. As all the other aunts stood around, enraptured by her. This was going to be a sisters' collective like no other. All there for each other, always, for their eternity—no problem is too small or large to be shared between them.

He slept right through one full night. Deep, long and intense. On awaking he finally decided to show an orisha, how to deal with a childbirth. Then in turn she could teach, instruct, develop all her sisters in that same art. Making all of them so much more self-reliant, more specalised, a coming together of womanhood, sisterhood and motherhood. A gathering of a unique set of deities, capable of anything.

He could hear they were all still in the chamber, with the mother and newly born baby girl. He put in an appearance, to be greeted by everyone. He kisses Ala, and his Nafisa. Not wanting to interfere with the bonding, he turns to the youngest goddess:

"Njoku, are you able to come with me?"

"Yes, ancient one."

She comes to him, smiling, her big, bold, brown eyes are alert, focused on him alone.

"Mighty, fabulous Njoku, I want to introduce all the sisters to midwifery. To show them how to aid, assist in childbirth, here and down below."

"That would be good. It would make us a lot more independent, make us more involved with our mortal women as well as each other."

"That is my thought. So I have chosen you. I am going to show you everything. Then I will leave you, to instruct all your sisters, in the processes that I show you."

"Master, I would love that. Can we start now?"

"Yes, come with me now, to my chamber."

Laying out all his medications, balms and salves once more, he first goes through the importance of being clean, so as not to infect the newborn or the mother. Then showing her preparations made with coconut oil. He tells her that the salve is good for wounds as well as sores. Then how the lauric acid in coconut oil kills off bacterial viral fungi, along with other infections. It is also used to improve blood cholesterol levels and prevents heart disease. Its moisture protects hair skin from being damaged from solar effects.

Then palm oil. Which prevents vitamin A deficiency, brain disease and aging. It can also be used in the treatment of malaria, high blood pressure and cholesterol, as well as cyanide poisoning. Its salve can also be used to treat and heal open wounds.

The soursop had its purpose too. The juice supported the healing of liver ailments. The flesh made a good poultice for wounds. The root and bark was a good antidote for poisoning. Its flowers alleviated catarrh. So many things she learnt.

So there they stayed, the young goddess, in obeyance learning everything she was taught. Demonstrating, repeating all of the creator's processes, both orally and physically, so that he knew he could trust her with that occupation, as well as teaching her sisters in this complex art. At the end of his tuition, he was more than gratified with the success of his student. The craft of midwifery was in very safe hands. He was jubilant. Njoku had been triumphant. The sanctity of life was highly regarded, even on the Plateau.

He puts his arms around her waist, lifting her up into the air.

"You are very clever, bright, learned. Njoku. I told you, a mistress in the art of midwifery. Let me kiss you in jubilation. Let us go, to tell all your sisters the good news."

Walking to the throne room, where all the orishas were all together, talking and discussing. Taking the youngest goddess to the centre, so everyone could see her.

"I have an announcement. Your youngest sister is a mistress in the craft of midwifery, the art of childbirth."

"I wish to thank the ancient one for his time. But it is also my wish to share all that I know with you all. So that we are equals, that we share in each other's knowledge and passions."

The seven splendid deities came to her, congratulating her in her achievement and pulling her deep into their inner circle. All wanted to know when they could learn the art, alongside her. He sits back on his throne, watching, glad all the sisters were mingling and looking out for each other. No one is shy or unhappy. This is his plan, so all are treated as exemplary, in their own right, or as a large collective of goddesses. One signifies all, all signify the Awon Orisha, who is shared with all her peoples, as a single entity, or as all eight astounding, marvellous orishas. The demure, reserved Njoku, now as bright as a star. Not a shrinking violet, any longer.

She so elated as he reclines back absorbed in their sheer delight. He leaves the ladies to their own ends. Standing aloft on the plateau he listens and watches all the life far down below him. He is rapt at how far advanced everything had become since he arrived from Helios, all those aeons ago.

A Ahon Ina dwelt on the past for a while, amazed at how it had all changed with his own influence. The people's fruitful existence now running in tandem with the smiles and guidance of Awon Iya Orisha. Fleet of foot, a changeling, shape-shifter, A Ahon Ina disappears to the Ngizim tribe to check on his physicians and see how Fidaussi is doing. She has created her own following, with all her training. She has surpassed all her dreams. Now she is at home on the council of elders.

Then again the shape-shifter turns into the agile, sleek bull shark, travelling as far he could along Obas' rivers. He thanks her for her gracious acceptability as he shape-shifts once again, this time as the incredible, beautiful yellow-casque hornbill. Flying over the Kwararafa Kingdom in the Gashaka Mountains. Overseeing the Jibus who were still in the very able, capable hands of Adesuwa. Alongside her still with all her zest for life is the impressive Kauna. She the physician, now sat beside her senior tribal elder, Adesuwa. They both worked together in establishing a training system that would entice young girls and women to school, to learn for the good of the tribe and their own personal empowerment. They were succeeding with great alacrity. So it was all going forwards. He flew far and wide, checking on all his alliances. They were all beginning to work together. On his wayward journey, eating the black pear, then spreading the seed, across the fertile savannah of West Africa. Along with the juicy supplement of the African star apple. Also passing the seed of this fruit across this beautiful, tantalizing portion of Africa. So loved by its people, who are learning to live together.

Then the changeling within the hornbill transforming into a vicious Lizard Buzzard. Playing with the undercurrents of hot air. Free flying, no restrictions, high above the sky line, filling his lungs, free falling. Once again the freedom, exhilaration of flight across the vast, open plains, took hold.

Finally having had his fill of flying alone, he returned to Mambilla Plateau, returning to his form as A Ahon Ina. He walks into the throne room where he finds all the orishas all playing, talking and spending their time with their young nieces Victoria and Nafisa.

"Why not use the spare rooms for their learning and playing? The throne room is good, but far better are those that are larger, less restrictive. Take whatever you need."

"Thank you we will, wise one."

"Njoku are you well?"

She stands up, smiling, joyous, happy he has noticed her again.

"Yes master."

"Njoku, I am not your master. Call me what you will, but not master. You are now mistress of your own destiny. You are all powerful, my dearest goddess."

"Then wise one, I am at your disposal."

As he approaches her, he picks her up, smiling and pats her gorgeous, round rump. He walks off with her. The other deities laugh, shaking their heads. As he waves, then winks at them all, as he has her cradled in his arms; she looks very comfortable there too.

CHAPTER FOURTEEN

A Ahon Ina walks into his chamber, softly putting Njoku, Orisha of the Yams, on his bed.

"Wise one, what have I done?"

"Nothing, that is my problem, you delectable young goddess. I thought you wanted to be a complete woman. I thought you wanted my complete and undivided attention."

"My sincerest apologies. I do more than ever. But I did not know how to approach you about the subject, Ina."

"I know. Perhaps you are still a little coy. So I thought I would do something for you, make the move that you wanted to make."

"I am most thankful you did. Otherwise I would still just be toying with the idea of being with you. Now I can get your undivided attention, guidance and teaching. The instruction I have needed for so long."

"That you will my tantalizing, scintillating Orisa. I will start by removing your robe, as well as mine."

Attending the reclining, supple, sublime body, of the young Njoku. He undresses her before removing his own clothing. Standing before her, her hand outstretched, as she is able to touch his flaying manhood.

"This is the organ of a man, that can cause all the damage, goddess."

"Why is that, ancient one?"

"It is the part of him that gives women the seed, that produces children. Makes them pregnant. As long as women know that then they can always put a stop to it."

"How do they do that?"

"I will show you, as you learn, Njoku. Come stand in front of me. So I can show you what I know."

She sits up, jumps off the bed, then stands before him in all her forbidden glory. Moving forward, he rubs his lips against hers while running his fingers through her thick, lush, silky hair. Then holding her neck as he parts his lips, he puts his tongue inside her slightly parted mouth. As they kiss they rub their nubile bodies against one another. He removes his mouth from hers, the tutor nibbling on her sensitive earlobes making her giggle. The softly diverting his tongue to the inside of her ear. Licking her with the very tip. Njoku runs her nimble fingers across his hairy body, squeezing his little nipples as she does so.

"That is excellent Njoku. You are joining in with me, already. Do you enjoy?"

"Yes wise one, my body feels different too."

He nibbles her fine, long neck as she offers it to him. Again leaving a love bite there for her—his mark. He picks her up, laying her on his large oval bed. Then kneeling over her, he joyfully sucks her mighty, large, round nipples. So sensitive they plump up almost immediately. Kissing her robust, firm, magnificent breasts; squeezing, twirling her already agitated teats. Making them so much larger and longer, he caresses her warm breasts. So magical, a brand new sensation for her.

"Can I play with you, wise one? How can I make you happy, pleasured?"

"Orisha, rub my organ. Softly, gently, however you like. Enjoy yourself, at my expense," he says with a big, broad grin on his face. Njoku smiles back, knowing she can do as she likes with the creator, as long as she pleasures herself, learns and most of all enjoys herself.

Then he strikes her golden honeypot. He rubs her sensitive venus mound with his finger in between her two hot, delightful love lips. Sliding gently so she was more apt and inclined to move in time with his stroke work. He then wants to taste her so much. So getting his face in between her warm, soft thighs, lashing at her tight, bushy quim, with his tongue. She, still a virgin, chaste, pure. Saving her some indignation, pain, with his longest finger, he inserts it; puncturing her tight, hard maidenhead. Applying extra pressure with his very active oral muscle. He pushes through; his vibrant, excited tongue tasting her instant sweetness. Her juices flow, very slow. But all the same he can smell her beauty, willingness; the overwhelming fragrance of a stunning, sensual woman.

She is totally absorbed in rubbing, cajoling and gently manipulating his manhood. Watching him grow. Amazed by her own ministrations, adept fingers, lost in the joy of what she is able to do to her wise one. She squeezes the hilt of his manhood pushing her hand up towards the crown. Watching in fascination as it seems to change its colour.

"Orisha, let me lay a while. You come on top, eat me, see if you like this!"

"How do I eat you, ancient one?"

"You have done half the job with all the playing and toying, the rubbing you gave to me. Did you enjoy?"

"Yes, I enjoyed all of it. I also enjoyed you enjoying me. Your tongue is magical, Ahon."

"Mistress I hope you will enjoy this. All you do now is put me in your mouth. Then suck and lick with your warm lips, use your tongue too. Concentrate on the bulbous, red crown. You can put all of me into your mouth, if you want. Just try, and see what you like, what you really find pleasure in. Also to heighten a man's pleasure, rub the pad of your thumb over, across and around the sensitive head of the erect, surging gland."

"Wise one, lay back let me tend you, I will try and find what I enjoy, what pleasures you as well."

Fascinated by his erection, Njoku tries all the variants she could think of. Sucking, licking, pressing, squeezing, pulling, using her lips, tongue and teeth. Making him submit to her will, she then tastes his saltiness, thick and sticky, licking her lips. Slowly she succumbs to the real enjoyment of her own sexual pleasure and passion.

"Ahon I enjoyed everything I tried, I hope you did as well? I'd rather not waste my energy just for myself."

"It is my honour, pleasure, delight mistress, that you dwelt on me for so long. Would you like to take my place?"

"Of course, my wonderous teacher, instructor."

"Will you lay face down for me, my sumptuous orisha."

She happily lays face down on his great bed, so comfortable.

"Goddess, would you kneel up for me, loving your cute tight body?"

Njoku kneels up, her delightful rump sticking up into the air. He places his rod against her tight, firm buttocks. Very softly he nudges against her, parting her well-formed cheeks, delving gently as his red, angry dome slides into her curvaceous derriere. Calming her as he cups her full, warm and splendid bosom with both of his hands. Pulling on her jutting, erect thick teats. Now planted into her tight gorgeous rump, he slides slowly into her hidden depths. She sighs, moans. He retracts, then heaves in again; slow smooth gently, his strokes drawing her closer to him. Both relish the intimate, physical, sexual contact. Her first penetration, the delights of which she has never experienced before. Filling, expanding her little orifice, accommodating him so willingly, fully. He thoroughly enjoyed her closeness, as he was up to his hilt, gently throbbing within.

"How was that for you, my very generous lady?"

"Hot, sumptuous, magical, explosive. I enjoyed every inch of your manhood."

"I just have to wait for my swelling to diminish, then we can continue, my adorable orisha."

Then as his hardness softens, he smiles as he withdraws himself from the orisha's round and fully developed bottom. Just loving her tight fit but needing to move on with her sex education. Keeping her in the same position. He lays his hardness against her mound and bush of short, curly hair. Gently using a rocking motion, he slips across her pink velvet, without actually entering her. Her love lips are swollen and aroused as he puts his sensitive, round crown upon her quivering quim. Edging down with applied pressure, he ushers himself congenially into her proffered, virginal pussy. He rubs haughtily against her exposed, naked love tunnel. Disappearing down, grazing and rubbing in direct contact with her walls. For him it felt out of this world. To be able to arouse himself, along with the gorgeous woman beneath him. His erection, upright, thick, powerful ploughs her fertile furrow. Colliding against her clit, his length fills her tight new cavity so completely. It took her breath away, gasping as she was.

"Ancient one, that muscle, that tool of yours is so lethal. But ohh so wonderful."

"I told you, so receptive, you captivate me too. Now, if you do not want me to plant my seed within your perfect body, just lean forward, with all your weight so that you just slip, fall off away from me completely."

Njoku tries this immediately. She falls away, off his proud manhood. Free of him, she turns to look. He smiles at her as she looks in disbelief.

"Then if a man tries to force himself into you, at any time, you just need to cross-clamp your thighs together, so he is unable to force himself onto you, however much he tries. Or, if you are facing him, slap his gland hard, so it dies and wilts almost immediately. Would you like to try this on me?"

"Yes, but it will not hurt you, wise one, will it?"

"You will not pain me, my glorious young Orisa, do not worry."

So he gets in behind her.

"Cross your thighs hard, force yourself to stop me. With all your might, here I come for you."

Njoku crosses her legs with all her strength and will, forcing her thighs closed. He tries to prize them apart, to find a way in, without any success.

"That is very well done, mistress. You did that with a vengeance. Now you turn around, see my hardness?"

"Yes."

"Hit my raised manhood with your open hand as hard as you can, with as much force as you dare orisha. Then just stand back and admire your work as the lust just evaporated before your eyes."

She hits his stout erection, quite hard with the inside of her hand. She watches as, incredulously, he goes limp, his hardness gone. He smiles, so surprised is she at this reaction that she rushes to him and looking up at him, into his eyes.

"Are you OK, Ahon? I hope I did not injure or pain you in anyway."

"Mistress Njoku, you did as I told you. If there is any pain, it is my own fault. It was to make you safer, to give you more control over all you do. He will recover, do not worry."

Njoku rubs him, kisses his bold, sensitive tip. She licks and sucks him, watching him regrow to his former stature and thickness."

"I feel better now that he grows again, with my help. I want more of him."

"My stunning goddess, I told you he would recover. Would you like to carry on with your instruction?"

"Yes I want your instruction, now, if I can. Of course I want to continue with you. I hope you are able to carry on with my lessons."

"My very dear sublime Njoku, you have seen you have not inflicted any lasting damage to me, so now we can enjoy each other some more. I am going to lay on the bed. I would like you to lay above me, with your legs by my head."

The goddess lies above him. He starts sucking at her inner thighs, lapping at her sensitive quim; he slurps as he enjoys her sweetness. Also he becomes engrossed with her amazing fragrance. Pushing his oral muscle along her divine cavity, He makes her wriggle, gyrate, as he hits her g-spot.

Her mouth is full of him, sucking biting, nibbling, then licking his throbbing, pulsing blue vein. Feeling it come to life, along her tongue. Then she takes his, raging, bulbous, shimmering dome to the back of her throat milking his saltiness. Both enjoy the essence of each other's body, sex and feelings. Both goddess and creator let their cream flow. Both are now moist, aroused, simmering, heated. A little wanton, greedy.

"Orisha when we change, I am going to approach you. I want you to remember how to stop me, then stop my advances, too."

"Yes wise one. I remember how to stop your wilful unwanted attention."

Njoku sat on the bed, her hands in between her legs. Her long, lithe limbs are both crossed. He accosts her, trying with all his might to part her crossed legs. She then lashes out, hitting his stout, hard, muscle. Watching it die, fade into its previous limp state. Her resilience overwhelms him. He fails once again to get his own way.

"Goddess that is marvellous. Well done, you get better and stronger every time we try."

"Thank you ancient one. But it is due to superb, superior instruction that enables me, to be as aware as this. Are we going to continue, now?"

"Yes we will continue orisha. Will you stand in front of me, bending slightly forward for me Njoku?" The orisha is enjoying her instruction and willingly adopts the required stance. The creator holding himself, slips in so nicely; Njoku does not realise he is deep within her until she tries to stand upright. Then she feels him, laughs out loud; puts her hands behind her, finding him surplanted between her loins, already.

"So smooth wise one. A pure delight, so deep and gorgeous."

"That is doggy style. How do you like this way. Does it satisfy?"

"I could thrive on it all day. Please stay there, just a little longer."

The creator jiggles and wiggles as he caresses her breasts. He cups those two beauties, so warm, smooth and angelic.

"Let me lay on the bed, my stunning Njoku."

He extracts himself and picks her up, laying her resilient torso on the bed, face up. He has her with her legs over her shoulders; he kneels over her, licking her labia. Enjoying it too, but not as much as she is, slowly she finds that her itch fades. Then standing above her, parting her sensual love lips, he rests his shiny, purple dome above her tiny, tight muff.

Then with downward pressure, gently, he sinks slowly past her pink velvet. All the way up to his long hilt.

Twisting his throbbing shaft as he sinks into her wet, delicious well of sensuality He then drives with long, slow, deliberate strokes. As he pumps, she jerks, unable to control her reactions to his purposeful movements. He pulls on her thick, plumped-up teats as well as massaging her massive breasts, all on his downward surge. He feels her get wet, now he ups his speed. It makes his erection bolder, more savage, more rotund. Njoku climaxing, her thick milk rolling down her nubile thighs.

"Glorious, erotic orisha, would you like to finish us off?"

"Oooohh yes please, my wise one. That would be very special indeed."

Again he withdraws, lying in an unguarded position on his back. She feels his manhood as it juts supremely in the air. Thick, rotund and excited, he guides her on as she straddles him, Her legs to either side. She grips his muscle, so demanding, angry and pulsing.. Lowering herself onto his rampaging weapon, She sighs and moans as she takes every inch into her quaking, resilient quim as it is pushed to her very limits. Enlarged with his ever-increasing thickness. But whatever was happening, she wanted to be part of it. Enjoying, engrossed in it too much, to give it up. She needed to fulfill her desires now. She moved herself up, down, up and down his imperial, towering shaft. She could not stop the infernal burning, did not want to halt the scorching between her thighs within her sweet, overly wet loins. Now she was just pumping for her own selfish, personal pleasure. She had climaxed, orgasmed more than once; but still had not managed to make A Ahon Ina release his cream, his seed.

"Help me, oh wise one. To make you release your seed into my willing body."

"Njoku, I am yours to command."

She leans forward onto his shoulders, he grips her hot thighs to hold her still. As she pushes down, he lunges up. Now they both strive to be sexually amplified; to reach nirvana, the pleasure zone. Njoku was besotted with the oracle that gave of his time freely to her. Instructing her in the ways of a mortal's existence, but most of all, enjoyed the education he was giving her now. Euphoria nearly achieved on the creator's part, as he pumps, grunting for his release. Her svelte, heavily breasted torso bangs against his mighty, unstoppable sexual lust, impetuous. Wanting the final release. He puts his finger in her, curling it back on itself, agitating her swollen clitoris. He makes her jump, ride him so much harder, faster. She kisses him, as he pushes even deeper. Feeling himself about to blow. Finally relaxing, her loins in urgent need of his forceful release. He erupts a powerful surge of cream; thick, white sticky. The sweaty orisha smothered in his cream and seed, loving every single moment. Taking his seed, as she asked. Now thankful, that A Ahon Ina was her first lover. Just like most of the other goddesses she felt more than complete, satisfied. She now knew she was a deity, an orisha, the same as all the other sisters. As well as having things to teach her sisters, she felt compelled to tell them of this great event in her life. Just waiting for his excelled, excessive, swollen gland to dissipate. Njoku focuses entirely on her needs, expressing her pleasure by brutally riding the creator as hard as she is able.

Her thighs smack against his, hearing him exhale on her every downward stroke. Finally, the carnal release she wants, she gets. She stays on top of him, milking the creator. Both pairs of loins covered in the thick sticky juices.

Triumphantly she rises from his very addictive throne. Flushed and so very rosy from her exertions, now smiling, showing no sign of her former shyness. With complete abandon, she bowed towards all her sisters, all of whom are engrossed, having watched her nubile frolics and antics.

"Sisters, how long have you been there? How long have you been watching me and the ancient one?"

Together they all replied by laughing aloud, seeing the joy in her eyes at having been able to share this with her family.

"Long enough to know you too have been enriched by the love, joy, pleasures of the wise one. Just like ourselves."

Naked as she was, she went over and fell into their arms, in the embrace of intimate sisterly love and affection.

"I am honoured to be called your sister. I am so privileged to be able to call all of you my sisters. Love abounds between us all."

Now all twelve orishas have been ordained by the love, passion and the wisdom of the one known as A Ahon Ina. Now the circle of sisters was complete. When their female offspring understood the importance of Awon Iya Orisha, it would become part of their lives as well. So much more than their sheer glistening beauty. The power of thirteen savant sapient deities would be overwhelming. All their knowledge and wisdom gathered from the whole continent known as Africa. Yes they were goddesses but no slave, nor subservient to another man or god. They were resplendent in their own right, respected and adored, not a secondary idol, but as the main divinity for their followers.

All thirteen goddesses were there to help all mortals that seek their advice at the Mambilla Plateau. Whatever they required they knew the Mother Goddess was there for them at any time. Their names shouted across the savannahs, the plains and the mountains. Their names are music in the air, travelling on the wind to every corner. The orchestra of drums resonates, through the vibrant jungle as they chant all their names: Yemeyah, Oya, Oshun, Njoku, Ala, Odudua, Aje. Also they rejoice in the names of Oba, Amirini, and Ochumare.

Casting their hearts skywards, they sing aloud, clear and in unison. Everyone wants to be heard by all their heavenly, majestic deities.

CHAPTER FIFTEEN

Watching over their people and following their lives, down at the bottom of the plateau, never ends. All seems to be going well. Peaceful communities, live side by side, having learnt so much from each other, and having traded, foodstuffs and precious ores with some degree of success. All concepts of being alone were put to one side. This increased bonds and ties between certain tribes and even led to mixed marriages. This causing even greater links between tribal trust and various communications. It also stemmed the violent hostilities, bloodletting and needless cruelty.

The aggression fades, love dominates. So with the Yoruba. Great expectations, with the forth coming wedding. Great joy, jubilation, festivities, with the alliance of the Yoruba and the Hausa Kano Borno tribes. The Nupe co-joined through the marriage of Oranmiyan, of the Yoruba, to the Princess Elempe, daughter of the Nupe King Alaafin.

The circle of eleven overjoyed at the prospect of a large wedding. All agreed they should attend with their daughters. Yemeyah with Victoria, Oshun with Nafisa, Oya with Sashantae, Ochumare with Kayefi, Oba with Uyai, Amirini with Halimat, Ala with Chichima, Njoku with Marziya, Aje with Lenu, and Ouduwa with Biebele. All will be supporting various hairstyles to suit their faces.

They stand tall, shoulder to shoulder. Already to descend upon the unsuspecting King and his stunning daughter bride. Wearing all their finery, he shape-shifts into a magnificent black kite. Seated on his back, all holding onto each other, he changes them all into little bee eaters. Swooping down from the heights of the Mambilla Plateau He takes them all for a ride, across the open, blue skies. From the plateau, using the warm, friendly currents He soars showing the orishas and his daughters the splendour of the heavens with a birdseye view of the earth, with all the people beneath them. Then they reach the destination, the Oyo Empire, within the boundaries of King Alaafin. The kingdom was alight with the adjoining sounds of the multiple music of the Ogene, Ekwe, Sanza, Balafon and the sweet notes of the ivory horn.

Joy and pleasure permeated the whole valley. The Hausa tribe who were the loyal subjects of King Alaafin, were celebrating and enjoying the preparations for the much-anticipated marriage of the young Princess Elempe, daughter of the Hausa King Alaafin, who was to be the newly wedded wife of Prince Oranmiyan, of the Yoruba. Thus binding and bonding the two tribes into one single family.

Everyone aghast, amazed, surprised as the superb black kite landed alongside the flock of smaller kites that preceded him. The eleven little bee eaters all sliding off his back, dismounted. The whole entourage then resumed their normal personas reverting back to the magnificence, regal splendour, of the almighty goddesses with the enchantment they carried everywhere they went. With the Creator, transmuting, back to himself. Their sensual orishas, being here for the great celebrations.

A Ahon Ina, the aura, his smile, his benevolence, affability, counteracts all the light. He stands so everyone can see and hear him.

"There is no need to bow or pay homage to us. We are here to help you rejoice in your wedding. We come to honour you all, in the joining of two tribes."

They all cheer, pay their respects to the creator, their orishas and their daughters. Then they go back to work, finishing the preparations for this immense event. The bride and groom appear, spontaneous cheering from the gathered crowds, waving and sharing themselves with all the tribal members. Smiling, laughing and talking they both look forward to the big moment. The sun smiles down on them, sharing his light and heat with all the assembled throng. There were festivities, but larger ones to come, on the actual day of the wedding, the nuptials.

With the sun at its highest point, the orishas in their finest abayas, their silken tresses of hair sparkle in the sunlight, giving all of them an added dimension of allure and splendour. They spent all their time ably assisting the bride with all her needs. Making her look as good as them, finishing with her hair in an impressive high bun. Draped in a fabulous purple and gold gele, which the orishas had made, especially for her wedding. This matched her lilac satin abaya, perfectly.

She was astounding! Elempe looked every inch the princess, every inch a woman of nobility, knowledge and worldly arts. She was at a loss, could not thank her deities enough; all were welcome, all were at the side of Elempe. Her radiance, regality and womanhood shone as a beacon for all to see.

A Ahon Ina was beset by questions from the young Oranmiyan. The Creator answered them all for him, not condescending but like a grandfather to his young, patient grandson. But he sensed that Ornmiyan, with his knowledge, understood all that needed to be done. That he would be as good a man as he could be, especially with Elempe at his side, guiding him along their path together.

In the Oyo Empire, the gathering of the Yoruba, alongside the Nupe; the great wedding begun. From the Niger in the east to the shores of the Volta in the west; all the joy, sublimations and celebrations echoed across the Edu. Flooding along the Lavun, the Nupoid spoken word could be heard, thus far! The joining of these two great tribes and peoples was a great, immense occasion in its own right. All the goddesses with their diligent, delicate daughters, all escorted by their proud father, who were only too pleased to be in their company, enjoyed the splendid spectacle.

As the bride and groom enter the fray to start this wondrous, memorable, perfect event. The music could be heard, was audible across the mountaintops, the plains, the savannahs; across over the treetops, from jungle to forest to wood. To even the smallest copse. All along the Shebshi Mountains, Udi Hills, Biu Plateau, the Abakaliki Uplift. Over the Anambra Basin. Echoing around Hamman Kankadu, the town of Edu. Reverberating in the canyons of the mighty Mandara and his sister Gotel Mountains. Flitting passed the

Erinta Waterfalls, rebounding off the Olosunta and Orole Hills of Ikere.

The drums reverberated along the rivers and across the mountains, with a hypnotic beat and a virtual life all of their own. Especially the Ibo ekwe,[3] singing soulfully alongside the powerful sanza.[4] All the water sprites and wood nymphs came to the party to be intoxicated with the magnetic life force within their jungle. The sprites flitted, riding on the vibration of the musical notes, taking the time to stop to inform the gentle Ikogosi warm spring why so much mirth and gaiety was abound on this particular day. The rhythm of the various African drums selling their song to everyone in this balmy, enthralling heatwavwe of music, people and dance. But let us not forget the presence of the supernatural, given in the form of the sprites and nymphs, who in fairness, could only be appreciated by the orishas and their daughters.

Then after the high ceremony, when the villages, tribes and peoples settled down to feast, to help consummate the marriage. The orchestra of the ogene, ekwe, sanza, the ivory horn along with the balafon, played a little less wild, to show the nuptials had been agreed. That woman and man had tied the knot in this very equal marriage where the woman was not a chattel, serf or slave but every inch the equal to her man, in every sense of the word. If servitude was involved, then the king was her servant too. They both smiled, acknowledging all

---

[3] A long drum. Traditional percussion instrument of the Ibo tribe, played in the east of Nigeria and the Cameroon. Traditionally carved from padauk wood.

[4] An African thumb piano, also known as mbira, kalimba and chisanji. It traditionally accompanies African praise songs honouring ancestors and revered chiefs.

the regards, praise and esteem showered upon them, in which they were both held. They both danced together, while everyone else joined in. All the children of all ages enjoyed the loud celebrations, running riot, playing, as the wedding feast carries on into the night, then into the early hours.

A Ahon Ina the changeling turns once again into a magnificent bateleur, seated on his back are all his daughters, those of the orishas. All turned into fire finches holding on as he takes to flight. Returning them all back to the incredible heights of Mambilla Plateau there he lays them in bed, singing, reading and telling them stories of when he first arrived here; to make them feel safe and not alone as he sits with them, enchanted by each and every one.

As they grow, they get drawn into the circle where they are safe, secure, indestructible, impregnable. The goddesses along with the creator, their teachers, tutors, knowledge base.

He sings a Yoruba lullaby *Iya Ni Wura*. All his daughters join in. They know the words, as he sings it to them all the time.

"*My iya dabi a diamond,
pe ko owo le ra.
O ti gbe me fun mesan osu,
in inu re.
E dupe!*
(TRANSLATION: My mother is like a diamond,
that no money can buy.
You carried me for nine months,
in your womb.
Thank You!)

They smile and laugh, climbing out of bed and jumping onto his lap, pulling at him, wanting his attention, all of them, all at once. They neither respect nor understand his prominence, but he is not concerned. He is their father, just wanting to be treated as such. Just overwhelmed, with their love, affection, adoration. Their complete faith, trust in his ability to keep them and their mothers safe secure, free, protected from any blight, insurgence, that might come their way, looking for some or all of them. So busy is he that he misses the call from all of his orishas. But he catches it, on the second time of asking. He flies down to Oyo as an imperious black kite. Shape-shifting, he gives his warmest wishes as he kisses the bride and shakes the hand of the groom. He bestows his blessing on the newly married couple.

Along with the goddesses he changes back into the black kite while they transform into glorious sun birds, all perfectly formed, in a train behind him. Swooping up, away they soar gracefully, aided by his massive wings. In no time at all they are seated upon their thrones, atop of the plateau.

"Ancient one, how are our daughters?" they ask as one.

"My glorious, majestic orishas, they are safe. Fast asleep. You can go, see. Or wait until they wake."

"We can wait, our very dear one. Come let us rest, while we can."

So peace and geniality prospered upon the heights of Mambilla. A serenity and calm fell as all were blissfully asleep.

CHAPTER SIXTEEN

We see and hear these strange invaders from afar. Investigating our shores they arrive with their vessels, they talk a strange, virulent tongue. Eager for domination, to strangle our religion, they attempt to replace it with their skulduggery. Prince Henry the Navigator is trading in spices, gold and silver. It was procured by any means possible. Also the slaves were treated in exactly the same way; just as plunder. Objects to be treated the same way as the rest of their cargo.

All the tribes of west Africa were overrun with misery, disorder and disease. These white heathens brought strange, distressing ailments with them as they journeyed inland. The Portuguese buccaneers ransacking, kidnapping, abducting, all forms of banditry imposed upon our peoples. All taken by force, against their will. All along the West African coast. Utter contempt for the slave; as they were put in fetters, loaded onto the ships, waiting in turn at Arguin Bay and Lagos. Then onto Lisbon, for their own markets. Then even further still, into the Americas, to Brazil where they were eventually landed, bonded into slave labour there.

The goddesses saved some of the mothers along with their children, who did not have a clue what was happening. The Mother Goddess with all her guile, thwarted these sailors by hiding away her mortal mothers and young daughters. So they could not be interfered with or molested by these pale-skinned mischief makers. She, like her people hated these marauders with a passion, and made sure they were missed. But there were so many that went, never returned. Tears were shed, families were torn apart. Their religion was absolute, they bowed to only a single god. One that told them they could go to any place and steal the treasures there, even if that included the people who lived there. They, the Portuguese, called the African people ignorant. But in all fairness, it was the Portuguese and their god who had it all wrong. But we left the decision of belief to our followers. As long as it was not forced upon them—if they took it willingly, then no harm is done. But if they were chattled and force fed, these untrue, unsacred words, then they will not last. Their religion, faith or belief is referred to as Catholic.

This regime is run by a tyrant, Francesco Della Rovere. A Franciscan monk, who became pope, the pontiff. He who sent these Portuguese Catholic pirates, here to steal our land, people, wealth, beliefs. Then to spirit them away. To replace them with such low morals and self-belief, we will never be the same again.

The time of infamy! In the time of Pope Sixtus the Fourth, the pirates landed at Warri. They were not well received. They did not find many converts. The artful, clever orishas putting their spoke in. Concealing the ways they hide the families. So the brothers, the monks moved onto Itsekiri. Where they were better received.

Sixtus the Fourth sat on the throne of disenchantment with his illegitimate children, having committed incest with his sister, Raffaelle Della Rovere. All his family were in positions of power due to his very open nepotism. Declaring war against, Florence. He the Pontiff instigated the Spanish Inquisition to act as a deterrent against all interlopers, any opposition against him and the Vatican. Especially in the fight, the final annihilation of the Jewish community.

Wherever they may hide. His open suggestion that nunneries should be converted to brothels. Himself a Satanist, worshipping Cybele the Queen of Heaven. Instead of concentrating on his own religion and beliefs. Taking himself, the Vatican the rest of his church and congregation, into a void of darkness, despair and depravity. With such an evil, immoral bishop at the forefront of this church, the circle are duty bound to keep our own faithful, safe, secure and protected from the spawn of the devil, itself.

So A Ahon Ina spoke to Helios, regaling their other life which now seemed an aeon ago. Asking his old patron if he would shine a torrid unfriendly kind of heat upon these rabid foreigners. Making the jungle a furnace, so unbearable and uncomfortable for these detestable morons. The orishas casting a charm over the female mosquitos so they would bite and disenchant only the palest of skin, swarm and enjoy the sweetness, given freely by these ill-intentioned brothers. Turning all that they could against them. Provoking all our natural energy against them.

Stopping, retarding the enslavement of our children. Rescuing them from the confines of such an unnatural belief. Protecting, safeguarding them, so they can turn to the succor, the relief, the love and mothership, of their own old, ancient religion; which they will always feel at home with, safe with. Who would want to be part of such a depraved, irresponsible cult! Where the figurehead worries more about his own personal fantasies than leading his church from the front. Downtrodden by a single man, with only his self-interest, at the forefront of his woe-begotten life. No wisdom, worldly knowledge, compassion, charity, hope, faith. Just greed, anger, contempt, opprobrium, enmity; along with no actual self-belief, in the doctrines of his own church, whatsoever.

He thanks Helios for his blistering, scorching power. The orishas! I hail their infinite wisdom. Gratified by their unified power, resolution, for this invasion. I kneel before them as well as our daughters; telling them what a privilege it is to be within the circle with them. With their wealth of powers. As they set about sculling the noxious female mosquito, as well as the tsetse fly, to rid us of this plague of pale-skinned rapscallion. The fly alongside the mosquito, eat such tender flesh until they throw all the invading force into disarray. Being felled with such disease and conflict, disease that we know as yellow fever, dengue fever, malaria, elephantitus, typhoid, leptospirosis, schistosomiasis and Lassa fever. Having laid their eggs within this soft, supple flesh. So the disease burns, penetrates, spreads, infiltrates. Killing some, infecting lungs, along with other major organs. The Portuguese suffered unfavourably in the extremes of the African sun. Swelling, rupturing, failing; they were not so resilient, when using our water, breathing our air, eating our food. The myriads of tics, fleas, bloodsuckers; their young being laid. Then hatching just about anywhere, on their weak bodies; on land, sea, sweet flesh. But soon they wished they had not arrived, on our strange, sunny coastline. After a short, unwelcomed stay they scattered to the four winds, returning to whence they had come.

The goddesses all now have daughters all partaking in the challenges of their daily existence. The care and protection needed in looking after our faithful, of safeguarding them, sharing the insight, wisdom and intellect with their young daughters. Showing how to be courteous, how to listen to the doubts of these mortals have when talking about their achievements or the lack of them. Showing their daughters how to instil self-confidence and boost their moral. So that the mortal can envisage her life and see for herself what she would accomplish by her life's end. Delighted and overwhelmed in sharing their lives alongside their daughters, with all of their believers. All knowing to be very careful, with the whereabouts of Ikaki and Eshu, the two tricksters. Both are born of the orisha, both very adept at most forms of deception. Both lead irresponsible lives. Both are unsettling, very wild, chaotic, both rebels.

Being there for our people, understanding their needs, paying your respects to them. When they offer a prayer, a token of their respect to us. We are at their side always, for an eternity. It will be us guiding, assisting, good times, bad harvests. We do not get shaken from our tree easily.

Even the two tricksters pay us servility, obeyance, at the moment. But they are still young and yet to grow. So things will change between us, I am sure. As they grow older, wiser on their terms; learn, gain knowledge. Their personal regard for us, will evaporate, turn to disdain. Obduracy will be their prime operative with lesser mortals. They will seem very recalcitrant. Both will be very iniquitous, obloquy—both a complete let down, to the mothers that gave birth to them.

But the circle is unbroken. Now having grown to include all our precious daughters. The fire they bring, emboldens their desires; their need to search the wonders of this rather small blue planet. So once they are all of an age, we have promised them all the chance to investigate, explore and get involved in everything, to their hearts desire.

My daughters Victoria and Nafisa are finding time to accommodate all their half-sisters that I have fathered, alongside them.

Nothing is futile with us. Our life force needs to be extended. This is done with new blood. All the young daughters have been named, then welcomed into the circle of eternity, life and creativity. Each darling daughter has been given her own name. each has been given the mark of her loving father. Until she is required to replace her mother, the orisha. Then and only then, does she sit on Mambilla, with her mother's name. Along with the responsibility, power, creative force, craft that is ordained upon her. But she does and will have everyone around her from the circle only too willing to help, assist, guide, tutor, at any time she may require it.

Islam has taken hold up in the far northern states. It victimises everyone especially their own women, no matter what their age. They have scant regard for the females and degrade them at every opportunity. They cannot rise up and rebel there is no one to support them. The caliph and imam shout and infer, whilst the husband treats his wife as a sabaya, abusing and beating her all the while. All the time keeping her hidden away in a dark place, mentally and physically. But it does not bestow any inspirational surges, dreams, ideas, for its women. They who tend the family, look after the children; downtrodden, forgotten, misused and beaten. So unfair, for the matriarch, who feels misguided, deluded and completely forgotten. So one sided.

The grace and enchantment of the orishas command respect with the joy and pleasure they bestow on their avid believers. When you feel alone or in a desperate situation, as a female follower of Awon Iya Orisha, she deems it her job to make herself available to you personally, so you have someone to listen to your troubles and quell the riot within. Your orisha will give you the compassion you desire, love and the chance to talk, and the need for someone to listen. She, they will be there to ease your pain. We still follow our ancient codes, our unwritten laws. This archaic belief it is for the people. Young, old, male, female, the blind, the infirm, the beggar. It has no great church, only the heart of its believers and a home atop of the great plateau. The deities always on entering a prayer or incantation of either a single follower, a small gathering or a multitude of followers, assure their people that they are there for them. No request or task is too small to attend to at any time. Without you needing or wanting us we will only fade from your memory and then finally not exist at all. So for us to be part of you it is you that needs to believe in us, so we can continue with our metaphysical existence. The Awon Iya Orisha is yours to be truly enjoyed. To prosper with, to ordain your life in however you wish to live it. As long as our light shines, we will find it and praise our devotees. Shed all our sanctity upon them and make their harvest flourish, be bountiful. Allow our spirits to eternally make their world prosper.

It is not for you, to aspire to us. But for us to help you to aspire to your own personal greatness, in any way that we can.

I am only too happy to take my two eldest daughters with me, when I go earthwards. To seek, aid, assist, generate the interest of the mixing of cultures and sexes, amongst all our peoples. Victoria and Nafisa hang onto their father. As they change from black kites into bush chimpanzees, becoming *oha ojii* being blown in the warm winds; to a gentle rainfall. We travel up to Jos Plateau as a warm trade wind, settling down just the three of us. Watching, admiring the tribes. Their comings, goings, interplay, interaction. Their respect for one another. We enter their busy lives, listening, learning, silently advising, endorsing ideas, along with my two supremely confident young daughters. Trying to enrich people, their lives. Imposing the idea of enriching, improving, empowering, the woman's life. Improving her status along with the burden she carries daily, the one she shoulders for the family. Hoping that she, the mortal female can find another plain of existence instead of being the pit pony of the village, enduring all the back-breaking work, the drudgery of a campaign of endless physical work, with no thanks given and nothing to show for all her labours at the end of the day. Except one tired, miserable body. What she would like in a perfect existence, is a life of her own where she makes her own decisions, is allowed to study and be educated. Then to go out into the big wide world and be empowered enough to stamp her authority on her own existence, thus being able to claim her life as her own. To have a reason for being here.

We three become part of the prevailing gusts that take us as if by magic up and across to the north-east corner of this vast green, fertile stretch of land. To the borders of Borno state, across Kano, Katsina. Where a passing of an age or two, Islam was introduced. It turned out to be the preference of the local courts and commerce; by Muslim traders and clerics. It was they who spread it peacefully. Adopted by the Fulani cattle herders, the Berber people in north Nigeria who migrate living off their herds, as well as corn, millet, sorghum and sugar cane. As well as wild fruit and nuts as and when they are available. This is good for the man who loves to control all about him. Not letting his wife, daughter, niece, mother or grandmother into their secretive lives.

She with a millstone around her neck. Even though the holy book of God, the Qur'an, states that women should be respected cared for. That they should be treated as equals in education and gaining knowledge. But this is rarely given any countenance of thought by their over obsessive male counterparts. In truth this is a divisive religion, made by men for men, to inflate their ego. It also states that she is allowed to own and have her own possessions. She must be present at any legal ceremony that involves her.

But in many eastern countries they are manipulated, controlled, abused by any number of incumbent, hostile male relatives.

As he sits explaining all of this to Victoria and Nafisa, they are transfixed on his every word.

It also tells you that a woman cannot be forced to marry, if she does not want to. When a girl does marry, she becomes part of the husband's family. But in truth, in all respects she becomes his chattel, his property. Treating her in any way he sees fit. Showing no respect for her at all, demeaning her, at every opportunity. Her life is his. She is not allowed to work, kept in the shadows, her freedom restricted, curtailed in all respects, spied upon. Then she has a purdah to contend with. Having her whole body shrouded, just like her meaningless life.

She is not allowed to mix with men who are not related to her. Even at their mosques and other meeting places, the men and women do not mix. So this is how they are treated as equals. At any time in her existence, she is told what to do, when to do it, how to do it, how many times a day to do it. She is not allowed out into the streets unless she is chaperoned, unless her husband gives her permission. She gets beaten for no reason at all, just for being a woman. She is encapsulated within the home, with no freedom whatsoever. A prisoner for the rest of her time, the rest of her life. As a wife, mother, grandmother, with no say as to what happens to her or her offspring. So the Qur'an dictates. But in reality, the woman is kept in darkness, freedom is not part of their role in his life, her husband, brother, father, grandfather.

"Father, this is not our way. Why are they so different to us?" Nafisa questions the wise one.

"This is because their god has made women to be the slaves, property of the man. He dictates how they live. To do his every bidding as and when she is told. Not to think for herself. To be cut off from reality. Not to use the brain she was given. Not allowed to question anything, not to think for herself."

"Father, our world is fairer, happier. A lot more colourful. Is that because women bring so much more life experiences, love, happiness and joy to us with their freedom of expression, ideas, words, care and closeness?"

"Yes my clever, darling daughters. This is why I want to bring you out with me. So you can feel all of this. The way different people live, survive, exist and endure these cults of hate and oppression. There are so many, some good, some bad." Then together they smile, telling their papa.

"We do learn so much, when we come out here with you. It is always different. So good to see all these other people, how they survive."

"Now we go to the Niger Delta. But first, I will change us all into the Nigerian killifish as we are going to travel down the into the south-eastern part of the country."

"Do we have to worry about anything, while we travel along the waterways?"

"No my beautiful young ladies. You will be in front of me. Are you both ready?"

"Yes, Father, we are in your hands."

As the three of them change into the shape and sphere of fully-grown Nigerian killi they are immersed in the warm waters of Nigeria. He kept his eyes wide open; not wanting anything to catch him unawares towards the safety of his two eldest daughters. They traversed brooks, streams, rivers, saltwater pools and freshwater lakes. Bounding over the Cross River, the Calabar River. Finally they end their journey within the watery paradise, the hidden haven that was Agbokim

Waterfall. Full of splendour, wild plants of so many varying colours grow there of all hues and tones. Young trees and old, the calls, chattering and the songs sung by the brightly coloured birds. The high wall of the Agbokim Waterfall hiding an entrance into a small warren of caves behind its fast-flowing cascade. The idyllic beauty and panorama of the jungle hideaway, was unspoilt.

"Father this is paradise, Eden! Hidden away, it is all so unspoilt."

"So it shall stay. As long as we can look after it, my dears. We have come to see the Kalabari people. Are you both ready for another adventure?"

"We are father," Victoria confirms.

"Let us hold your hands, please," Nafisa asks her father. He holds out both his hands. As Victoria takes one, Nafisa gripping onto the other. Walking through the waterfalls, being cooled by its very fine spray, the droplets produce a small perfect rainbow that sits contentedly above the peaceful haven. Thus, they cross the Calabar river. Marching through the salt water swamps. Trekking across the dense sweaty subtropical rain forests. Marching high up, onto the hill above the river; alongside a lakeside oasis.

The Kalabari a friendly, joyous people. Their markets are full of pineapples, banana, plantain, cassava and palm oil. All trading from the mangrove swamps. So friendly, they are instantly given the warmest of welcomes. They are invited to sit, to eat with them. To partake in the communal meal. They are offered *Tomina Fulo* (soup of fresh sea food, thickened with cocoyam). Alongside which they serve another dish, *Onunu*, (boiled plantain and yam, finished off with palm oil).

A Ahon Ina asks the young lady who serves up the meal if they know where Ikaki is. Whereupon Agbani, the young girl's name, tells him he is no longer here, with the Kalabari. He told everyone that he was going to make his way up to the north. Perhaps as far as Borno state, so he could meet up with Eshu.

"Then Agbani, there will be problems when these two tricksters get together. Thank you for telling me."

"It was my pleasure, Ancient One. Be safe on your journeys."

"You young lady, will have a good life. My blessings on you, Agbani."

"Father, why will there be problems with Eshu and Ikaki, if they meet up?" Victoria asks quietly.

"Surely as sons of orishas, they are unable to cause harm, or any mischief?" Nafisa, confides with both her father and Victoria.

"It is because they were both born to create havoc, chaos. It is in their mix of blood. It should never have occurred. But it has happened. So I need to find them to discover what they are both up to. Now you can come with me, or return home to your mothers. So you can go with them to the festivals, carnivals; that are due very soon. I will try to get you back in time to come with you."

The two precious young daughters both reply at the same time:

"We want to come with you. To further our experiences. To spend more time with you. As we feel that we do not spend enough of our life, enjoying you, what you can teach us, show us. So if it is not to be a hardship, we want to be with you for as long as we can."

"That is fine. Then the three of us will once again travel up into the northern part of the country. We will travel by various means. All that I am sure you will both enjoy, be exhilarated by."

"So we can come with you, Father?" Victoria cries.

"Yes, of course."

"When do we go?" Nafisa shouts, wanting to leave this very moment.

"First you can both enjoy the hospitality of the Kalabari."

"Then the day is ours, darling Papa?"

"Yes, Victoria. We shall leave early in the morning. I will go and inform your mothers and aunts that you will both be staying with me for the continuation of the journey."

"Can we explore while you are gone? Can we talk to these gentle people?"

"Of course, my beautiful Nafisa. I will not be gone long."

Transcending his physical body, in complete control, he leaves his two devoted daughters in the safety of the Kalbari. He makes a straight flight as a black kite, to the Mambilla Plateau. There he is greeted by everyone, as they knew he was on his way back. He transforms from the big dark bird back to the ancient one that everyone relishes and loves so dearly. They all ask as one voice,

"Where are the girls Victoria and Nafisa, have you forgotten them somewhere?"

"My beloved orishas, they are both safe. They are in the Calabar. I have come to tell you that we must go to the north

144

to check on the two tricksters, as they are finally trying to meet up."

"Will you be back in time for our festivals and carnivals?"

"Yes, we will be back in time to celebrate with you all. Our daughters want to come with me and spend a little time with me. But we will all be back, as both young ladies want to share these special occasions with you."

"Can you stay a while?" Yemeyah asks him.

"No. I must get back to our daughters, I cannot leave them alone too long."

So they all kiss and hug the wise one, not wanting him to leave, so soon.

"My darling delectable wives, I shall miss you all, along with all my other sensational daughters. Yet the time will soon pass. We will all be back together again, in each other's company."

Changing into a lizard buzzard he sweeps, swooping up high. Then he dives down, across and over the heads of his glorious goddesses and his amazed daughters. A raucous bellow from the buzzard is his sign of a fond farewell. As he flies back to the Calabar He lands in the dense tropical forest. Transmuting into a thunderous, ill-tempered and raging silverback. Then as he arrives, emerges into the market place, everyone backs away from him. Then he reveals himself once again as the peaceful, wise one.

He bumps once again into Agbani.

"Sir, your two daughters are off with the older women. They are discussing medicines, cures, treatments, herbs and the like."

"That is fine. It is all that they learnt from their mothers. So I will sit and wait for them."

"Come old man, wait with me. I am just about to have some fresh *Tomina Fulo*. I would be very happy, to share what I have with you."

"Agbani then show me the way. I love fresh *tomina fulo*, along with the company of such a beautiful young lady."

She blushes, a little coy, turning her face for a minute to recover.

"You are very generous with your compliments, thank you."

Inside Agbani's home, the smell of fish, cocoyam and herbs fills the air. The sweetness of the fish makes his mouth water. Silently he blesses her and her house.

"Ancient one, what can I call you? It would seem we are destined to spend time together, whether it is short or long, in each other's company. I can feel your knowledge and wisdom. It comforts me. I feel drawn in towards you. I am compelled to get closer."

"I am A Ahon Ina, perhaps that is why you feel a closeness, a familiarity towards me. Tell me what you call your own father, what name do you use as a sign of respect?"

"I never knew my father, he left before I had a chance to know him. If I had a father, or knew my father, I would call him Papa or Dad, a term of love, endearment, a closeness that I would have loved."

"Then Agbani, call me Father or Papa, call me whatever your heart desires to call me. You feel like a daughter to me, even after such a short time of knowing you. So it would be my honour to be your father, guardian, whatever you want me to be; whatever you feel most happy with."

"Then you will be my father from now on?"

He nodded smiled laughed aloud. She came to him; hugged him very close pulling him to her. Putting her arms around his neck she kissed him repeatedly.

"Then Agbani you are my daughter. From this minute, we are tied together as father and daughter. I must go north, to check on two young boys who may cause trouble. But if you ever need me, for anything at all, call for me. I will recognize my name along with your voice. I will be with you at your side, in an instant."

"Then Papa, will you pay me a visit, on your return, from the north?"

"Yes, my dearest Abgani. I will come to you, before anything else."

She serves her father with the hot, fresh fish stew. They sit and eat, talking about Abgani's missing father. How her mother brought her up, how the father left without telling anyone. It has been hard, without a father figure to look up to. But her mother has been astounding, making sure they both had everything. It was a struggle, forlorn at times. They waited patiently for the return of his two daughters. Abgani smiles, as she asks her father:

"Would you, Victoria and Nafisa like to sleep here with me, before you all depart, early in the morning?"

"Your sisters and I would love to spend the night here, with you, my dearest daughter. We can all get to know each other so much better."

"You say *my sisters*! Do you mean that?

"Yes, you wait and see. Your sisters are the daughters of Yemeyah and Ala. So they will receive you with open arms, and all their love."

As they talk, he hears voices, instantly recognizing them both. He jumps up, moving to the doorway,

"Victoria, Nafisa we are in here. Come, meet your new sister. We will be staying here, with Abgani tonight."

"It is good to see you, we have just been talking to the tribal physicians," Nafisa tells him.

Victoria adds that, "We have just been giving them some ideas, on how to improve their medicines, treatments and care."

"That is excellent, both of you. Now I would like to introduce your new sister to you both. This is Abgani, now she will never be alone."

Nafisa and Victoria smile, rush over to her side and cuddle her, bringing tight into their circle. Hugging and kissing, making her welcome, making her part of their sisterhood.

"Sisters, I want to sing the praises of the orishas your mothers. Yemeyah, Ala my aunts, my mothers. I hope they value me more than my father ever did."

"Abgani, you also have other sisters, their mothers now your mothers, that will always be at your side." Nafisa tells her.

Victoria also tells her, "You honour us too, by being part of our family. It is a privilege to have you at our side."

The three of them cling to each other, dancing, singing, laughing and crying. Happiness, joy and love abounds and overcomes them. As colour, worth and family now enters her drab, dark, lonely life. They stop. Looking at him, he gets up joining them in their small circle, to make it complete, for all of them. As all the goddesses' sisters smile down upon them. Not regretting for one minute, the new addition to their ever-growing family.

CHAPTER SEVENTEEN

Before anyone else thinks of rising and waking for the start of a brand new day, the wise one and his two daughters rise. Not disturbing anyone else, all three of them changing into a small family group of chimpanzees. Scaling the dense, tropical forests they make progress, swinging through the foliage, leaves and branches, always keeping his young daughters in front of him, in plain sight. Once through the vast complex of the sub-Saharan forest, the blue skies beckoned. Using the various rivers, tributaries and even the smaller waterways, including an unknown underground river. The freeway to the north, virtually unused by the mortals. Changing all three of them into various shades and sizes of the glorious red finned barb. Finding themselves swimming in the nearest fast flowing river gaining the required direction immediately, so as not to draw any attention upon any of them.

Having gotten as far as they could, by means of the various waterways. In an instant, they change into the big, raucous Bioko batis. Heading up the warm currents, soaring high, heading straight as an arrow, to Borno state just as the sun begins to rise. It appears large, bright and yellow, just above the horizon as we come to land, on a cluster of Ayan trees. As they gather their breath, they watch, wait and observe.

"There is Eshu. I recognize him. Running wild, tormenting, teasing and bullying all the other children, as they play their games without him. Theses tricksters play a hard game. Then they grow up, become more odious, iniquitous, so full of rancour and spite."

His two daughters look at him. As always they ask him a question in unison.

"Why is that, Father? Surely, they are just like any other child?"

"Because something tells them that they are different to the others. They think their birth gives them some sort of right. But it does not. There births were forced upon two of your aunts, when they were both younger. They were forced to tolerate the deliberations of some wayward men who raped them. Not knowing who the father was at their births, they were given away, to other families. Resentment sets in. They feel they have to make a statement, one way or another, to be noticed. A statement of power or intent, that everyone else will take notice of. Being bullies, despicable young men, obviously just like their fathers they need a following. So if he meets up with Ikaki, then all this will happen, in the very near future."

"Dear dear Papa, they are still so young. Come, you will know when the time is right to come looking for them again."

"Yes, at least we know where they are. Come let us go back to the Kalabari. To see your sister Abgani, before we go home."

They all transmute in to the spectacular, impressive Bioko Batis, returning the Cross River State. Alighting just inland of the Calabar river, They walking into the village, to be greeted by all its people. Abgani shouts, smiles and waves trying to attract their attention.

"My papa, such joy you bring with this day along with my two beautiful, glorious sisters. I want to introduce you to my mother; she is the one who cared for me, still does. She is Rayowa."

"It is my privilege, honour to meet you. To be in your presence Rayowa, mother of Abgani."

"Ancient one, it should be me, bestowing praise upon you and your enchanting daughters, for taking her into your fold."

The three sisters catch up, as all the villagers are interacting with the three, vibrant and joyous young girls. A Ahon Ina is left alone with Rayowa. As they look at each other, he asks, "Rayowa, how long have you been left to look after your daughter?"

"Since I knew I was with child. He left me, I have never seen him again. She has been a burden to me. But I have struggled through. Now she is on her own."

"Do you think that is fair? After all, it was not her fault she was born, into this world."

"Wise one, come with me."

Rayowa takes his hand, taking him with her. They stop outside a single-roomed dwelling.

"This is my home. This is where I have lived, since I was pregnant. I have worked hard, struggled, toiled such long hours just to keep the two of us together. I did not want, nor do I want to lose my precious daughter. Yet I am afraid it is going to happen, it will be so. Because we cannot survive together, in this tiny hovel. Come in and see for yourself."

He goes in with her, stifled by the small single room. He wonders how the two of them, could possibly survive here, in such cramped conditions.

"Wise one, join me here, if you would."

He goes to her, sitting close, almost on top of her. She takes his hand, putting it inside her buba. He softly cups her pert, warm, desirable breasts. Rubbing, soothing, comforting. He feels her hand gently massaging his crotch. She pulls him forward, their lips touching, grinding. She eager to taste him; then she realises in her hunger and need, her impudence, she may have been just a little too forward.

"OOOHHH, wise one…"

"Rayowa, do not apologise or feel embarrassed. I am not a shy man. But I also feel your want. Having been ignored and bypassed for so long, of no interest to anyone. We can enjoy this together, here side by side, if you still want to be satisfied."

He loosens her buba, lowering his head. He takes her nipples in turn, sucking, licking with his long, eager tongue. Gently tugging them with his teeth. She puts her hand down, so she can physically touch his rising manhood.

"Would you feel more comfortable, if we disrobed?"

"Rayowa my deceptive beauty, I think we both would. Allow me to undress you. Then you can give me the same service, if that would pleasure you, make you happy?"

"Yes, it would satisfy me, no end. It has been such a long time, since I last touched a man—let alone had sex with him."

He stands up with Rayowa, who smiles as she disrobes him. She touches him everywhere as she does so. So excited, as she holds onto his hardness, so pleased she has aroused him to her own satisfaction. Kneeling in front of him, she takes his jutting shaft in between her sensual, lush lips. Sybartic stroke work, firing up his senses. His blood boils with the intensity of her motions. She gleans his saltiness across her impudent tongue. He offers his hands to her; she gladly accepts, taking them both as she rises from her bended knee. He puts his arms around her neck, kissing her ears, lips, eyes. He removes her gele, his hands running through her thick, luxuriant locks of auburn hair; loving the feel of her across his sensitive fingertips.

Finally releasing her iro, letting it fall to the floor. Now his turn to go on bended knee, before this delectable, stunning woman. Then he licks at her bushy soft quim. She thrusts herself forward, for so long untouched; only by her own hand and fingers. This is so welcome, wanted for so long—the attentions of a man. To be enjoyed by a man, once again. To have a man interested in her and her barren body, a miracle. A sensual, erotic pleasure she had given up on. Now she just wanted more, she did not want him to stop.

She closed her burning brown eyes as she felt his oral muscle enter her sweet loins. Her eagerness showing, she feels no shyness, as she pulls herself open for him, so he could really penetrate, gain the depth she required, to fulfil her needs. He delves with his wild, lashing tongue, sucking with his lips. His tongue now as deep as it could be, tasting her sweetness, lapping at her cream.

"Oooohhhh, wise one I want you inside me now, please."

He lays on his back, his eyes all aglow.

"He is all yours my Queen Rayowa. I hope he serves you well, that he satisfies you, completes all your desires and needs, as a woman."

"He will pleasure me, way beyond any of my expectations, I know."

Her hands wrapped around him, stroking, rubbing, teasing; filling her mouth with his overgrown shiny dome. Then removing herself, she climbs over him, rubbing her moist loins up against his erect, throbbing shaft, wanting to savour every little touch, enjoy a man once again. This is beyond her wildest dreams, thinking this day would never come to her again. He is rampant, hard, wanting her now to encase him within her supple thighs. Now to enjoy his manhood. Holding him upright, rigid, hope triggers her thoughts of lust, lost love and wasted dreams.

Smiling, her wanton brown eyes are fully alight, her senses fully charged. Her thighs tremble, her loins moist, wanting his hard muscle now, grinding in her depths. Impatient, greedy, but wanting him, oooohhhh, so slowly; so deliberately. Needing to feel his every inch, as it ignited, fired up her wanton, over anxious, quaking body. Wriggling, jiggling, gyrating, enticing his already red, swollen crown. Inch by inch, she lets her body slide down his erect, rotund, pulsing tower of flesh. As she fills herself with him, he in turn caresses her firm, round majestic bosom. Running his fingertips over her counter sunk nipples, he tries to pluck them out, of hiding.

As she sits on his hilt, her tight quim full of his thundering organ; she leans forward as he traces his oral muscle around,

around her large, coarse and uneven aureoles. He loves the texture, the feel on his tongue and the taste of her sweet, tender breasts. Slowly her nipples rise to the surface. She gently squeezes his man muscle, with voluntary contractions, from her tantalizing thighs and groin, arousing him no end.

Rayowa again leans forward, taking his head in her nimble hands, kissing him with an overtly hard and long buss of wilful passion. A kiss she thought she had forgotten how to give. Rayowa in the realm of fantasy as their lips touched, feeling his surge of desire instantly satisfied that she was still able to light and stir a man's fire at a single sitting. She had all but forgotten the delight of being impregnated by a man. Not any man, but one that knew the art of lovemaking, and used it to its fullest extent; used to enchant the woman, delight the woman, make the woman feel good about herself.

She sat on him, feeling him grow, fill her, so endeared to his manhood as it throbbed. Emitting its warmth, succour, power through her whole body. Refusing to let him go, she makes the most of him as she had him all to herself. She was now wet, dripping, over-indulging her soft torso. Her gentle motions engaging her with his virile, thudding muscle. She pays reverence; her nubile, besotted torso infectious upon his. As they kiss, he plucks her vibrant jutting nipples. He is so generous letting the sensitive and provocative Rayowa take the lead in her display of sensual and sexual craft. Her hunger to satisfy her own need was paramount to give her back her self-confidence and self-esteem. The aroma beatific between the perspiring bodies. She is overpowered, absorbed by his electricity is unable to sit still. She writhes, gyrates and pumps uncontrollably. She shrouds in her own love juice, body heat and has the biggest, sweetest smile on her face.

Now fully lubricated, so very wet, she rides his erect hot manhood. Willing him to leave his gift between her loins, to fill her, to satisfy her, to instill his milk into her body. Then to make her orgasm, climax, he rubs her G spot, as she bounces, nay jumps on him. She cries out, shouts and screams, calling him names,

"Old one, wise one, ancient one, release yourself into me. Please, I want all of you in me. Make me a woman; make your maid, your hand servant, your wife, creator. Fulfil my desires, then I am yours."

Finally she feels his turbulent rush. His life force enters her, his stickiness abounds and overflows. Unstoppable, cascading, filling her as she sits on him. Letting him erupt deep, so deep. She feels her body, his mix become a single entity. His flood is unstoppable, ceaseless. His love is not shy, he gives it all to her.

After his swelling fades, she climbs off him. Her arms around his neck, her kissing is remorseless as he smiles, at her love for him, he holds her close to his torso. Returning her myriad of affectionate pecks, they dress, exiting her dwelling. She turns to look. Now the single squat, a complex of six rooms. With a large garden, where she sells, with her daughter, her fresh fruit and vegetables. She along with her daughter Abgani do not realize how their lives have changed slowly, since the chance meeting with A Ahon Ina. Nor that mother and daughter had been living apart, now they once again live side by side in this glorious house.

"Rayowa, would you and Abgani like to join us for a while, to meet the orishas and their daughters?"

"Ahon I would love to. I think we should ask Abgani, to make sure she is OK with this idea."

"There you are Papa, greetings fair Rayowa." Both Victoria and Nafisa smiling with their greeting.

"Mama, Papa, have you spoken, since we left you?"

Together Rayowa and A Ahon Ina reply, "Yes Abgani we have spoken at length."

The creator adds, "And done so much more besides."

"My dearest Abgani, would you like to visit your other sisters, your aunts, now?

"Will you be coming as well, Father?" Victoria, Abgani and Nafisa all ask as one.

"Of course, my loving daughters, I will be there to show you all off. I will take you all to Mambilla Plateau."

"In that case, I would love to come with you all," Abgani retorts, as she cuddles both her mother and father.

That being said, in a flash they are all in a family group of gorillas. The large silverback, seeing them safely through the dense, subtropical jungle. Then changing form dramatically. Into a shoal of Tilapia Croaker; swimming the depths and torrents, of the fast-flowing rivers. Then the final lap of the journey, the ancient one again, shape-shifts one and all, for the last time on this journey into a flight of erroneous black kites. Transcending plains, hills, savannahs, mountains. Enchanted, in awe of the power of flight, Rayowa and Abgani stay close to the wise one. In the fear that they will fall out of the sky without his continual guidance. Slowly they gain some independence and are then capable of enjoying the spectacle.

Abgani joins her two sisters for the rest of the flight to Mambilla Plateau. But Rayowa, keeping so very close to her new protector feels the safety, security, of being within a heartbeat of his great wing. With a mighty, majestic swoop he takes her with him to the massif, the protectorate that is their home, Mambilla Plateau.

As he lands with Rayowa at his side. They instantly resume their immortal and mortal substances. The youngsters stay longer in the clear blue sky. Playing, daring the with the warm air currents. Sweeping them high one minute, then to the heights where they are unseen. Then next, diving, diving swooping down, over everyone's heads. A Ahon Ina bows in reverence to all the orishas, all his attentive daughters.

"I have returned safely, with our daughters, Yemeyah, Ala. We must wait for them to stop playing. But here I have with me, a mortal wife, for all of us to enjoy. This my darlings is Rayowa. Mother of Abgani, my latest dearest daughter."

The creator, whistles a loud deep whistle, carried by the wind, high into the ceaseless sky. Within a minute, all three black kites land on Mambilla. All smiling, happy, full of joy and love.

"Victoria, Nafisa, Abgani, you all returned very quickly."

"Yes Papa, Aeolus told us, that you required our presence as soon as possible."

"My friend Eolian never lets me down, he is good and remembers me."

Abgani was standing next to her mother and father; a little uneasy as she is not sure how she will be welcomed. As an interloper, a fraud, a freeloader, a carpetbagger. But this was not her intent. It was her very dear dad, that invited her here, after all. But she need not have fretted, nor worried.

"Now let me introduce everyone, so that you will all know each other, and get acquainted, as sisters, aunts, mothers. You know Rayowa already, this beautiful child is Abgani our daughter. Make them both very welcome, so they can make this their home to. Now we have Yemeyah, mother to Victoria; Oshun who is Nafisa's mother. Sashantae, belongs to Oya. Kayefi is the daughter of the rainbow goddess, Ochumare. This is Oba, her daughter Uyai. The other beauties are Halimat, the child of Amifini. Ala the orisha of fertility and her infant Chichima. Njoku has in her arms, her daughter Lenu. This more than happy pairing, is the orisha Oduduwa and Biebele. This is my family, that you are now part of, Rayowa, Abgani. Now come join us and eat."

The orishas all gather around Rayowa and Abgani making them both feel the centre of attention. Wanting them both to be and feel part of their large family, to integrate, to be one of them and to join in, to feel welcomed. Then Victoria along with Nafisa, take Abgani their newest sister, between them to meet all the other excited sisters, wanting to know all about the new member of the fraternity and everything that happened when they were with their father. All talking at the same time, all wanting to know everything, they all did together. Just as sisters do. So one big happy joyous unit, as it should be always. Everyone seated, Rayowa in between the goddesses and Abgani in amongst all her adoring sisters. While the ancient one sits back, warm, appreciative and satisfied in the knowledge that no one feels out of place. That the addition to the family has been a good one. That the mother and daughter will now bond as they should. They can live together, be happy in each other's company.

"Orishas, daughters Rayowa, we will shortly be going to your festivals and carnivals. All in your honour. Please tell me, will my new wife and our daughter be able to come and join in all the excitement, as one of us, to celebrate with all our peoples?"

There was a prolonged loud cheer, waving of hands, excited loud voices, all as one. A definite climax of yeses.

"Yes, of course they must come."

"Rayowa must dress as one of us."

"Rayowa must have the same material, I have some spare."

"We want Abgani, with us, we will dress her."

"Abgani is now one of us, she shall have what we have."

He smiled his knowing smile and sat back down to enjoy his fresh pineapple, picked from Rayowa and Abgani's garden. So now there was lots of chatter and giggles amongst all the mothers and even more so amongst the gathered daughters. As they all mixed in with each other, discussing what to wear, how to have their hair. But he sat at the table, warm in the thought that no matter what they did, nothing could improve on perfection. He here sat, alone, but with such company that no man could compete with—the most perfect, united, iconic deities, in this land. Not one of them needs anything to make them any more so perfect, adorable, sensual or attentive than they already were.

But he did not say a word, he did not want to spoil the moment, did not want to spoil their ties of sisterhood or the unison they had forged as strong, virile, nubile, independent women. Women who were even stronger when undivided, when they were together as one.

"Father, Papa, husband, dearest one, we are going to get ourselves ready. Will you miss us all?"

"Of course, my precious beauties, I will miss you all. You are all part of me. But you go, enjoy yourselves, be happy. I shall get ready also."

CHAPTER EIGHTEEN

The Oba, a king who can claim direct descent from the most mighty, alluring orisha, Oduduwa. They alone can wear the sacred regalia, the conical bead crown and beaded slippers. They also carry the all-important fly whisk. The war between the Yoruba for supremacy raged on for a mind-blowing four hundred years. But finally sense and relief prevailed. The final sixteen years of the war, led by the warrior general, Ogedengbe, of the Ekiti army; had triumphed. To the adoration of all his followers. But eventually, all twenty-four Yoruba Obas agreed to the cessation of the war, between all the tribes, at the Kiriji battlefield. It was overseen and settled by a Captain Bower, amicably. He being commissioned at Ibadan. These were wild times for all twenty-four tribes fighting, not giving anything to anyone. Warring to the very last body. Not good for all, but satisfaction to the victor; there goes the spoils of war, any war. But any act of contrition affects everyone involved. Peace comes at a price and all Yoruba paid that price. The sun still shines, calm settles over all our villages. As all the Obas now respect one another. Cherishing their friendship and unity once again. After the prolonged four hundred years, of trying to vanquish one another.

But as the twenty-four Obas, put their mark, stamp, authority to the cessation. A Ahon Ina was there, to satisfy all the people. Hopefully, never to be in this situation ever again. So the faithful prayed. The orishas along with the ancient one listened, learnt and acted upon their wishes to keep the peace now, for as long as they could.

As they all stood high, aloft on the roof of the world that was Mambilla Plateau, they watched, listened, as all their people sang, were joyous and happy as they started to get everything ready for all their festivals, carnivals and village celebrations. Collecting all the fruit, soursop, pawpaw, avocado, limes, African pear, mangoes and melons. Harvesting their vegetables and spices, along the way. Yams, plantains, semolina, with pumpkin and jute leaves, African efirin and shuwaka, and so many others. Ensuring they had a supply of ogogoro, made from their favoured raffia palm tree. There was also a large selection of the local sea delicacies—crayfish, crab, tilapia, Nigerian killi, vundu and Niger tetra. On the day, they would go out hunting with the good fortune of the orishas behind them. They would seek, find and catch an abundant supply of flying termites, caterpillars, giant silkworm, dragonflies, crickets and the palm weevil. Then either roasting, drying, in white hot sand. Boiled, or sun-dried, skewered, fried or roasted over an open fire. Then either eaten alone, or with freshly made foni yan. At the same time, they clear away all the local threatening spiders. The likes of the Hercules baboon spider, cello spider, dark option spider, six-eyed sand spider, along with the jumping spiders. Last but not least, they spit roast freshly killed meat.

All to make these days very special to the villagers. To show they are still as loyal as ever to the goddesses. Which in all cases, was their very own powerful, enchanted orishas, no one else's. That the believers hold very close and very dear. The Orisha, anyone one of them, is like a mother. This is what they want, feel, need, to guide and instruct, so this is what they give to their peoples. Each and every one of the significant and outstanding orishas are in their own right a lewa woman. Breath-taking, outstanding, all motivated by the love, adoration of their followers. The orishas give it in abundance, their all; in whatever way they decree, to receive it.

So far above the plateau, the excitement is rife. The daughters, the Orisas, the one very special mother, are all getting ready for the celebrations soon to come. They each attend to each other's needs. The collective of orishas known as Awon Iya Orisha, have their own therapies and make-up regime. It all incorporates black soap and the very special properties of the coconut and its restorative milk. Once they have deemed each other to be at their finest, they journey to their very own mortals. They love to mix, learn, show themselves to all the believers and followers. Hoping to make a difference to and, in their lives. Their way of living, their survival, health, their welfare. This is another reason to be able to look stunning, to be at their best. To be the deity that is required, The orisha, the mother that does brighten the rather dull, humdrum life of the villagers. Attempting to cast some soul and colour into the bleak life of the downtrodden female. To sow a seed of charm and enchantment to anyone that willingly clasps at it. To bring the sun into their lives, leaving it there, for as long as possible.

Once the orisha has left there is a hive of activity up on the plateau. A Ahon Ina regales himself in his best trousers and buba. Then he dons his finest Oba regalia, his softest beaded slippers and his gold conical beaded crown upon his shiny bald head. Then he takes up his outstanding, impressive solid gold fly whisk crafted by the goddess herself.

Then finally, the most important part, the entrance of all the deities, their daughters; along with Rayowa and Abgani. All look supremely regal, resplendent and eye-catchingly beautiful. All wear the same colour abayas, purple and gold. But the purples are all of different hues, tints and tones as they flashed off in the sunlight. Their hair all different styles, all locked into place. The hypnotic roll, cute curly, curly braided, single flat twist, frizz free, Bantu knot, milkmaid braid, the big high bun. No geles this time. The orishas wanted to be noticed, acknowledged in all their finery. Their long, thick, lavish auburn hair, in particular. Their feet dazzle in the glinting, sparkling shoes they wore. Complimenting the abayas, as did the purses they all had clutched in their hands. The feathers adoring the orishas hair, were all given freely from adult sunbirds, rock firefinches and the gorgeous, glamorous yellow casqued hornbill.

"Can I say you all look fabulous, out of this world. Looking like deities from some African myth. Truly breath-taking, captivating, extraordinary. It is truly my privilege, to know you all. To be in such glittering, powerful, majestic company."

166

"You too, look every inch the creator. Masterful, a father to us all."

They blow kisses in his direction, then as one united woman, they tell the ancient one:

"This is all for you. To show our regard, in that you let us lead. Be at the forefront of this belief, doctrine, of the orisha, us your wives. Where no one else lets us lead, apart from you, wise one.

"My glorious orishas, This is your time, believe me. These are your carnivals, festivals. The people love and adore their orishas above all else. So it is you that must lead. I merely follow in your wake. So all of you enjoy, long may it be this way. I am here to do your bidding, to grant you knowledge, skill, craft, the art of leadership; to help turn you into the goddesses you all want to be. This is the way of Mambilla Plateau. You must never let it change. Here before stands, the mighty, all powerful AWON IYA ORISHA. It is not a single goddess. But the name for the collective, the full circle, of all ten orishas. their combined authority, accomplishment, to do good. Help their followers, prosper at every stage of their life."

"We enhance their life already, wise one. How can we do more?"

"To be able to improve their circumstances, come what may. Make sure they do not have to hide their support, or following for you. Make sure they can openly display their belief in you in whichever way they find easiest. Whichever way suits the individual. For you to enthral them, to interact with them, to assist at every possible moment. That is their enjoyment, their life, their vital responsibility. To the mortals down below, their voices and songs that enchant you, the orishas, every single day. Especially the good fortune of the women and their female offspring and their prolonged happiness, a right. A gift to every deity on the plateau.

Now everyone was ready, excited and filled with absolute joy. The creator stood amongst his bevy of beauties, overwhelmed by their magnificence. Those that gave the stars their life, their light, their brilliance. His mighty, delectable goddesses—they shone! Their combined radiance was all consuming, all powerful. They were above, on the high exalted reaches of the Mambilla Plateau.

CHAPTER NINETEEN

The next instant they were on terra firma. Below amongst their followers, their people of faith, understanding. A cloud of purple seemed to descend upon them all, to enshroud everyone close enough to the haze. It was no magic, no trick of the eye nor an illusion created by the ancient one.

But merely the fact that all the orishas were draped, in the same beguiling, alluring colour, which was purple. People stopped, stared, pointed, shouted praises, the children enchanted by the luminous exuberance of the orishas. Running up to them, taking the deities by the hand and walking at the side of their own personal favoured goddess. Then the whole village forming a tight circle, enclosing them, so they could be adored, revered. Applause. Quiet, a hush, not a sound. Then! Just at first it was a lone voice, then two, then fifty, then three hundred, the whole village was swept along in the adoration of this amazing spectacle. That of the purple haze produced by the Mother Goddess, having descended from Mambilla Plateau. So that they could relish the festivities with their followers. The more the orishas tried to calm the village and its people, the louder the idolisation swept through the gathered throng. Louder, LOuder, LOUder, LOUDer, as they all as one chanted the names of their very own orishas. Then, to the extreme joy and admiration of their daughters, their names were chanted and praised alongside their mothers' as well in thanks and adulation. Expressing their own happiness, in a very fruitful harvest. A good year, alongside a very peaceful one. Their crops a salute to the closeness of the goddesses and the mortals that tended, tilled the fields. How they looked out for one another. Not disrespecting, but praising, thanking, giving joy, in what they received, bestowed upon one another. So at last, the circle of delight, the orishas The Mother Goddess, took the front of the procession. The crowds, music, bands, the food, followed them all along the village paths to the great open square. Here they celebrated Ovia Osese, in Ogoriland, Kogi state. The attractive Ogori women transforming from puberty, adolescence, into adult womanhood. The festival symbolising the rites of passage for all the young maidens of the right age, to enable them to pass over the threshold from child into the state of puberty. To gain the respect from this point forward as a fully-fledged adult. A strong overpowering sense of womanhood, that would enrich their lives.

The deities dance with and alongside the virgins, the daughters enjoying and joining in the celebrations as well, all one big merry throng. It was savoured by the whole village. Followed by song and poetry from the vibrant, strong-willed young women. All hoping to be accepted as members of the adult world, all wanting to find their own place within this village, or another. Wanting their independence, as a rite of passage. Not having to fight for it, or work towards it. Wanting it given to them, on reaching adulthood.

Victoria along with her sister Nafisa stand to give short speeches on how women are strong, intelligent and resourceful people. How they can improve the life of the village, the state, their country. This was followed by a similar recitation, from the deity, Odudua. Infusing their lives and how the Plateau, apart from the creator, is the centre point for feminism. Wholly dominated by women, freely, such a pure environment with no animosity, just love. Freedom of every kind is rife. Even our daughters, they are all included in this rite of passage. No one is turned away. Our power lays in being open with one another. So regardless of what anyone else has to say, women do deserve to have a say in how everything is run and is accomplished. Fresh ideas lead to a new existence. Not for women, but for everyone. This is not a control concept, but freedom for all.

As Ala, Yemeyah and Odudua sit down, the applause, recognition starts loud, very audible. Stays loud, long. First the young women shout their approval, consent, to the injustice that occurs. Cheering, chanting; then all the other women, mothers, grandmothers, sisters and aunts and the youngest female child to the eldest teenage girl, shout their agreement— solidarity with the sisterhood. Stamping their feet, they sing the names Ala, Yemeyah and Odudua, then using all the other deities too. Eventually all the orishas and their beloved daughters rise as a single purple cloud, to the acclaim of all their joyous, happy women.

Then as the cheering subsides, the orishas, their daughters mingle with all the very attentive crowds. As the music starts up again, the eating commences. The maidens that have crossed the boundary into adulthood now have the chance to express themselves by standing before the village and reading their poetry, prose and stories, so that everyone can see they are learned, respectful and able to communicate. Having read their poems each young maiden in turn, seek the company of Victoria and Nafisa, to speak to engage, to know how it feels to be part of the adult society.

Everyone was happy and content. The wise one sat quietly eating, as he listens happily to the whispered words and all the other communications between the orishas and all the women. The love, equality, feeling it, sensing it; at one with his people, followers, believers. Rayowa left all her exalted company to find a little peace, comfort and partial solitude. She found the food very much to her liking.

Then she found he who should not be left alone, enjoying his own company.

"Oh wise one, can I sit at your side?"

"Of course Rayowa. Join me please."

"You should be out there, with your goddesses, A Ahon Ina."

"No not me. It is time for women to come together. To find themselves, they know the way forward. Now they have to do it together, as the Mother Goddess. Then the mortals, must do it too. Who better to do it with, than the deities, orishas, they all love, trust adore and idolise."

"You do love them all, mighty one, alongside your daughters. Do you have a favourite?"

"I do love them all. They are my life. They need strength, determination and willpower. They must not let anyone

172

repress their free will, their need to go forward, to shine, to expose and exonerate womanhood in all its glory and at its most powerful and exuberant. But then I try to help them, in my own way, to further their cause, make them more approachable. This is why we come and mix, socialize. So no one is too shy to talk, to walk, to enjoy our company whenever they can, whenever they want or desire."

Rayowa leans across, kissing the creator hard and long with extreme passion, ardently in fact. Soft then harsh, lingering in purposeful contact.

"You are a powerful attraction. I have known that since our first contact. I hope to see more of you, now that you have brought our daughter so much closer to me."

"Rayowa, both you and our daughter will see more of me, her sisters, as well as her aunts, OK? Go now, enjoy your time with them all. I will get myself more food, with some of the ogogoro."

"You stay there, I will get you food, as well as the palm wine before I go back to my circle of sisters."

What actually happened was that six of the village maidens paid attendance to the wise one. With them came the food, with the ogogoro. Then as he enjoyed the food and the pungent palm wine, the maidens read their poetry, danced and sang for the ennobled one and for him alone. Then when they had finished their recitals, their folk dance, eloquent songs of the forest that kept them safe, he stood and laughed with such joy and merriment at their works and words and dance. He applauded loud, long and with such conviction and love. They thanked him, would not stop thanking him. He kissed each one on the cheek. He strolled over with them, to where the orishas sat with their daughters. He introduced the six, individually, to his wives and daughters. Whereupon the six maidens went to the centre of the circle, to recite their poetry, give readings and perform their dance, and give their recitals, for the joy of being in front of those from most high.

It was a lovely time, immersed in the village. Especially appreciated by Odudua. The altar was shrouded in black, adorned with big, bold lighted black candles, all in her honour. The Orisha of Fertility, Devotion and Love. Humbled by their exactness, humility and devotion to her, she rose up from out of the crowd, walked forward and blessed the altar, casting her name upon its cloth as well as the candles that stood aloft, burning. But not as a flickering light. It was a bold, sacred purple flame. The wax not burning, the candles not shrinking. But the sweetest essence filled everyone's nostrils—frankincense, myrrh, lime. All the maidens rushed forward to touch her in the hope of being blessed by her unearthly radiance, aura and magic.

"Come touch me, one and all. Do not fear me. I am your goddess. I am only here for you, my very own people, my believers."

She stood there, so that everyone that wanted to touch her, kiss her, touch her dress, or just to bathe in her radiance, was able to do so. Then when everyone was satisfied, the chant began:

"Odudua, ODudua, ODUdua, ODUDua."

Lit up the night. Along with the gangan, ikoko, calabash, the ivory horn, took over the silence. Completely absorbed, by the ministrations of one lone deity, to her favoured, trusting people. The respect, adoration, idolization, from both sides; completely sealed forever and a day. Having delivered ourselves there, we decided it was time to move on to our next destination. To the next festival on our calendar. With cries and tears of joy, the ancient one, all his wives, and his daughters, form a circle; then they are gone.

They are away to the Leboku Yam festival. A tradition of the Yakurr people, in the Crossover State. A tradition long held by the Yakurr. Hoping in turn to receive the attention and favour of their favourite goddess, especially at this time of year. The yam festival collected the finest, then offered to her as a sacrifice, for another good harvest the following year. On their arrival, they were overwhelmed, by the peoples of Leboku. The women, all the women begin mobbing Njoku, wanting to touch her, feel her grace and favour coursing through their veins.

The young orisha, was the centre of their attention. She loved it, absorbed all with her admirers, followers and believers among her peoples. She sat speaking to all those that would listen to her, those that asked questions, she answered. She gave of herself freely. The women that gathered around her were of all ages the mothers bringing their infants to be enlightened, their newborn to be blessed by this special deity. Young girls wanted to hear her words of wisdom. The men celebrated the goddess, Njoku, by eating the yam, by drinking its potent brew made from last year's plump, juicy yams. Everyone happy and joyous, the music loud, so very loud, filling the air with song and dance. The heavy vibration of the Nigerian drum makes the spirit writhe and contort, the body move, to its very infectious beat. Love instilled, all the daughters along with their mothers dancing, with their beautiful people; long into the hot, delectable, sultry night. The villagers are joyful, without a care for in the world. A very memorable night, once again. They silently disappear, in readiness for the next celebration and festival.

CHAPTER TWENTY

They all travel with his voice resounding in their ears, for a moment. Then a stillness in the void as they travel together in an unreal silence. Then as single entity the all imposing purple Awon Iya Orisha enter the sanctuary of the Oldkun Deity festival. In this blithesome, congenial reception in Ilajes, in Ondo state—for the orishas Oshun, Oya and their associated influences

She is the Goddess of Diviniation, of faith, belief, hope and redemption. The ordination of strength in self, supporting those that need your strength. Then there is Oya, the Warrior Orisha of the wind. The primeval Mother of Chaos, the Creator of, Changer of, Distributor of Fortune. Her power associated, aligned in complete harmony with lightning, tornadoes, earthquakes and other storms that beset her, when she is troubled. Her lines cross death, cemeteries. Her motherly strength inspires us to embrace change, to learn from it. Using her machete or Sword of Truth, she cuts through stagnation, untruth, lies and hidden desires. Clearing the way for new growth, ideas, plans to go forward and advance. She is the Wild Woman, the force of change. Also the Queen of the

Marketplace. A shrewd businesswoman, not to be beaten. She is adept with horses. As the wind she is the first breath and the last. The one who carries the spirits of the dead home from whence they came. To her and all the other Mother Orisas, Oya is tall, stately, fierce and ferocious in protecting her own in battle. She is the Goddess of Creative Power and Action. She tells us:

"Every breath we take is the ultimate gift of Oya, the Warrior. She will reclaim it at any time, that suits her."

A Ahon Ina changes into a steed of war. Its colours are black, silver and flaming red. Black is the colour of death. Silver is her control over of lightning. Red is to show her power over the earth. To be able to disrupt its peace, at any time she likes, with the strength of earthquakes. She sat atop her gallant steed, her long, thick hair, to her back. Her Sword of Truth she thrusts high into the air. Thus she spoke warmly to her multitudes:

"I am here, to warmly accept your offering of praise, homage, warmth and adoration to me. I offer you all my protection, sanctity and eternal motherly love. I respect you all and the way you lead your lives. I give protection to your mothers, sisters, daughters, grandmothers, aunts and spinsters. Love and cherish them all, they are the sacred ones. They who bind our lives together. Forget them at your peril. My sisters and I bequeath our warmth. We look forward to seeing you all, when we take you to our bosom, after your final breath."

The cheering was fanatical as the crowd adored, mobbed and idolised all the women once again clammered to shower her and all her sisters and their daughters with gifts, tokens of their loyalty, devotion and self-belief. The circle of sisterhood, always held in high regard, especially when they turn up as a stately physical presence. No one taking precedence or seniority. They, the orishas all bound as one, only happy to serve each other as handmaiden or sister. Taking a backward step so that everyone can attend Oya or Oshun at their own festival of thanksgiving. Their every whim heeded without disdain or hate. She was happy to talk to all that wanted her undivided attention, to question her knowledge and prowess on all things sacred, domestic, carnal and personal.

A Ahon Ina sat in the shade of an old jini jini tree, sipping his ogogoro as he spoke to the wise, unencumbered spirit of the woodland. They talked of their lives, which stretch back many aeons. Back to when only the two of them lived side by side. As they spoke, a woman came to sit at his side.

"Are you the one they call the ancient one?"

"I am indeed. But due to our age, I think we both are."

He and the tree spirit both laugh. But the woman can only hear A Ahon Ina laugh out so loud.

"You laugh so loud, do you enjoy being alone?"

"I apologise. But the tree spirit was laughing with me, at my last few words. I do not mind young lady. I spent so much time alone, in my existence. It does not come as a discomfort to me."

"Could you tell me, how I must find a man, when my face scares even myself?"

"Biebele…"

"You know my name, how?"

"I know many things, my precious lady. I have been sat here, waiting for you, to come to me. To speak to me of this."

"Can you help me? Will you help me, oh wisest one?"

"It will be my pleasure, an absolute honour, to quell the riot within you."

"Then I am at your disposal. Please tell me what to do. How to do it."

"First take me to your home. Whilst everyone else is busy, they take no notice of us."

So hand in hand, she leads him to her hut. She takes him into the darkness where with a snap of his fingers, his aura lights her home.

"Biebele, please remove your gele, buba and iro."

She starts disrobing, along with the wise one.

"Young lady, I know you are of thirty years, as well as being a virgin, you get ridiculed, which does not help your confidence."

"You know me too well. I love Oya immensely. She was the one that told me you could cure my problem, oracle."

"Biebele I could, it is well within my powers. You could have gone to see Ala, orisha of fertility, or Odudua, the deity of love and devotion. Oshun the goddess of love and sensuality would have been more than happy to give you her wonderous touch. But you decided to approach me, therefore I will solve your problem for you. As A Ahon Ina talks to the woman he starts to get very aroused, upright and starkly erect. Biebele looks overly concerned, points as she eyes the oracle.

"Ancient one, what is that pointing at me, so proud and fierce?"

"That, my gorgeous woman, is my manhood. It is you that has put me into this condition. You have made me want you so much. Feel him please, it is this weapon that will take your virginity. Turning you into a complete, satisfied woman. Then because I sated your desire so you in turn will become desirable to other men. They will be enchanted with your charisma, then you will have no shortage of swains. She timidly touched his penis with her finger.

"No Biebele, like this. Give me your hand."

He puts her hand at the base of his staff. Running it up, keeping a tight grip all the time. She smiles.

"It feels so hot, he is so thick too."

"Yes, you make him thick, by attending him, rubbing him. His heat comes from my body. Let go just for a while."

She lets go. He kneels in front of her, up very close to her warm, tentative thighs. Putting his face towards her mound, his tongue softly caresses her small labia, the tip agitating both. He pushes up, into the tight V at the top. He licks, kissing and teasing, against this erogenous zone, her tight sensitive spot.

"Are you enjoying the interaction, between my tongue and your very sweet body?"

"Yes creator. I have never felt anything like it before. My nerves tingle a lot."

He now stands up. Again with his mouth, he engulfs her thick nipples and sucks long and hard. He makes her already thick, long nipples, plumper, juicier.

"Now would you like to eat me?"

Yes I would like to try, creator."

"Then just hold him, like I showed you, Biebele. Put me in your mouth. Then suck me, lick me, run your tongue over my ripe, glowing, bulbous dome. Just enjoy."

Kneeling in front of him, taking hold of his organ, she runs her small hand along his thickening rod. Keeping him hard, she then puts her mouth over him, deep throating him straight away. Running her tongue all over his erection, She enjoys his saltiness along with the power she has to control him.

"Would you like to experience a man deep inside you?"

"Of course I would. Will it be you?"

"Yes, Biebele it will be me. With what you have in your hand and mouth. Are you ready?"

"I think so, just be gentle with me, take your time."

"I will my darling Biebele. Just kneel on the bed, on all fours. This is called doggy, it is very popular."

Biebele kneels down on the bed. A Ahon Ina gets behind her, up very close. Rubbing his rigid, turgid weapon in between her tight buttocks, She takes the secretions from his manhood, rubbing it into her, lubricating her small, tight anus. Then softly he eases himself into her. All the way in. Staying there, locked into her curvaceous derriere, he leans forward, he cupped her full, heavy, round breasts. Stroking, caressing and rubbing. He enjoying, she just sighing, moaning. As she could feel him grow inside her.

"Now I am going to plough your most important furrow, with my erect thick blade."

"Plough me all you want, make me fertile, satisfy me please, Creator."

Slowly his urgency subsided. Slipping out of her tightest orifice, he sidles down, slipping into to her sweetest. Thrusting in with his plunderer, he splits and renders her hymen useless. She squeals and snorts, feeling his ravaging, thick throbbing plough push in deep, deeper, filling her furrow. Again he leans towards her, fingering, tweaking and squeezing her enormous, firm nipples. Wanting them to set her virginal body alight. To fill her with desires, needs she did not know she had.

"Biebele, do you feel good?"

"Yes, at last a man to satisfy me. I love the feel of you throbbing within me. Your fingers manipulating my nipples. I adore all that you do to me. I just want to feel your hot white seed course through me. I want you to make me cum, to have your love fill me. I feel your hairy body against my silky skin. It is not something, I will forget in a hurry."

As she spoke, he was rocking and pushing deep, long strokes into her craving, wanton, very forgiving body. He is slamming against her erogenous zone, that little G spot. Then she grunted, started bucking, moving until they are together as one. The faster he went, it drove her wilder, more frantic. His shaft rammed against her honeypot as she pushed backwards, against him. Now wet and sticky she climaxes. Erratic, she loses all her self-control. He extolling his expertise, continuing to ravish her. Riding her delectable, warm body. So carnal was his desire, he felt his bulbous, red dome swell; then gush with such force, heat and electricity. Their juice from their carnal effort, given back her self-confidence, self-esteem. Just loving his organ erupting, exploding in her.

As he knelt there, overflowing on her thighs, loins and waist, her firm buttocks. All her body is satisfied by this one immortal. She smiles, laughs out loud, tears of joy, extreme happiness.

"I need to kiss you. Can I, before you go anywhere else?"

"Biebele you can kiss me wherever you like, for as long as you like. First, let us enjoy each other. You have such a lovely body, such an amazing big bosom and tremendous, lively nipples."

"I know, but you are the first to enjoy all of them properly."

His semi-rigid, spent muscle, slips out of the bountiful, brown eyed beauty before him. She kneels in front of him kissing him hard and long with such passion, desirously. Tongues in each other's mouth. Her eyes all a sparkle, glistening. Those brown beauties are like hot embers. Her whole body burns, along with them. She felt so much different to how she felt before, she had even set her eyes upon him. He bowed his head, sucking her swollen, red-hot nipples. They really were juicy, like big overripe morello cherries.

"Wise one, have I changed, since I have been here with you?"

"No, you are the warm, sensational, provocative young lady I met beneath the jini jini tree. Why, do you feel different?"

"Yes I do. But I do not know what has changed. I will go and get my mirror."

She leans across to her bureau, picking up her small mirror. Looking into it, she sees a face she does not recognise.

"This is not my face. Whose is this face?"

"This is your face. The one that was hiding beneath the mask, you had before. Do you not like your face?"

"Yes, it is a beautiful face. I am just not used to these looks."

"But Biebele, my gorgeous woman. You are stunning. I can assure you this is your face. I have given you, the looks you deserve, that were hidden from you, in the first place."

Again she faces him on her bed. She takes hold of his face, kissing him so preciously, softly and warmly. She bites his lip, stroking his still semi-hard manhood. Making him erect once again, she licks and sucks, kissing his emboldened flesh.

"I thank you almighty, for your concern and your constant love for me. You are my deity, along with Oya."

Biebele looks at her face in her tiny mirror, not believing that the face she sees has been hers all along. Regarding it as a miracle but not daring to to out alone in case someone accused her of making a pact with some degraded incarnate. Smiling at her new self, putting on her most colourful abaya. She notices her oracle waiting patiently by the entrance to her home. She walks out of her house, without noticing it had transformed into a four-room house, with a garden. But she would at some time or other. So she took the arm of A Ahon Ina, as they took each other back to the festival. Everyone just looked at the couple, not one of them recognizing Biebele, the young woman, that was attached to his arm; she was not going to let it go, at any cost. Except the orishas and his daughters, who all came over to welcome them both to the celebrations. Once they had accepted her, then everyone else wanted to know her, who she was. Especially the single men of the village, they queued up to court her. She smiled so warmly, but waved them away, preferring to stay with her immediate friends, the goddesses and their daughters, and of course the creator. Who helped her to become the woman she is now.

Oya takes Biebele to one side:

"Biebele, you look utterly amazing, delectable, elegant and provocative. Does this make you happy, joyful?"

"My most honoured orisha, I am happy beyond this world. The most noble creator has changed my life, more than he really knows. He has given me more than one divine gift."

Biebele rubs her thighs together remembering the fullness of the oracle's gift, of his hot seed. Then smiling as she kisses the charmed and vibrant Oya squarely on the lips. Then, arm in arm, they rejoin the celebrations that were there to rejoice Oya and Egungun—the collective ancestral spirit. Now Biebele keeps the most elite company, for the rest of the festivities. Before they leave the village of Ilajes, the wise one found Biebele in her home.

"Biebele, I wanted to see you, before I left. Do you feel any better, than when I first met you?"

"I feel more than better, more than good, I feel privileged, with the honour you have bestowed upon me. My home seems so much bigger than I remember. Everyone speaks to me now. Then men look at me twice, after wishing me a good morning.

"That is good. Now we have this shared bond. Any time you need me, just call my name."

"Which name should I use?"

"Any name you wish, I will know it is you, calling me."

"Then I will call you My Love. For that is what you mean to me."

With that she kissed him on the lips, refusing to move them until he returned her kiss. She took his hand, putting it on her breast.

"These await your attention, on your return, my most auspicious creator."

He smiled. As the long kiss was met with all his passion, affection and force. He bowed before her, then joined the throng of goddesses and his daughters, Rayowa; as they journeyed to the Odun Agbon Osara Festival. In praise of the simple fruit of the palm, the coconut.

The celebrations were loved and enjoyed by all. For the ancient one, the orishas, all their daughters to turn up unannounced, for them to join in was an added privilege for everyone. They were all treated like queens of the village, the ancient one as a very respected Oba, in all his finery.

The celebrations went on all through the day, then long into the night. It was an epic show of respect to all the holy ones. Then once again in the early hours of the following morning, came the purple haze of spirit transformation; A Ahon Ina takes them all to the outskirts of Onwasato. Aha Njoku leads the way with her daughter, into the vibrant, loud, overstated Onwasato Yam Festival. Aha Njoku, the Goddess worshiped by the Ibo of Nigeria. She is responsible for the yams. A central ingredient in the Ibo diet. Just as important, she looks after, tends to and loves the women who care for them. The procession stops in the village square, they all stand silent, standing a ritual, a mark of respect physically for the yam, which is held in high regard for its nutritional value. But more as a sign of thanks to the orisha of the harvest and yam, Aha Njoku. To give her praise for an excellent crop of yams this season. He tells everyone that it is taboo, forbidden to touch, steal hide any yam, or part of the yam, until it has been blessed by him. When he has eaten of the soup and foofoo, to show that everything has been blessed, then and only then can the yam be enjoyed by all the village.

So after cutting the goat's throat, letting the blood flow over the orishas' sacred symbol, the carcass is handed over, to be cooked into a soup. Yams are pounded in front of the priest, to create the magic that is the creamy foofoo. All that is left of the skinned carcass is the bones. The soup is now ready, poured into a dish along with the foofoo. The priest smiles as he eats. Then he declares:

"Great gracious Njoku welcome. We all bow before your magnificence. The yams have been blessed, as you have decreed. Sit with us, enjoy your harvest; as we enjoy your select company.

"Food for all, the yam has been blessed. Yet another great harvest. Praise be to Aha Njoku."

"Priest, people of Onwasato, I welcome your blessing, as I do every season. I mark my respect for my women, who care for my yams. You are in my care eternally. My love is yours. Anything else you need, just ask me, I will provide."

The cheers resounding, the music and rhythm alive with the drum sanza, ekwe, ogene, they all join in with the dance. The village is full of joy, gaiety, laughter and love for the sacred ones overflowed. In turn that love returned, again in more than equal measure, without any inhibitions. Sensationally everyone is comfortable, in each other's company. The priest offers Njoku, the highest placed orisha of his beliefs and his followers, his bowl of the creamy sanctified soup and foofoo. The deity supping the congenial mix from his sacred mouthpiece so everyone could see the two of them use the same bowl and same mouthpiece.

"Highness, Sacred Goddess, receive from me our offering to you. This is your food that sustains us through the year. We offer this in the hope our harvest will be as strong as it was this year."

"I accept your offering, as always. It is very special to me, as are the women that tend to the yams throughout the year. I promise you that your harvest will be even better, on the next season."

As she is standing, she holds the bowl up high so everyone can see. Then she slowly drinks the soup. Before eating the sweet red foofoo, with her delicate fingers. She enjoys both thoroughly. As she drank and ate, the calabash, udu, dundun, and igbin played. Slowly, softly and low, they pick up the pitch as she drank. Upped the volume, as she ate the foofoo. The sound stretches, echoing, still resounding as a natural sound. The drums were stilled only as the orisha Njoku finished her meal. Then it was time for everyone else to enjoy the meal, the company, the entertainment. The whole congregation of the village having enjoyed been enthralled, by the great festivities. Everyone intermingled with the purple cloud; they were the mild-mannered goddesses along with their beautiful, attractive, very receptive daughters.

As A Ahon Ina kept well out of the way, so all his orishas and their daughters could bask in the limelight, which they all deserved. He ate his food in quiet anonymity, so as not interfere in their glory and the aura of these very strong, powerful women. He is more than happy to make his deities stronger, more vibrant, more challenging, more willing to lead and be at the front, to help all their people.

So one last festival to attend, which will bring all the remaining orishas to the forefront, all of which makes it so much more enjoyable. But let us enjoy Njoku, while we have the chance. The sun shines strong, the sky is a deep resilient blue, the yams are sweet, juicy and very good to eat. The whole village sings its folk songs, of war, peace, heroes and of days gone by. Sadly none of them are about females, heroines, women of power and influence. The women of the village, mothers, sisters and daughters who have helped enrich the community, the wealth of the village. Have nothing to aspire to they have no way of knowing their worth, because no one takes the time to tell them of their importance, of their input into their society. They just go about their duties unnoticed and under-appreciated, keeping the family together, peace, the art of living and staying alive. Which women are more than capable of. In fact they show men up.

That is why men would rather they stayed at home; unseen, unheard, forgotten; controlled and kept in the dark. But here within circle of purple, the woman is more important than anything else. Now is the time to let them feast, to eat the atmosphere and dictate the way of the world.

But enjoying the soft beat of the drums, the soft undertones of all the other instruments in the jungle orchestration. The proximity of so many voices joining in with the tribal songs, or just idly gossiping with one another. The chatter of the birds in the canopy, the clicking of the crickets close by. All making this a very magical moment. The joy of the warm vibrant atmosphere was not lost on a single person present. All enveloping the forest, as all the villagers present, got lost in its enchantment. The day was long, but full of so much fun, love and wishing that it did not have to end. But again time has beaten them. As night turns to day, the circle is complete, they all feel the surge of the ancient tone. His latent power, magic and mystic abilities come to life, filling all of them. As in a wink of an eye they are completely refreshed, revitalised and full of energy, joyful once again to be amongst their people, followers, believers and friends, their blood. They all smile, surrounded by light, beautiful bird song. All the birds know the orishas. All the bigger birds sit, talking to the wise one, they all talk to each other. After all this is the sacred forest. Where everyone, everything is a friend, compatriot. Even the old silverback, bows to the revered deities; along with his cousin, the alpha chimpanzee. All stop to greet, enchanted with each other's grace, manners and charm towards each other. The trees, flowers and the whole forest environment sings out with its perfume, scent, unheard voices, charms and chirps. This attracts the attention of Aja, the forest orisha.

We have come to the sacred Osogbo Forest, for the Osun festival. Now Osun, shares the forest with all her sisters. Osun the orisha of love and sensuality. She is a tall, tanned and erotic young woman, with all her sensuality shrouded around her. She is the patroness of rivers and the bloodstream. She wears seven brass bracelets and she has a mirror at her belt to admire herself. She is accompanied by the primping peacock and the cricket. Carrying river water in her pot. Powerful spells are worked, through the Lady of Love and Sensuality. She sustains rivers, is the goddess of all the arts, especially dance. Beauty belongs to Oshun and represents the human ability to create beauty for its own sake. She is the knitter of civilization, since great cities, for the most part, have been founded for the most part along rivers. In order to supply water for all of its populations.

There is Yemayah, another great goddess of Nigeria, the orisha of the Ocean and Motherhood. She has been venerated for centuries, as protectoress. She is also the avatar of Mama Wata, the Mother of Waters. Even as she slept, she created new springs, which gushed forth each time she turned over. The first time she walked on earth, fountains sprang up, that later turned to rivers, wherever she rested her feet. The cowrie shells represent her wealth. They are also the medium through which her priestesses can hear the voice of the universe. The shells were one of her gifts to her people. She is the deity of the fishes, the power of the ocean and she wears the insignia of alternating crystal and blue beads. She has a strong nurturing nature, life giving and yet a furiously destructive nature. She is considered the Great Witch, the ultimate manifestation of female power. Her name originates from Yey Omo Eja, meaning 'Mother whose children are fish'.

The deity Ala is the Earth and Fertility orisha and goddess of the underworld. She is the mother of all things. In the beginning she gives birth. At the end, she welcomes the dead back to her womb. Then within the circle Aja, the forest goddess. She instructs her followers in the use of medical herbs found in the African forests. Aje is also the goddess of Wealth. Ochumare was also there, orisha of the Rainbow. Amirini is an early goddess, who has always been with us. But not quite as ancient as A Ahon Ina. The sacred orishas now arrived. Oshun takes the lead into the sacred Osgobo forest, to unify the culture and art, identity of the Yoruba, who have survived for four hundred years or more. Oso-Igbo goddess of the Osun, with magical powers, which inspired all her people, who were frightened, filled with dread and the desire to die when facing their enemies on the battlefield. She was the one that stood at their side, then marched into battle to face their foe with them. She was the shield-maiden they all prayed for, to be with them as they fought. But at the ceremony, carnival, festival, all were her friends, people, followers, smitten with love, adoration, idolizing Oshun, her sisters and all their daughters had for all the Yoruba, all their people, was dynamic. They sat as one; the unflinching, unbroken circle. Their people approached were welcomed, no one was turned away. The circle grew in size, then another circle formed around the first, then another. As the villagers, followers and believers all paid their obeyance, asked their questions, kissed, touched, were inspired by their own personal deities. They moved from the inner circle to an outer one, to make way for another follower. Such was the deliberation, the calm, the peace, the solitude, the serenity, the love, the joy permeated. The overwhelming experience of the visitation continued.

The music started. First the ivory horn made its low, heavy sound, the heartbeat of the sacred forest. Then it was joined by the calabash and udu, the blood flow, the life force that made it grow strong. The energy within the forest slowly formed an electrical pulse, a force all of its own making. The sanza forming an incomparable duet with the ivory horn. Then not wanting to be left out at any point, the gbedu and batu joined the musical network and inspiring the nervous system of this incredulous ancient and sacred forest. The gangan, the talking drum, and his friend ikoko stands without ceremony as they talk to one another, looking for freeloaders that would contaminate this wild woodland. The ekwe and igbin gallivant, having a nose for trouble, wanting to protect the mild gentle air that flows all around these ancient trees. Then the balafon, igbin, for listening; long hard for the interlopers, the destroyers, the pillagers that want to rape, disrupt and destroy this hallowed place. The pigs of our society. The Asikereje, the hands with whom, it protects itself. From any harm, from any outsider. Finally the legs, the ilu ipesi, dundun used to run forward, impeding the way of the violent transgressor who tries to lay claim, to any part of the Osogbo Forest; or any part of this wonderous land of Nigeria.

Now the whole body of the sacred forest is awakened, alerted and able to dance to its music.

The ancient one, the orishas, his wife Rayowa, all their daughters, the people of Oso-Igbo; those that are not, all unified by the music. The need to dance, to sing along with the forest. To be in step with its needs. To create a bond with this ancient gateway so that it knows that it can feel we need its purpose in our paltry existence. Instead of plundering its wealth, the serene magnificent resource of the Osogbo Forest should be savoured by all. Not devoured and consumed by a few ignoble transgressors who are so selfish they only think of their own personal welfare. We should all, Igbo, Yoruba, Hausa and Ibo be attuned to its welfare and desires. So that our caring reflects well in the eyes and heart of the orisha Aja. All that she and her enlightened sisters bring to their lives and mortality. This sinuous celebration of life, love, eternal joy and happiness is infectious. Everyone can feel the music, the rhythm, the beat within them. The very heartbeat is injected into every soul present. One great big throbbing, thudding, pulsing sound, bringing the forest to life. All the trees move to undulations. The very soul, its inner depths of the Osogbo, comes into being, having a life all of its own at the behest of the wise one. It encloses around them, bringing every living thing to a closeness that befits the energy, power, electricity and the pulse of the forest. That provides a life, security, redemption for all that enter the sacred forest, paying tribute to its sanctity. Its love, spirit and well-being are cared for by all that are of the living core of Osogbo.

The sun shines bright, sharing its light with the big full moon. Everyone can see life at its best, shared by every life force that frequents the safety of the Osogbo.

Oshun, her sisters and all their daughters pay homage, chanting loud and clear

We grant you life in all its forms,
our love committed to your very
survival.
Our first breath we give you life.
our last breath we reclaim it.
But to our bosom,
you will always return.

All those gathered sing along with the goddesses. Filling their lungs with every word. Letting every word linger within the forest, to enchant its well-being, to show their love, adoration. To give it extra intent, meaning, wanting everyone to understand, once it had been translated, so that every life form could understand, in its own way, in its own form. That pleasure, joy and desire had been granted by all, for all. So come enjoy the company, the food, the drink. Friends, family, whatever notion they existed in, whatever dimension they lived in, their open arms embrace one and all. At no expense to anyone. Just the love for everything, to exist side by side, for an eternity, if not longer.

The chant fills the air with static, awash with a strange show of star bursts, flashes and various types of lightning. The fragrances of the flowers, trees and shrubs are all intermingled, entwined. The older trees, the new vibrant blooming flowers. The shrubs and undergrowth, the spectacular miracle of the flora and fauna of this stunning forest, all now take a bow. Let us all be as one for this day, for this sacred muse, the enchanting Osogbo Forest.. The display, all thoroughly enjoyed by the chimps, gorillas and pygmy hippos who are awe-inspired as they watch from the trees and the pools within the forest. The wood nymphs, daughters of the tree spirits, join with us all. Liking to fireflies, lighting, filling the sky with such wondrous colourings. Thrilling us with their displays, of flights, paths of glory. Bestowing upon us their glamour, embodiment of chant and charisma. Such beautiful creatures, such grace and perfection.

The feast is here for everyone to enjoy. The cousins come from the trees, to enjoy the harvest of the orishas. The pygmy hippos feed with all due reverence to all living things, living and surviving side by side. Happiness spreads through the forest. A young woman sat on the lap of the wise one; hugging him close, kissing both his cheeks, wishing him good luck, as she moved on. All his daughters come to find him:

"Papa?"

"Father!"

"Dad," they then all tell him together, as they always seem to do, in an attempt to get their wishes and their mother's wishes across to him, so he understands, and does not misconstrue their intent, he thinks to himself.

"We want you with us. All our mothers, your dear loving wives, want you, in their exalted company now. Please come, sit with us. Join our circle, so we can all be one."

"My darlings, my beautiful daughters, thank you so much. I will come with you, sit, eat and embrace each and every one of you. I am proud, so proud to be in your company and your mothers, of course. To be part of your eternal circle."

All the daughters crowd round him, escorting him to their pride of place. Sat in the centre all the orishas—spectacular, regal and magnificent, in their purple and gold. As if by magic, a pathway clears for the daughters, as they take their father to the sisterhood. He stands humble before all in front of him.

"I give myself to you. I am here because you all believe in the sanctity of your beliefs. Keep this true, then we will always be here for you."

He bows to his people, then to the sisterhood, his loyal and very understanding, gifted and intelligent daughters. He sits, as his eldest daughter Victoria gives him food from the banquet.

"Father, can Nafisa and I spend some time down here to study, to be mortal? Just for a short while, until I am, or Nafisa is required to return to Mambilla Plateau, for whatever reason."

"I will talk to your mothers. I will also have to check on those two tricksters, Ikaki and Eshu. They are beginning to become more than a nuisance down here. But if it is at all possible, you can spend some of your time here, amongst our loving and generous people."

"Thank you Papa. We will be very careful, we promise."

"I know. But we will ensure your safety too. Our eyes will be on you at all times. To secure your infantile mortality. It is not something we would dare want to lose, at any cost."

"We know we are so very precious…"

"You both, Victoria and Nafisa, are more than precious. But let us eat, with your mothers and aunts. Discuss it with them. So you enjoy now, your dreams will be fulfilled, we promise."

Oshun, Yemayah, Ala Aje, had all spoken to our wise, forthright gathering. Now everyone wanted to mingle with all the other beings within the forest. This did not happen very often. All was entrusted to the sacred forest itself. To keep hidden its secrets from prying eyes. This magical moment when all bodies, metaphysical, corporeal, physical and spiritual, were allowed to mingle within the boundaries of the Osogbo Forest, were known to happen but very rarely. All the kindred spirits made the most of the time they spent in each other's company. Before going back to their own dimensions or existence, hopefully before the portal called them. Otherwise it meant staying in this existence until the portal re-opened. So if at any time you see something you cannot explain, this may well be the reason. Remember they are friendly, they are lost. So please do not berate them just help them as best as you can, and do not reveal their whereabouts. Those that see it. Only to the spirits of the wise old trees, the wood nymphs, flowers and wild animals, when no one else was close by. Or if they ever visited the sacred forest, again during their lifetime.

It was a tie to the universe, to nature, to all things natural, to all existing life forces. A heavy burden, but one endured by all recipients.

The time of Oshun and her sisters seemed like a blissful eternity. A splendour without end, where the mortals were always enthralled. But once the sisterhood, including all their daughters, blithely entered the confines of the sanctuary that was the sacred forest of Osogbo. Time was motionless and meaningless within the divine, green oasis. So that the orishas themselves could stop for a moment and be just who they wanted to be, without changing the courses of any mortal's life. Time stood still, so that everything could be absorbed, by all that had made the special journey. The eyes, the heart, would never reveal the disclosures. The cost of revealing all or any of the revelations was an imperfect soul that would not, could not at any cost, be replaced. Once the charm was broken by the Sisterhood, time regained its momentum. Everything moved along at its normal pace. Everyone stopped and stared skyward, to watch A Ahon Ina, take the sisterhood, back to the plateau. He then let Rayowa and their daughter, Agbani, say all their fond farewells and goodbyes. The Sisterhood tells them both, they either come and visit, "Alone or together!"

"Rayowa, Abgani, if you want our services, or feel the need to come and visit us, just call out Awon Iya Orisha, or call us by name. then we will happily come and attend to your needs. Our love is yours always."

Abgani, a little unsure of herself, but with the sweetest of smiles, asks:

"Mothers so regal and rare. Could I perhaps travel with Victoria and Nafisa, on their journeys?"

"Yes of course. But why not ask them yourself, dear child," Yemayah replies.

"Honoured sacred sisters, Victoria, Nafisa, could I your lowly sister Abgani, join you on your travels, when they start?"

"Abgani, you are not our lowly sister. You are as much a sacred sister as any one of us here. Yes, we would love your company. Especially as you know your way around, already. Our father will take the three of us together when we are ready, when the time is right."

"I look forward to that day, my divine sisters."

The three of them hugged, then a last final hug of all; a group hug with Rayowa and Abgani in the middle. To confirm the bond that they were all definitely sisters, so that nothing would sever that holy kinship, that eternal feeling of togetherness. A Ahon Ina shape-shifted himself, Rayowa and Abgani into the most colourful, auspicious, outstanding streptopelia. They dived from the plateau, dropping low. Then by using the warm currents of warm air, the thermals, they regained their height. Flying low over all the sisterhood as an adieu, they flew, following the wise one to the Crossriver State. They soared into the heavens, until they could see the Calabari river. Swooping and diving, finally they land just outside the village. Changing back into their normal form, Abgani looked deep into his eyes, such adorable eyes they were too.

"Father, do not forget us. Please remember me, when you bring my sisters here to learn. I must go to my friends, whom I have not seen, for such a long time."

"Remember where you live now, Abagni."

199

"I will Papa. With my mother."

"I will come and collect you soon, my dearest, cherished daughter."

They hugged and kissed each other very affectionately, then she left.

"My very own wise one, will you stay for tea?"

"Yes Rayowa, I will thank you for your kind offer."

They both went to her house. She led him to her bedroom. The softness of her bed, catching his fall. She on top of him, rubbing her enflamed crotch hard against his jutting masculinity. She removes his trousers, taking his aroused manhood, stroking him softly, slowly. Then violently. She watches the crown swell and redden, his shaft elongate. Putting him uncensored, into her open mouth. Sucking, licking, enjoying his boldness, his manliness, heat; his pumping blue vein, now in between her eager lips. Then releasing the knot of her abaya, letting it fall away from her onto the bed. She is now naked as she removed his buba and trousers completely. Rising like a spire from a cathedral, the lure was too much for Rayowa.

She scrambled back to her bed, holding his pole in excitement. Her quim was instantly wet, as her juices were flowing with such intensity. She rubbed both her breasts hard, against his mounting erection. Then sitting over him, her anxiety almost quelled, she massaged his overgrown, bulbous dome against her sticky snatch. She writhed against his eagerness. Then she force feeds his jutting prowess past the pink velvet of her quim. She rose above him, slowly, silently, slipping down his entire length until she had all of him snug, tight and throbbing in between her joyous, welcoming loins.

"Lord, I will call you lord, because you are extra special to me. I will sit here, realising your charm, hardness and thickness, along with all the magic you have granted me. Just in case I never see you again, in my lifetime."

"My beautiful, sensuous Rayowa, you will see me again. When I come to collect Abgani. Then when I return her back to you."

"In that case, I want you now anyway. So we may both be satisfied, in each other's arms."

As they spoke, he reached up, caressing her large, fine breasts. He teased her hot stumpy nipples into life. Running his fingers around and over her large, unrefined aureoles. She came down to him; his mouth swooped engorging her enormous nipples, one at a time. suckling, nibbling, pulling them from between his teeth. Now licking feeling the coarseness of her large, darkened, round aureoles. Also, being able to kiss, languish over her mighty heaving bosom. Feeling himself swell, even more within her. She could feel him as well; sighing with pure delight. The heat, power, surge of electricity was sweeping through her whole body. Slowly she started to bounce, up and down, on his live, uncontrollable, thudding pole. Loving the sensitivity of his opulent, radiant, glowing crown as it stroked against her swollen love lips as it grated against her vaginal walls. the G spot gave in, all her erogenous zones tingled as if enclosed by some erotic fever.

She was now bouncing on him, as hard and as fast as she could. Her loins quivered with a feverish spasm, Rayowa could not help herself as she lost her self-control and orgasmed. The oracle smiled at her radiance as he teased and tormented her with his prowess. He knew not to get carried away with his carnal pleasures. He made his play as he pushed up to her, he smiled at the enchantress before him, then blew her a kiss. Made himself thicker, harder. She moaned, snorted, grunted, transfixed by so many climaxes, orgasms. She cried in sheer joy, unable to stop herself, wanting more of him. His organ so hot, her thighs were unable to contain him, so much physical, liquid love. She could not slip off him, he was so big, filling her. His manhood struck her clitoris, making it swell redden. Her cream covering them both. Her carnal kiss, hot on his lips. Their tongues struck one another. He finally succumbed to their torrent of love embraces. An uncontrollable eruption of his milk, white and salty, bleaching both their fatigued bodies in the success of their lovemaking. Endorsing the happiness, they exerted towards each other. She still on top, ecstatic beyond measure. Not wanting him to fade straight away. Enjoying, luxuriating in the satisfaction, warmth and stickiness over her entire body. Too exhausted to move, they just lay there enhanced by each other, not wanting to be anywhere else at this precise moment in time.

Perfection, equilibrium, he holding her hot, generous hips. Reaching up he kisses her curvaceous, sweaty, tantalizing, glistening breasts. He draws her enlarged nipples into his waiting mouth, sucking long, hard and deep, He enjoys having her there, tasting her for even longer. His swelling begins to fade as she glides off his now semi-rigid organ.

"Rayowa, let us go together and wash each other, my sweetness."

"My lusty lord, it will be my honour to bathe with and wash you."

Off they go to the washroom, to freshen up before getting redressed, just as Abgani returns.

"Come Mama, Papa, the food is ready. Have you made some time for each other, held each other perhaps, before Dad goes away again, for a short while?"

"Yes, we got very close, we talked amongst other things. Your papa goes tomorrow, to find Eshu and Ikiki. So make the most of him, today my child."

The three of them eat together, enjoying the small private meal.

"Rayowa, Abgani, I will be back, as soon as I have found the two tricksters, where they are, what they are up to?"

"I understand wise one. Will you visit me, before your return to the plateau?"

"I will make special detour, just to make sure I do."

"Papa, when I am with my sisters, will you make sure that we are all safe and secure?"

"Of course. Along with the Circle of the Sisterhood, all our daughters, we do not want to lose any of you while you learn, explore and achieve, together."

Abgani hugged her father. They all laughed loud and clear. There was no hiding their feelings or affection for one another. The wise one told them again:

"My daughters, along with the serenity, might and knowledge of the circle, are far too precious, to fracture, in any way at all."

Having enjoyed the food, they all went for a walk in the village; all hand in hand, in the cool of the evening. The sunset was spectacular as it waned, as Helios went down. Giving way to the splendour of reds, golds, ambers and bronzes along the vast horizon. The ball of fire, glinted to the very end.

CHAPTER TWENTY-ONE

Just as the peace of the day was settled, a rush of feet, noise and pandemonium upset the evening. A small band of unkempt, scruffy, rueful young men, vociferous and unruly, uncaring and selfish, entered the small village. Eshu led the way, intolerant of anyone getting in his way. His followers with their machetes, handguns and small calibre rifles deal harshly with any transgressors. Eshu cannot show his intolerance and loathing to his followers quickly enough. He rouses the whole village getting his band of caitiffs to get everyone out of their dwellings as quickly as they can. Once all of the buildings have been declared empty, Eshu gives the command to torch the village. There everyone stands in shock as the village burns to the ground. For the single minor infringement of accidently walking into Eshu, the female child was shot in situ. In this way the village was held to account for the child's mistake of encroaching on Eshu's space. The population butchered, it is now a ghost town. With two of his henchmen holding strong within, guarding the exposed, freely accessible oil line. Truly a thug in the making. Not a word was spoken, everyone knew their place and acted accordingly.

Ikiki with his legion is further north, in central Nigeria. Extremists, fanatics everyone, Jihad or to struggle was not on Ikiki's mind. Just a brutal passage through any settlement of village that dared to delay or restrain him in any way. He wanted his own caliphate no matter what the cost to anyone else. He just had to find a deserted plain somewhere out of the sight of the government. He wanted complete male dominancy under the umbrella of Islam. So if anything did go wrong he could accuse or blame that religion of its misogynistic tendencies. To suffocate freedom in all its forms, to suffocate the very will from the people. To quash idealism, any female freedom, expression of individuality, chance of work, to smother their imagination. But with these tyrants the chance will never be. To toil and never see the light of day, would be the only pleasure with wasters such as these.

A Ahon Ina slowly wakes early. Leaving the warm bed of Rayowa, he decides to go south. Starting there, then going north, looking for the two tricksters. Leaping high into the sky, he traverses the plains, savannahs, forests, farms and grasslands. A closer look at the mineral-rich Niger Delta. Yet he has a very uneasy feeling. So he alludes detection as he changes into part of the oil line. Gradually he works his way down, coming to the fire-damaged homesteads along with the scattered dead bodies. He moves stealthily, listening to the loose talk of his avid followers and devotees.

"Eshu is a strong leader, he will find our fortune for us."

"Yes, then we can find a settlement, create our own caliphate."

"Then slowly transform this country, into our own."

So this is Eshu's work. So the south and the Niger Delta will be out of bounds, the ancient one thought. Quick as a flash, faster than any mortal eye could envisage or detect, he is gone. A quickening, looking about him, at all times. Questing up to Lagos, central Nigeria. Again he feels it is right for Ikiki, who hides, building up his following. Nothing untoward as yet. But Ikiki is leading towards something big. At present the only safe area, for his three daughters, is up in the very north of the country. A Muslim stronghold, but nonetheless friendly. So there is the starting point for his three eldest daughters. Now he wends his way back to Calibri. He soars as the largest black kite ever seen by the villagers.

Rayowa, Abgani cheer, laugh and wave, telling all the others:

"That is our wise one. Do not be afraid. He has come to visit us all, before taking Abgani to the massive heights of Mabilla Plateau. So she can be with her sisters. So welcome Abgani's papa, to our village."

So everyone waves, cheers or stands agog, allowing the kite room to descend and land. Then, before them all, he slowly changes, back into his more recognisable form of the wise one. The whole gathering enjoys the spectacle he has just performed for them, his beloved people. Helping them believe that they are special and with his help, they will always be that way. He bowed before his large, enthralled and excited audience. Shaking their hands, he holds them close as his dearest friends. Hugging those that wanted to hug him, he returns the kisses of those who kiss him. Picked up the young children, that were given to him, those that came to his open arms freely, casting his blessing, his love, his warmth, to them all. They gathered around him, beseeching him to return to them again soon.

"I will see you all again my beloved people. Do not fear. You are in my heart, now I know that I am in yours too."

He walked away, with Rayowa and Abgani on either side of him. Led by both women to their house, they have their meal together.

"Dad, when we will go to the plateau, to pick up your other two daughters, my two sisters?"

"My beautiful, clever Abgani. We will go first thing in the morning. So you can get a good night's sleep. Your mother can have a man in her bed, to keep her warm."

"Wise one, you do me a great privilege by coming to my bed."

"Papa, then I will see everyone tomorrow!"

"Abgani, you will touch your beloved sisters and aunts, very soon. Rayowa? It will be a pleasure to sleep with you as well."

So Abgani rushes off to her bed, so full of excitement at the thought of seeing and talking to all her sisters on the morrow. Then actually exploring and being taught, along with two other young ladies. So much better than having to do it all alone. So to sleep; the master of recovery, rest and relaxation.

Rayowa kisses A Ahon Ina so forcefully, he feels very inclined to return the kiss with just as much vehemence which he does. Pushing his hand up under her very loose-fitting top, He loves the feel of her full, round, boisterous breasts within the grasp of his fingers. Also twirling those fine, thick nipples; drawing them out gently, squeezing. Withdrawing his lips from hers, he neglects any finesse. He curtly removes her iro, buba and gele. Watching her thick, lush auburn tresses of hair fall across her shoulders. The thick juicy nipples are on open display and really excite him. He puts his arms around her back, supporting her as he gorges on her big, fat, plump cherries. Taking each in turn he sucks and licks, masticating, teasing with his infuriating tongue, lips and teeth. In turn he tastes, licks and caresses her impressive breasts, loving every inch of her warm flesh. He traces his tongue around, her large, round aureoles that are coarse, uneven and splendid. Then her hands got busy too, deep inside his loose-fitting trousers, toying and pleasuring with his aroused, ample, pulsating muscle. She loves the transfer of body heat and control, from him into her hands. Feeling him expand due to her manipulations, she removes his shirt as he steps out of his trousers. He lays on his back. Rayowa lies on top of him, facing his erect, taunting manhood. She encloses the bulbous, shiny crown within her sweet lips, sucking on him straight away. He is only too happy to eat Rayowa's tight honeypot. Teasing, lapping and licking, he tastes her sticky sweetness. Feeling his hardness, so firm, round, rotund she longs for it to be inside her hungry, wanton body.

"Rayowa, would you like me now, my sensuous woman?"

"Yes, creator. I want you now. I want you in between my hot, ready thighs."

She rises from his coarsely haired groin. Squeezing hard against, against his pulsing blue vein. Her mound lubricated, her labia swollen, she pounces on her very active creator, astride him in a flash. Writhing with such glee as she slips down his entire length, She luxuriates at his ability to fill her completely. Both are very comfortable with each other. Their carnal desires are alert and profound, the hunger needs feeding, appetite quelling until it is completely sated. Rayowa and her wise one, fulfilled, slowly fall asleep in each other's arms. Content, sticky and very happy and pleasured.

Abgani is in their bedroom very early.

"Mama, Papa? Breakfast is ready. Come both of you."

They both rise, not shy of each other or their daughter. Getting dressed, they all share the meal with no rush. Every morsel is enjoyed, all share a long, tight, very affectionate hug. Squeezing, they share kisses.

"Rayowa, I am not sure when I will bring Abgani back. But return she will, to her glorious mother."

CHAPTER TWENTY-TWO

"So my dearest daughter Abgani, you tell me how would you like to travel to the plateau?"

"Which is the quickest way to get there, Dad?"

"If I transfer us instantly."

"Papa, let us do it…"

Then before she has time to finish what she wanted to say, there they were, high above the savannahs, on Mambilla. Not alone but with all her sisters and aunts around her. Taken aback by all her aunts and sisters as they take hold of her, they led her to their charming leisure area. There there was comfort beyond compare.

"So my charming, dearest daughter, just so that we do not lose you, I am going to bless you; just as I have done with all my other daughters. See for yourself."

All the other daughters are either seated, or in the arms of their stunning mothers. Abgani is shown where to look by Victoria Ngozi. She smiles as they all very willingly show her their feet. She can see the word NGOZI embossed within the creases, at the back of their delicate, tiny toes.

"Papa, surely that will hurt. I will not be able to walk for days. What will you brand me with?"

Before he could answer for himself, all the Orishas, daughters, of the circle, the true Mother Goddess replied:

"Our sweet love, it is blessed with his and our eternal love. There is no pain, no torture. Just a kiss, along with the touch of his hand, that is all it takes our dearest daughter, our loving sister."

"Papa then touch me with your love, everyone's love, make me one of you. Give me your eternal countenance. I will be yours now and forever. Please do not forget me, never lose me and love me for an eternity."

"I promise you all that and so much more. Also, to commit to you all, if it should ever happen. I will never give up the search to find you, redeem you, bring you home safely here to Mambilla Plateau, to the joy of us all."

Abgani sat in amongst her sisters, removing her shoes. Her father knelt before her. He kisses each little digit on her foot. Gently he places each fingertip into the little crevices at the back of her toes. With an intake of breath, he could feel an instant kinship with his newest daughter. She felt a new force within her, but not one she could explain to herself. It could only be the presence of her father, of whom she was so proud. She checks her toes. There it was! "NGOZI", in its place, on her body.

"Abgani, do you, did you feel or sense, a sensation, a change at all?"

"Yes my Papa. I can feel you and the sisterhood within me. Making me feel safe. My toes tingle, I feel so very special;

protected by some unseen force. I feel an internal connection. If I look at you, I can see through your eyes."

"Was it as painful as you thought it might be?"

"My dearest papa, there was no pain, no discomfort. Just your love and essence flowing through me."

"Then when we have eaten, rested and arranged everything, we will start your education. So just enjoy everything we have here. Your sisters will help you, I am sure."

He goes to rest, for a short while; not noticed by anyone as he leaves the women to eat, chat and decide what the daughters need to take with them.

Yemeyah disrobes at the foot of his bed, gently climbing into bed beside him. Holding him close as his arms encircle her, he draws her tight, close to his body. They sleep undisturbed, until they are both completely rested. The allure of his hot, hairy torso, so close to the orisha, awakens her passion, her wild desire to mate yet again. With all her uncontrollable urges, that have been contained but consuming her, all this time. He is naked, nestled into her soft, nubile and wanton flesh. His hand gently, tenderly cups her bosom. She loves the physical touch. She feels his hardness grow beside her. He rubs her mighty nipples as she parts her legs, his staff rests in between and against her soft warm buttocks. The goddess squeezes herself against him. Luxuriating in his erection, the turgid, heated power, she wants so much more from him this very minute.

Sneaking beneath the covers, holding him preciously, she sucks his whole jutting member; his body heat transfers to her eager lips, tongue and mouth. Enjoying his gentle throb as she slips down his raging pole, she knows he is stiffening so much more from her very close ministrations, from her expertise and very close eager practices. Her tongue laps at the very apex of his swollen glossy dome. He gets a little tacky, small globules of him being teased out by the very happy and obliging Yemeyah. She tastes his so very fresh saltiness, knowing he is just about ready for her.

She resurfaces, only to find him wide awake with a big broad smile on his face.

"My supreme Yemeyah, that was absolutely divine, delectable."

"I am so glad I pleased you, learned one."

She knelt over this amorous immortal, wanting him this very second. So breathing in, she lowers herself over his erect, turgid, rigid shaft. Absorbing him inch by inch, her thighs ripple with the intense joy and power, she feels coupled with him once again. Now he is completely inserted, she talks to him in her soft, loving tones.

"Ancient one, Ahon, with our beloved daughter, Victoria, when you make her mortal, then leave her down on earth—you will not leave her and our delightful daughters, alone will you?

"Yemeyah, I do not plan on leaving them. I will put them into school together, far away from the clutches of the tricksters. Let them find their feet. I shall be very close by, at all times, never fear."

"How long will you leave them, down there?"

"As long as they are enjoying the learning process. I shall proceed with their quality of progress. Unless at any time they are required back here, at the plateau."

"That should not be necessary or a problem. Is there any way you can let Oshun and myself see their progress in any form, while it happens?"

"Of course you will be able to, enjoy their life, their ups and downs along with them. I will see to it. All you will have to do, is think of them. Then you will be able to see where they are, as well as what they are doing. Try it now."

Yemeyah thinks of Victoria, then plain as day she can hear her daughter as well as see her.

"She is with Abgani and Nafisa, talking to all the other sisters about their upcoming adventure."

"Does that make you happy, my beautiful orisha?"

"That makes me feel so much better. I will tell all my sisters, they will so thrilled too."

Feeling his organ expand, throb and lengthen all at the same time, she is excited. She leans forward, allowing him to suck her hot, heaving, hard nipples. He sucks so hard as he hoists his thighs up, penetrating his goddess deep, deeper, as she pushes down on his erect tower of flesh. Feeling his petulant blue vein gyrate against her eager flesh. Her nipples grow as he sucks continually, drawing the plump tasty morsels out in between his warm lips. She humps her thighs, now wet and juicy, splattered with her thick cream. Driven wild with desire, trying her hardest, she wills him to ejaculate. Her firm, svelte body bangs his. That still tight venus mound is sopping and sticky as it grinds and twists, losing what little self-control he had left. He grasps her thighs and rolls from side to side. He pulls her down onto his enflamed organ. Giving way to his own excitement, he erupts! His lava flows. The orisha loves his compliment to her, with so much love spilling from him, mixing with hers. It splatters both their thighs, loins, pubic hair, groin.

They reach a tender carnal finality as she sits on high. She glories in his hot, sticky affection and passion. She is not willing to dismount. He is only too happy to have his goddess there, enthroned on him. Such a regal moment, not shared with anyone at all.

Having freshened up, Yemeyah leaves to talk to her sisters as well as spend time with Victoria before she leaves for her studies.

Just as Ahon opens his door to leave, Oshun takes his arm, turns him around and walks him back into his chambers.

"Can I call you Ahon?"

"Oshun of course you can. You can call me whatever you like, whatever makes you feel comfortable."

"Ahon, how long are Nafisa, Victoria and Abgani going to be away?"

"Until they feel that they have reached their full potential."

"Is there any way we as mothers can watch them from here?"

"Of course. I have just told Yemeyah that all of you can. Just by thinking of them. You will be able to see them, hear them, as though you were with them at that moment. Try it. Think of Nafisa now."

"I can hear her talking to Victoria and Abgani, about the school they are going to, in the north. I can see them, discussing it, with all their other sisters. That is amazing, wise one. Now will they be left to their own devices?"

"No, I will be staying down there with them, to ensure their safety and mortality."

"That makes me feel very good."

Turning to him, kissing him dead centre, right on his lips.

"Oshun you have the sweetest, softest lips."

"I bet you tell all your wives that, wise one. I believe you though, because I am one of your wives."

The ancient one smiled, his eyes glinting at her.

"I was going to tell you, I will be staying down there, with their knowledge. For their own safety. Also I will not get in their way of their personal enjoyment, they are young and need to spread their wings while they have the chance. I will be their personal bodyguard and attendant."

"So ancient one, after this short break, we will not see you for a while."

"Only if you need me. But you my glorious powerful orishas, will be here on Mambilla Plateau. I know of your fidelity, charisma, knowledge and charm. I could not be leaving it in safer, more capable hands than yours, the Mother Goddess."

While she had been listening, her hands had been busy. They had slipped to his groin, softly rubbing and massaging. Getting him into a state of flux. Releasing the bow of her abaya she revealed her perfect, sensual, erotic torso. He knelt before her, running his finger across her soft, fine, downy hair atop her perfectly formed quim. Licking his lips, he ran his impatient oral organ along her tight, crisp crease. Softly, gently he teases her labia, applying a little pressure to make them swell and open. First using the tip of his tongue, then using the flat of his tongue, he traced it up and down her snatch. Slowly she relaxed her tight little love lips. Seeing them swell, partly revealing her delicate vulva. He lavishes his whole oral muscle on her prime groin. Inserting it into her oval cavity, he pushed down and in as far as possible. Feeling her body heat, his face tight up against her pelvic girdle, enjoying her golden, irrepressible honey pot—sweet, sticky and plentiful. A joy to eat her, just like a hummingbird he fluttered over its flower. Feeling himself harden and energize, he rises to face Oshun as her hand dips into his loose-fitting trousers.

"My very excited wise one. That is how I want you, hard, strong, impatient and throbbing. Ready for me." They walk over to his bed, where he lays on his back. Oshun climbs over him, parting her long legs, she lets A Ahon Ina pierce her tight, moist pussy. She loves the grating of his excited muscle against her pristine pink velvet. Feeling him swell, he gets more turgid and robust, as he penetrates ever deeper. She smiles, now having all of him settled in her, loving every inch he has to offer. She wants him badly, so much so, she was willing to do all the work. She was jostling his joystick, squeezing his rotund, erect manhood with her powerful thighs.

Forcing herself against him, she wants to agitate, arouse and feel him thicken, throb. Feeling him lunge up, along her loins, he fills her to capacity. He drives her desire with his willingness to make her climax, first. She is overwhelmed with one hell of an orgasm. With her sweet cream already flowing, it now turns into a torrent from her twitching loins. Already a muskiness, a male scent has arisen from him. Which seems to make her even more sensual, desirous. She rides him hard, with a severe intent. Every time she goes down, she can feel him pulse. Just luxuriating in all her deliberations, exertions.

She smiles, her will not quite strong enough to overpower his. Both pairs of thighs are covered in her thick, sticky love juice. Then he takes hold of her thighs, then her curvaceous hips, pulling her down on him and holding her there. As he blasts his physical love into her hot, needy body his white, sticky, salty milk overflows instantly. He lays there with his regal, wonderful orisha, perched high above upon him, enjoying all that he gave her.

"My stunning goddess, will that satisfy you, until my return?"

"Yes, my darling wise one. I will not forget this ever."

"The orishas will be the power up here, as they have always been. You only have to intervene, at any time at all. The power is within you to make the right decision. But if you need to talk to me, just speak, as though I were next to you. I will hear you, at all times."

"Do you know where you will take them, for the start of their new adventure?"

"Yes, I will be taking them far up into the north. Away from the tricksters, they are split at the moment. One in the south, the other fairly central."

"That is good. You will make sure all of our precious daughters are safe and secure at all times?"

"I will, I promise Oshun. All is within my power. Come, let us go and see everyone else, see how far they have got with getting ready."

"Come on wise one. We will miss you. We will look forward to seeing you all, on your eventual return. I will definitely be looking forward to your return, I know."

Arm in arm, they go out into the large lounging area. They all smiles as Aje, Njoku, Oya, Ala, Amirini and Ochumare join them, talking of his upcoming escapade. He was the centre of attention, enjoying it as well. They asked him what it was like at the very beginning. So he gave them the story, from the start, right up to this very moment now. Amirini and Oba talked about their beginnings and origins too, so everyone felt at ease in this very august company. All shyness was gone as the deities gathered on an equal footing. All are proud and happy to be up here, on Mambilla.

"What I will do is travel by air. We will all travel as the wind. I will ask our daughters how best they would like to get to their destination. But I hope they will enjoy whatever they ask for. What do you all think?"

They replied as one, unified voice:

"As long as they are safe, secure and protected and, of course enjoy their journey."

"Then it would seem everything is in place. The mothers are all happy, the father is protecting his daughters. The orishas all look and smile down on the welfare of our divine, strong-willed individuals."

Sitting down and talking, all in agreement, all stoically accepting the long-term void that will be left in their lives by the three daughters along with the effervescent old man, A Ahon Ina. But in turn, they know without a shadow of a doubt that they will all return, better equipped to have their say up here on the plateau. He receives kisses, hugs and other platitudes from his esteemed wives. He gains his full stature and mythical size and encircles all his orishas and daughters, hugging them as one, all at the same time. As a father, husband

and protector, to show his eternal gratitude, respect and love for his complete family. As Victoria, Nafisa and Abgani come back into the room, they join in the encirclement, feeling the love and in return give their love back. The tears flowed, but soon dried.

The three daughters make ready for their great adventure. Looking forward to their imminent departure, which Nafisa, Victoria and Abgani thought would never happen; thought the day would never arrive. But here it is, just about to start. So there is no turning back. Plus they have each other to depend upon along with Abgani, who has some knowledge of how to exist, being a mortal herself. The three are overwhelmed by their sisters, mothers and aunts. All want the last kiss, touch, hug and word, the last fated eye contact. None knew how long this excursion into the unknown was going to take. A Ahon Ina kept out of the way, letting all the deities have all the contact they need for the bonding of their unbreakable, eternal ties, along with their natural love and regard for each other. So he sat patiently, in no rush. He knew time was on their side. That there was no inexplicable rush to do something. He smiled, knowing the girls were going to have the time of their lives. This would be an experience, never to be forgotten. He could see they were all in a group huddle with the three in the middle of it. He could hear his three delighted daughters shouting for him to come and join them.

"Papa, Papa! Come and complete the family. Make the circle tight, unbreakable."

"I come my beloved darlings."

He rose, Odudua, Ochumare and Oba releasing their arms, drawing him in so very close and into the very heart of the huddle. That way every single one of them could feel one another's closeness. So close they all felt a unity, closer to one being rather than many. So in the sanctity of this closeness, they closed their eyes for a split second that seemed an hour. He let them all truly feel and see each other's heart and immortal being and how much they mean to each other. Thus they left the frail mortals below, with nothing and no one to guide them along their rocky path, to live the life they wanted and not the life someone else wanted them to partake in. The continuity of the circle, was paramount. Breathing as one, surviving as one, was the same for the Orishas, as it was for their followers.

"My dearest daughters, I would like to ask you how would you like to travel to your new home?"

"How far are we going Papa?"

"Abgani, we are going to the very north as far as Zaria, Sokoto and Katsina. Your schooling will start in Zaria. I am hoping you will enjoy it there."

"Dad, do you have a school there for us?"

"Yes, the Mother Goddess Centre for Universal Learning."

"Then father, we would love to travel part of the way, as the wind and part of the way as a powerful bird, so we can view the land as we pass, high above it. If that is possible," the three daughters said as one.

"Of course it is possible. Would you, Abgani, like to see your mother on the way?"

"Of course I would, Dad."

"In that case, we will travel as the wind, as far as Calibri, so we can all see her. Then from there, we will change into the

Bateleur, finishing our journey as majestic birds. Such as you all deserve."

"That should be awe inspiring."

Victoria shouts out, "Sensational, breath-taking, Father dear!"

Nafisa laughs, unable to hide her joy. "Rayowa my mother will not know what is happening, my glorious papa."

"Come then my young ones, hold on tight to me," he says as he offers out his hands. Victoria then jumps on his back. Everyone watches as they fade into a strong breeze. Racing off Mambilla, they head along the Calibri river. The gusting wind is headstrong, wilful and determined. His lungs are full, as his brother the wind guides them to their first destination. As they hit the village, the breeze comes to a complete standstill, outside Rayowa's house.

"Mama, Mama, where are you?"

Rayowa comes rushing out. "Is that you my beautiful Abgani?"

"Yes, my glorious mother. Papa let me stop over, to say goodbye. We will call in again to see you, as soon as we can."

"Is your papa there to, with you?"

"Of course I am, Rayowa. I am here to keep them secure."

She rushed over to him and the three daughters. She holds them all very close to her, so very tight. Love binding them together. A few tears, the pain of separation. But solace, in being a member, part of the larger family group.

"Rayowa, if you need anything, you just have to call upon any of the orishas. They will be at your side, or you can be with them."

"I thank you my dear husband, I hope my faith in you will keep me well. But I know my glorious goddesses are up above, keeping me in their sights."

"All will be well. But even so, they are they there, waiting for your call, at any time."

So final kisses are given and taken, the hugs lasting longer than normal. But finally, everyone is ready to continue with their long flight. Once again all four of them change into a small flock of bateleurs. Rayowa watches silently as all four of them take flight. Soon off the ground, they oversee the stark natural beauty of West Africa and of the mighty Nigeria. His three daughters flying, they eye the country as no one else has ever seen it before. They enjoy the undercurrents and slipstreams that take them so high, they nearly lose sight of the long coast line.

But flying high they get short of breath, enjoying the luxury of the beauty and the panorama beneath them. Then suddenly they dive from this great height, swooping and chasing one another in the freedom of the air. They feel such joy, such expression and love of life and of each other. Nothing spoils the pleasure of the freedom of the air, actually being on the wing. But all too soon it was time to come down to earth. Again all four landed together. He knocked at the door of the school and the headmistress opened the door.

"Sir, are these the three daughters you spoke of?"

"They are, Madam Mbebe, wanting to learn as much as possible, with your fine teaching establishment."

"Come, come welcome, let me show you around."

"Come with us, Papa, please. Just so that you know where we are."

"Victoria, if you want me to come with you, then I am with you all."

So he goes in with his daughters, allowing them to take the lead. He enjoys the interaction between the four women. Abgani turns around to her father,

"Papa, where will you be, if we get into any sort of trouble?"

"I will be very close by to you all. Do not worry or fret. But if you are unsure, just think of me and I will be with you all, wherever you may be. Does that make you all feel better?"

"Yes Dad. We just wanted to make sure you are going to be close to us at all times."

"I will be at your very side, but you will not know that. You may not always see me or recognize me. But I will be able to see you all."

"Why will we not recognize you?"

"Nafisa, I do not want to scare away any thugs, extremists, fanatics or lunatics. I want to catch them, so they cannot harm anyone else."

The three girls face him, asking him unison:

"Do you have anyone in mind, anyone in particular?"

"Yes, two tearaways, who seem to be causing carnage all over the country. They were down in the central and southern part of the country. I plan on making sure they do not know of your whereabouts."

"Who are they?"

"Two tricksters, Eshu and Ikiki, who may know of you through their mothers."

"Are they dangerous?"

"Not at the moment. But if they ever get together, the outcome could be catastrophic or at least violent, with carnage everywhere."

"Are you keeping a check on them?"

"Yes, I plan on finding them, tracking them. Once all my daughters have settled in, I will be off on my rounds. To find out exactly where they are."

"You be very careful Papa. Keep safe, so you can keep us, all our mothers, your wives, our aunts, sisters and Mambilla Plateau secure from anyone trying to destroy it."

"That has been my concern all along, my precious young women."

"In that case, we will be very happy here, with Miss Mbebe."

His three darling daughters crowd around him. They all love him to bits, saying their goodbyes, knowing he will back soon, to keep an ever-watchful eye over them.

"You all study hard, make us all proud of your efforts."

While his three daughters were introduced to other female students, A Ahon Ina was off to the Niger Delta. He paid a visit to the town of Onitsha, where he shape-shifted from bushes to rocks to part of a pipeline. Working his way through the small township to finally finding him, hiding away in a tent, far outside the boundaries of Onitsha. Eshu the non-conformist, administering his form of radicalisation with his fanatics at his beck and call. His pressure techniques, of either joining him in his fight, or going to an early grave. Still resolutely offering his extremism, or running from his thuggery. Knowing where he is, at this moment, means his three glorious darlings are safe.

Now he shoots off to central Nigeria, to the village of Borgu, which is a real rural area. Flying around as a black kite, he finally finds Ikiki. His tyranny is rampant. soaring, swooping, watching, listening, as he addresses his sidekicks.

"For as long as I can remember, I have never had to work. I see what other people have, then just take it from them, breaking them in the process. I do not ask. I take it, with or without force. So if you are going to be sentimental, because this is your village, then I shall not require you. If I do not require you, then you are dead my friends. Do you understand me?"

"Yes, Ikiki we fully understand."

"People fear me, I do not fear people. I do not live to be popular. I survive by the way that I live."

"We understand Ikiki."

"You need to, otherwise your lives are of no use to me. Do as you are told, if you relish your life. Or, you will not have a life to hold precious."

"We are yours. You lead we follow. You command, we obey."

They hold the village as their own. All the occupants are evicted and sent on their way. The tyrant, his thugs and cohorts dream of bigger things. It would seem that no one is willing to stop these aggressors, not even if it is their own people, encroaching upon their diminutive lives. They are hardliners trying to disrupt the smooth running of their country. They attempt and succeed in exhorting their own countrymen. The mineral wealth was being taken by the powerful, the hierarchy of the military, ministers of parliament, state governors, petty tyrants and despots, everyone in fact. All of them deserted the man on the street, leaving normal people with no protection, no job, no income and no future. Even the heredity royal families fleeced their own subjects. So no money filtered down to the people that needed it most.

But somebody's father most dear goes back to Zaria to ensure he keeps focussed on his family. Somebody less focused on the greed and sniping of the mortals, here on this planet. Corruption is rife, at everyone's fingertips. Dictators and despots keep the country down and backward. Poverty, sickness and suffering lines the streets. Perhaps wealth is a drug that only the impoverished can only dream of affording? But A Ahon Ina does not interfere. Only if he is asked to. As yet no one has asked him for his help. So until then, he can only look on in disgust as the poor are treated worse than the rabid dogs on the streets. He resumes his place as the Akoko tree, outside the institute, where his three gorgeous daughters are being taught. There is no conflict, no hardship—just the sheer joy of knowledge, to help improve their understanding of their followers. As the three daughters were taught, their learning abilities grow sharp, precise and very impressive.

The rival guerilla groups were gaining more momentum. Ikiki is more than happy with what he had, what he controlled and who he controlled. But Eshu, wanting to extend his hand, grips and take more, regardless of the consequences. Needing, wanting more of whatever he could lay his hands on. Knowing that with mob rule, the tendency is that everyone moves out of their way because there is no one brave enough to step out and confront the vile attitude of said mob. So Eshu can have whatever he wants, because he has the backing of his band of armed thugs. He traverses along the coast, then inland to

Eleme, encroaching upon Ogoniland, Which is rich in oil, poor in wealth. But Eshu was not interested in the villages. They were just a way to make the oil his, or at least some large part of it and to impose power, distinction upon his roughriders regardless of what it cost anyone else. Having bled the people and the land, of all its resources, wealth, cultural wisdom and custom, they all moved on to greener pastures. There they would sustain themselves at the expense of the nearest village. Life was good on the open road, taking what you want when you want, from any passing traveller or small village, farmer or shepherd. Killing anything that moved for your next meal. If nothing else was available, then they ransacked the nearest building, raid a lonely farm or even rob a passing tradesman. What did it matter? Eshu only considered himself at any given time—a great lifestyle. Larger than life, not a care in the world, no restrictions, no ties, no kinsman. The only family the brotherhood around him, which he had to keep in check. No love lost, no love gained. No pain or torment, if one of his thugs had to be sacrificed, for the sake of the brothers. The travelling done, the village reached. Let everyone sleep, as the reprisals would take place in the morning. The elders would be dismissed, the women bedded, the men forcefully taken into the brother-in-arms. The children indoctrinated into a belief that is the way of the prophet they are following. But in actual fact it is infamy, rebellion, servitude, tyranny, the false religion of Eshu. That is the creed of these despicable blinkered wastrels. An apparent life of ease, with no ties or regrets. The only bond is with a heartless crew of olid, ordure mujahids, where all avenues of escape are denied and forbidden. No life of their own. A gang of tyrants and bullies, flouting the weak government, who along with military are too soft, incumbent to actually deal with the problem.

So when morning comes the village is woken by a vicious attack on the school. The teacher is struck dead, in front of the children. The elders capitulate immediately; but they are garrotted, their bodies left where they fall. The old men and women look in defiance, they have nothing else left in their personal armoury. The young men are afraid of losing their freedom, as one attacks the thugs. But the main band hiding in the bushes fire openly on the young cadre, fatally killing all of them. The old people are allowed to go their own way, they do not cause any problem. The children still sat at their desks, not daring to move, not even sure of where to move to if they had of done. The thugs laugh aloud, slapping each other on the back as they take hold of the young maidens and drag into the huts, either to force themselves upon them, or let the young girls help them to be taken willingly. Which is probably the lesser of two evils. The older women, the ones untouched almost know without question, instinctively, that food will be on the agenda. So they start cooking, as they have no one to turn to, no one to support them.

Ikiki has heard of them, Eshu and his band of thugs. He likes what he hears, the way they operate. Suspecting Eshu in some way is the same as him, he decides he would like to meet him. So he abandons his camp for the time being. He gets his troops together, travelling along the backwoods and along hidden droves, making their way towards Eshu's encampment. Travelling warily, point men at the front, back and both sides, they engage the whole village, encircled, with no room to escape or evade, the trap, they slowly tighten their grip, until they can see all the that is happening. Eshu is caught with his trousers down, unawares. Ikiki walks in unannounced:

"I thought the thugs were a clever breed. But no, it is greed that pumps through their veins. No, no do not say a word. Let me look, pigs in a pigsty. The hogs mating with the sows, with no thought of keeping the sty safe. The smell of swill on you all, just as pigs wallow. Because they do not know any better. Who among you is Eshu?"

"That will be me," Eshu admits, as he trips over his loose trousers, unable to catch them as they slip to the floor.

"Is this how the thugs intend to take over and then rule the world?"

"Who are you to question my methodology?"

"I am Ikiki. It is I that stands over the hog in his sty, as he lays face down before me, with his breeches around his ankles. It is I Ikiki, that questions your tactics and methodology. I had heard and thought you a strong, unbending resolute force. But I find schoolboys trying to be men!"

"You are right Ikiki, you have found us out to be amateurs. Just playing at being hardliners, much to our disgrace."

"I place you below the hogs. Because they have no choice. But you, with all your vile intent and behaviour, are nothing but cowards and bullies. Thugs? I do not think so, imbeciles and eunuchs, certainly."

"Would you take us in hand, show us the way to excel at what you do so well? Use us as you see fit."

"I could use you. But we need to be out of sight, where we can train properly. We need to trek up to the other end of the country, away from all these prying eyes and ears. So we can learn to sustain ourselves, live the hard life and fend for ourselves so as to counter wayward temptations within our ranks. That way we will get respect, so others want to come and join us and our cause will summon them, of their own free will. We need to show the way. Where there is light we need to cloak in dark. Where there is love, preach and redeem hatred, loathing. Where there is freedom, we create bondage. We bring everyone to believe, we follow the teachings of the Qur'an. But in fact we follow our day, our way. The road to destruction, piety, war and chaos. The female to be kept out of our way. We want our freedom our way. The infidel locked into the earth. We, the brethren, follow the road to ruin, to genocide and to annihilation. So brothers, are you with me?"

"Yes Ikiki, we follow you, to the path of darkness, the path of dread, the eternal path of martyrdom. To our life's end. Our life is nothing without the blessing of Allah, our creator, your destroyer."

"Then follow me to our destiny. The road takes us to Mokolo, Damaturu where we learn to hate, to fight to destroy. To wreak carnage on everyone that is against us. We will be Boko Horam."

"The brotherhood, Boko Horam will infiltrate and destroy from within. We are not afraid. But you will fear us soon!"

"Eshu, get everyone ready to travel. We the barbarian will go now to the north-east, to Borno State. To the Sambisa Forest. We shall take it over. It will be our home. ALLA-HU AKBAR, ALLA-HU AKBAR. We are the soldiers of the one true god."

So those who were not quick enough get left behind as the soldiers of the one true god, march on now. Towards the prime natural Sambisa Forest. A large movement of men is under way, all under the same banner, the same will and the same determination! The same war, to rid themselves of the infidel. Devoid of any morality, only self-achievement the goal. To kill or become a martyr. The art of death was to become their way of living. It started now. Ikiki stopped his stormtroopers, there and then and addressed them:

"We do not console ourselves with the beliefs outside of ours. It is not run by religion, or other beliefs. It is to do with what we want. We will use Islam as that front. We do not avail ourselves of the preachings. We use only what we need. If we need more, or something seductive or imposing or more direct, we create it ourselves. Feed it into the mythology, folklore or legend of Muslim belief. Our existence will become a song of freedom amongst the slavery of Christendom. We will populate wherever we go. We will create an empire of our own. The women will remain unseen, locked away. Only used when they are required. We march on towards greed and carnage."

The surge forward carried on, leaving everyone in high spirits. They force their way upward to the forest that is to be their home, their settlement, their statement of intent. Their barbarism, unrivalled, set to overwhelm, enslave and indoctrinate all who come in contact with the brotherhood. The stomp of death, the rise of spite and the control and detriment of womankind is the aim of these brutes with no brain, consistently killing all those who deride their nightmare existence. The sun is dead, defunct. An abyss of despair and retribution beckons this unconstitutional mob. Carnage is the god to all who commit to this, malign hall of thraldom.

CHAPTER TWENTY-THREE

He is called the wise ancient one. He could hear the footfall, of impending doom, destruction and annihilation approaching his front door. He could no longer be the miracle tree, the tree of life, the Akoko, standing in defence of the safeguard of the Blessed. The blessed refers to his three virgin daughters, that are studying at the school. The creator's three daughters not one of them know as yet of the impending radicalisation that is heading their way, by virtue of the fact that Eshu had heard a whisper that divine intervention had made an appearance at one of the many female-only schools with three young maidens. But response to this dire interruption was to move his daughters and Mrs Mbebe to another location. To move the "The NGOZI", away from the northern states. Regaining his form from tree to human. No one able to sense the speed at which he is able to work. Exceeding the size of any imagination, nothing seeming to change physically; A Ahon Ina moves the "Mother Goddess" establishment from Zaria in the north; to Ilorin, in Western Nigeria. The creator ensures that there is no upset, in the equilibrium of things.

As Ikiki and Eshu pass through villages in the northern part of the country, they keep hearing of "The NGOZI". Everyone talks of it. But no one willing to tell the meaning of it, this religious deity. Eshu finds a holy man in the town of Sokto. Taking him out of sight, taking his right hand, he cuts the nerves that control his fingers, one by one until he finally cries out in anguish, telling Eshu,

"The NGOZI" are the daughters of the Mother Goddess and A Ahon Ina. They are studying in the village of Zaria. In the Mother Goddess Learning Centre. Three of them were together, using the facilities. Showing interests in all sorts of things. Mainly ways of helping their followers. They are beyond your reach and your provocative, inane ideals. They are pristine, chaste, pure and untouched. The likes of which you, will never see nor touch."

"Thank you old holy man, but even they will not be beyond our curse or spell."

With that, he slits his throat. But within that instant of cutting and the holy man dying he is received into the arms of his beloved orisha. She smiles as she coos, soothing his brow, and with a touch of her warm lips, his throat is restored. His home now the Mambilla Plateau.

Ikiki, Eshu and their unruly rabble march on forward to the forest of destiny, where they will hide, practice, steal, rob and ensnare anybody and anything that will help their cause, even to the point of finding corrupt military governors and statesmen who will help them to destabilise the powers that run the country. Boko Horam the guerilla, the terrorist, the fanatic, the extremist, will never buckle or give in to outside influences. So within the forest the power is asserted, welded

234

and organised. The two tricksters rise to the top of the pile. Extortion by every means possible is used to gain influence and weaponry. Seizing power where possible, killing and obliterating personal possessions to impress upon all and sundry, that there was no tolerance for the free thinker. Your pitiful life belongs to Ikiki and Eshu, they decide what you did with your meagre life. Misjudgements were dealt with a very public, humiliating decapitation.

Eshu was now a little more aware, more assertive with Ikiki second-in-command. He was off on his own mission, to discover the whereabouts of the orishas' three daughters. The trio had been named "the Blessed" because of the markings on their bodies. So far he had not been able to find a thing about any of them. Not even their names! But for his own ends and satisfaction, he continues his valiant search. In the meantime Ikiki, who lingered at the hideaway within the forest had abducted four young girls, aged five, six, eight and nine, for his own ends. Giving each of them a coat to wear, wired with explosives, he sends them each to a market square, entering the local villages, unperturbed, unknowing their cruel master's intentions. He alone has the control button at his fingertips. The four children wander aimlessly into the busy village centres. Not knowing exactly what to do, how to act. He never knew what dread they felt or what their last thought was! Not knowing when, but that eager finger of Ikiki pushing down on that red knob, signalling mayhem without provocation. The final moments of those four young lives. The torment of the villages; the upset, the carnage, the waste, the destruction. The vile oppression the tricksters had begun. The plunder, pillage, by the extreme unseen coward had begun in earnest. Amongst the chaos, the panic, they came helping themselves to whatever they required, taking it all back, along with their female captives, to Sambisa Forest in Borno.

Eshu stopped at every town along his way, bidding his henchmen and thugs to do the same, to discover the whereabouts of "the NGOZI". If anyone had seen or heard of their whereabouts. Just as he attempts to enter a female only school, one of Eshu's cohorts sees a local Imam. Rushing up to him and giving him the greeting of salaam, he then gets into conversation with him about the presence here in mortal form of the three dauhters that supposedly belong to Awon Iya Orisha. The Imam tells him of the story that three young girls all of divine virtue, study just as the other students do, somewhere in the vicinity of Ilorin. Thanking the Imam profusely, he scuttles off to see Eshu. So now the trickster has a name of a town. With his band of cutthroats , they head in that direction, in the hope of getting there, unannounced, with a chance of capture.

Ikiki is in the process of demoralising and devastating all the people in the surrounding villages. Again using suicide bombers, all at the ages between five and twelve. Who are they to know or understand what they are doing? Kidnapped, abducted, the explosives strapped to their young bodies. Then cast alone into a village, to disrupt and cause mayhem at the cost to themselves. Then they are blown apart, to extoll the virtues of a way of life that Ikiki wants to impose on everyone. To get his own way and a caliphate, he must incite this desecration, to show to all concerned that life will not be peaceful until they agree to his will, along with his dream of empyrean here on earth.

Feeling the advance of terror looming, the father of the NGOZI informs his gracious daughters they are to go to another country, to learn even more, from another culture, with another outlook. So having made way for them, he asked all three of them together the same question.

"Would you like to be split up, or stay together as you are? Where would you like to go, to further your education and studies?

All three look deep into his unfathomable blue eyes:

"You really mean this father, don't you?"

"Yes."

"Why?"

"Because it would seem you are of some interest to a couple of tricksters I know about. The further away you are, the safer you will be."

"Are they the ones to do with our aunts? From such a long time ago?"

"Yes, so it is either your freedom to learn and gain knowledge, somewhere else. Or, as your mothers have told me, I have to return you all home to the plateau. So it is your choice my darling, impressive young ladies."

They nearly always answer together without hesitation. They tell their very optimistic father:

"Papa, first of all we three want to stay together. To carry on our search for instruction so as to be able to talk, judge, make decisions of so many and varied subjects."

"Then Victoria, Abgani and Nafisa, tell me, do you want to stay together, for the duration of this adventure?"

"Papa, we do. We feel so much stronger and safer with each other's company."

"Then there is only one more detail, I need to know. Where would you like to go, to further your tuition and training?"

"Dad, we had already decided that. If ever we got the chance to go and study anywhere else in the world. It would have to be London, England."

"In that case, your wish will be granted."

"How will we get there? Will you still be looking after us?"

"I will be your private jet. Yes, I will still be safeguarding you."

"When will we be leaving?"

"Tomorrow, so I need you all to pack whatever you need in these suitcases."

"Will you come for us?"

"Yes, I will pick you up. I have registered all our details at a private aerodrome. So you will be flying to London in the morning. Does that make you happy?"

"Of course, Father dear."

They rushed to bathe him in their warmth, hugs and kisses. Each picked up a suitcase, ready to pack their belongings in.

"I do already have somewhere for you all to stay. As for what you want to study, you can decide on that when we get there, OK?"

"Dad, that was superb. We are looking forward to this immensely now."

The circle of orishas paid a visit to Calibra to see their sister Rayowa.

"Rayowa, we come to eat with you and share our food with you. We know Abgani and her two sisters are going to another country to learn so as to become fonts of knowledge, to help us move forward."

"My dearest sisters, is our dearest husband still with them, still protecting them?"

"Yes, the ancient one still stands guard over them."

"Then I can feel at ease."

"But we know a thug is trailing them, Eshu. Who is not a forgiving man but a cold, resolute fanatic. We know he and his friend Ikiki are not just wayward. Yes, resentment bubbles underneath."

"Come sisters to my home."

"No dearest Rayowa, we have come for you. You will eat with us, live with us, so you are secure. Be with us on Mambilla Plateau, until our daughters and dearest wise one, return."

"Then take me glorious resilient orisas. I am yours for as long as you will have me."

So becoming part of the circle, the appreciation flows from Rayowa into her very receptive sisters. But then she receives the warmth, and love from her fraternity, almost overwhelming her and supersedes her own thought and ideals. But on returning to the plateau, her sisters sit her at the head of the table full of food. But more important than the dazzling display of fine dining laid before her, was the display of love and contentment given to her by the orishas and all their daughters. The sense of belonging, the warmth precipitated within the sisterhood overtook her, locking her into the circle.

A sense of family which Rayowa had never really known, after being deserted by her parents at the very tender age of five. Now this overwhelming sense of having a family with so many sisters and nieces, she cried tears of sheer joy, as the orishas could feel her pain. They drew her into their circle, cried with her, easing her discomfort in an instant. Over the food, they talk about all that they have seen. Aje and Aja explain to her about Eshu and Ikiki. How the two orishas were taken by force, then the two babies being given away to other parents. Now after years of no direction, no constructive learning, they have turned out like this. Heartless, cold, insincere, wanting everything. But not willing to work for it. Just taking it, acquiring it, keeping it from everyone else. Stopping them from ever having it again. Giving out false dreams, fake ideals, disputed methodology. Using religion as a false front, as a scam to draw willing and susceptible youngsters and troublemakers to join their gang of instigators.

CHAPTER TWENTY-FOUR

Nearly every day now all the villages around the Sambisa forest of Mokolo and Damaturu, even further afield in Katsina, Sokoto, Zaria, young vulnerable, innocent girls are abducted being kidnapped. Then within hours, they are returned into various village squares, markets, mosques, temples or churches, indeed anywhere that is thriving with life and people. Where they can do most damage. They just stand there, then press the red button. As the ignited detonator is set into action, the explosion released! The young girl expired from her captivity and into the arms of Yemeyah, Oshun, Ala and Aje. Fed, looked after, cared for as if nothing had happened to their young bodies. Led to play in the company of the daughters of the circle.

The people now tire of these needless guerilla attacks led relentlessly by the Boko Horam. They are trying to lead everyone into the belief that they fight for freedom, against Western education and learning. Now they are trying to deploy their ramshackle army within the furthest state, away from the centre of government.

The soldiers of freedom are committed to their war. They struggle to enslave anyone that gets caught in their vile, personal oppressive web of hate and rancour. The elders of Mokolo tell their people, the villagers, that the Boko Horam are the animals that should be abhorred and treated like termites. That the bigger the gun, the smaller the penis. The smaller the penis, the smaller the brain. So swat them, tread them underfoot, if you get the chance. Thus the leader of the council, tells them all,

"Boko Horam, my people it means hate, shackles, captivity and death. I tell you that Boko Horam, means 'men with no balls'. Cowards, bullies, charlatans, they wallow in perfidy. They bathe in iniquity. They think they walk into battle with an arcane part of the Qur'an, in their minds. But it does not exist. They look recalcitrant, but they bleed, just like everyone else. Mephitic every single one. But we need to stand strong. Not just for ourselves, but for our children and the future of Nigeria."

The congregation clapped and cheered, knowing the elder was right. Capitulation was not an option. Knowing that as a village, they will not be able to fight or fend off 'men with no balls' by themselves, they will need help to rid the township of these parasites.

The NGOZI are up bright and early, packed and stroll outside.

"Dad we are ready."

"OK girls."

One second he stands in front of them. Then a sedan in the road; shape-shifting with all the comfort they could want.

"OK in we get. Then we are off to the hidden aerodrome, for our journey overseas."

He drives them away as far as Kainji Lake. A superb natural setting.

"Stay where you are, please. Leave your seat belts fastened."

The changeling changes into a small private jet. They take off there and then.

"Ladies, if you look out of the window, you will see all the countries below you belong to the continent of Africa. Then once we pass over, we go on past mainland Europe to the island of the United Kingdom."

He lands just outside a large London airport. Shape-shifting back into the white sedan, he takes all three of the Blessed to East London. They park outside 23 Sussex Street. There Victoria, Nafisa and Abgani will be staying. Tomorrow he will show them around And they will enjoy a day of leisure. The highlights of London await. Plaistow is not so glamorous, but a good hideaway. Where should they go to learn, what should they learn? All that will be decided by his daughters. Here they will be safe and unlikely to be followed, because no one has the means to trace the NGOZI.

Ikiki and Eshu are still locked away in West Africa. They have no clue as to where the Blessed are.

Eshu has lost the trail. Soon he will journey back to the north. He and his thugs turn on villages, simply because he has lost the scent of the NGOZI. He has no idea where he lost them, or where they gave him the slip. As he passes through the town of Ilorin, he goes to the Mother Goddess Teaching Centre. Knocking on the door, Mrs Mbebe answers, her arms held to her side. Being questioned about the three sisters, She is then taken into her office, manhandled, mistreated and abused physically and made to perform sexual acts for Eshu that disgusted her. After he had finished with her, he left her dishevelled and sickened, feeling bereft of any human decency a broken woman. Now she is locked away, alone in her office.

The thugs round up all the schoolgirls, keeping them all together as they start the march back to the forest.

Ikiki is now surprised at their new name, 'men with no balls'. Apparently they are not scaring as many people as they used to. Or not as many as they want to, or need to, to keep them suppressed with their own kind of fear and desperation. So now the plan was to start robbing and raiding banks, then they attack mosques, stealing from those within, forcefully and without guilt. But with guile and extreme provocation. And not in the least bothered by the age of the worshippers, or their sex. Just wanting the means to buy weapons of any sort, anything to enable them to enforce their means of terror, as wide as possible. They had contacts across the border, so cash was all they required to gain the larger armaments Ikiki wanted. This was to increase the scare factor so as to initiate control over villages, towns and the populous within. The pariahs that are Boko Horam that want control of the heart soul and body of each and every person, within their grasp. They want them as captives, to do their bidding. Not as devout Muslims, but as cannon fodder for someone else's war to make them wealthy and in the aftermath, someone else's concern. A religion of hatred and physically owning your believers. Having the power and persuasion to dictate what they have to do for you. All sacrilegious and profanities, too scared to rebel, the followers of Ikiki and Eshu degrade each other in an attempt to get noticed and gain recognition. Thinking that the higher you are in the band the safer you will be. Belief in his strategy and self-determination has seen Ikiki gain a large, loyal following, who will follow him anywhere and commit these grievous acts for pure pleasure. Hate is the enemy of love, joy and freedom. So Ikiki instils hatred as the bond in the Boko Horam, so that nothing actually matters, there is no value in anything, unless you own it and hoard it.

Who else would sneer at 'the men with no balls'? The old men and women would, they even threw rocks at them. They knew in their heart of hearts they had nothing to lose. Their lives were done at their age, so rebellion against these carpetbaggers was the right thing, the only thing they had left to remonstrate with.

Who else would go around stealing young innocent schoolgirls! Then systematically send them back into towns, villages, populous areas and open markets among people at prayer. Alone, unsure, insecure, nervous, no one to turn to. A so-called suicide bomber on her first and only mission, not actually understanding, why she is losing her life, fear in her wide eyes. As her finger pushes down, ending her existence; all for someone else's greed. Or else they are sold off as slaves, child brides even forced to marry in no official ceremony, the incumbents of the self-defacing mongrel Boko Horam.

Toothless, spineless men who are cowards, thugs, bullies, destitute wasters, who hide behind the skirts of schoolgirls, innocents; are 'the men with no balls'.

All these innocents dying, affected the orishas and Rayowa. Daily their fragile, unblemished bodies were arriving in such a distressed state, not knowing if they were still alive, recovering or dead. Gently the mother inside each and every one of the goddesses talked softly and quietly to them. She informs each one in turn what had happened to them, who made them do this wilful thing and why. She then told them where they were, how safe they were. If possible she showed them how their families were coping, reacting to the aftermath of their wasted life. Also various orishas, along with their darling daughters, if they were walking, paid visits to the villages that had been affected. Calming the believers, they helped them where they could. Supplying food, warmth and comfort for all those that wanted and needed it. They knelt and prayed with them, casting visions within them so that they knew that their goddesses had taken the time to come and visit them, console them.

Eshu arrived in the forest hideaway. Informing Ikiki, that he had lost the trail of the Blessed in a village called Ilorin. But he had found the school they were meant to be attending. They had debased the headmistress and had taken all the other students prisoner. So now they had a ready supply of young suicide bombers in the camp.

"Eshu, what we should do is go into the mosque in Damaturu, get these girls converted into Muslims then get them married into our flock of dedicated freedom fighters."

"That is a wonderful idea. To change their religion, in a mass conversion. Then in the same breath, a mass Islamic wedding."

"No time like the present. Get the girls all loaded, we will go now."

The drive through the forest, which was dry, dusty and hot. Along the deserted roads, ghost villages, poverty-stricken paupers and everybody else suffering from the greed and isolation of their own ineffectual government. Their situation has been brought about, by the despots, tyrants in power. They were unwilling to share any wealth, with the people, especially as they needed it the most. Finally in Damaturu they stop outside the local mosque. Ikiki jumps out of the of the lorry, going to the steps of the place of worship just as the Iman came out, to see what all the commotion was about.

"Yes young man, how can we help you?"

"We would like you to do a conversion for us."

"What type of conversion do you mean?"

"To convert some girls from Christianity to Islam."

"How many of them do you wish to convert?"

"We have ninety-eight on the back of our trucks, all ready for you."

"Are you 'the men with no balls'?"

Ikiki dislikes the term used for him and his followers, but answers him anyway:

"Yes, old man."

"It is you that are the defilers of Islam. You use it as a weapon of trepidation, perfidy and malignity. It is you and your followers that are the true paynims and kuffars. You bring shame on Allah and will spend the rest of your days in Gehenna."

"Be careful old man. We are the soldiers of Islam, of Allah. *La-Illah-Illalah*."

"Words come easy to such as you, the disbeliever, the defiler of life itself. You are the Devil's spawn. It is right you shall be martyrs. That day you will be in the arms of your father. You be will held lovingly by Satan himself."

Ikiki tires of the imam's insolence, plus it is making him look weak and ineffective in front of his soldiers. He fires at the imam's shoulder, taking him down. The imam looks up at him smiling:

"You are hijacking my religion, for your own ends. For greed, envy, hate and jealousy. Regardless of what harm you do, you bring dishonour to my mosque. I feel sorry for the innocents under your control. May Allah spare them any pain. Begone Devil's child. Lucifer will have his day with you eventually, martyr!"

"Silly stubborn, imam."

As Ikiki snaps his neck, shooting in between the eyes just to make sure.

"We have no need of conversion, or any marriage. They are spoils of war and ours to do with as we wish. So we go back to the forest, to enjoy the fruits of these virgins. Those that are too young to lose their flower, will be our suicide bombers."

CHAPTER TWENTY-FIVE

Oshun and Yemeyah softly whisper to their husband. They think of him this way, since he told them all that they were his equal and always had been since he created them. They are capable of doing exactly the same as he does. If they see an injustice, or a one-sided fight, they can intervene at any time to correct, or infer an unfairness that has been committed against any person or persons. If they feel they can correct that wrong, or multiple wrongs. Then to make it right. But do not cause an imbalance. His final words:

"The power is yours, use it wisely, as I know you will. As I know only an orisha can. The Mother Goddess is all knowing, wise, courageous and beautiful. My knowledge is yours for an infinity."

At 23 Sussex Street, the paint peels, the taps leak, the locks on the front door broken and damp rages through the whole building. There were even cracks across the ceiling. It would seem the whole structure was about to give in. The two-up, two-down terraced house, hidden away in a cul-de-sac in East London, was not a safe haven for three young women after all. Probably somewhat small and stifling for a trio of energetic sisters. Luckily, they had not settled in properly. Papa had them moved to just around the corner, to a larger house. Still in East London, 44 Alexander Street Lay down a narrow road, not far from Upton Park. It was a bus ride from their university.

The joy of mixing with all these mortals, going to theatres, cinemas, cafes, studying. The unifying of whoever you live and mix with. They bond as never before. Through late nights and early mornings they burn the candle at both ends. But first and foremost, their studies are to be accomplished and endured. Certain levels they reach and achieved. Also their father bought them a small car, enabling them to move around. He drives them wherever they wish to go. He takes them to Tower Hill, to see the Crown Jewels at the Tower of London. They visit Trafalgar Square for all the restaurants, galleries and theatres.

Arriving home late one night he was just kissing his daughters good night. When three young men began shouting and calling the three sisters such vile, inopportune names. Obviously either drunk or on drugs, perhaps a mix of both. Who could tell? They with such boldness began to approach the stationary vehicle. Then father intimating to his very worried daughters,

"Quickly quickly, get back in the cars girls."

They all jumped back in as their father drove out onto the main road back out of town, heading towards the A13. The three young men jumped into their car, giving them an instant chase. They wound down their windows, leaning right out, shouting, screaming their curses, shaking their fists, because the car would not stop for them. Once on the A13 heading towards the Queen Elizabeth II Bridge, they were right behind us. The Ancient One shot down one of the exit junctions, approaching a set of traffic lights, that were on amber. Putting his foot down he drove straight through the light, just before it changed to red.

The car with the three drugged-up hoodlums, came to skidding halt at the red light. As now the flow of traffic was against them. Luckily enough we never saw the again, nor did we want to. So Papa took it nice and gentle, going back onto the slip road to pick up the A13 once again, but now it was London bound. Returning his three daughters safely back to the number 44, "The Blessed House."

So the young ladies could go back to their home, to calm down, sleep and regain their composure.

"Victoria, Nafisa, Abgani, you all go indoors, lock the door behind you, feel safe.. I will be here in the morning, to escort you all to university, for your exams. Have a good night's sleep."

"Dad, you take care. But please keep us all safe."

"I will, my NGOZI."

He hears all the locks being secured, then resuming his shape-shifting stance. He resumes his mode as the car park outside his daughters' dwelling for the rest of the night. When the sun shines brightly, smiling down on him, his three daughters emerge, all ready for another day.

"Come my ladies, get comfortable and I shall chauffeur you all to university."

"Do you think we are ready to sit and take these exams, Father?"

"My very dear daughters, I know that all three of you have studies hard and long. Let that be your salvation. You have all the answers within you, now you just need to understand the questions. Then the result will come from your learning and understanding."

"A Ahon Ina are you there? Can you hear us?"

"Yes, you only have to whisper my name and I am with you. Wherever you may be."

"The people that were chasing our daughters, back here in Nigeria, have subjected all the other students from the school to all sorts of horrors. The younger ones were committed to being suicide bombers. The others were raped, and married off into the Boko Horam. We have reinstated their lives. Returned them to their families, who are overjoyed to see them in one piece again."

"That is superb, my glorious, majestic orishas. An amazing job, such motherly love and concern."

"Thank you so much, our dearest husband. But what do we do about the men with no balls?"

"Our daughters will complete their studies soon. With that they will all get their diplomas. I think we should all be there, to celebrate their achievements to be there for them. To be with the circle, to show this is one more major step in the process of life. Then I will get you to take our daughters home with you so that we know they are safe, secure away from any sort of harm. Loaded and instilled with all the learning, experience, charm and spirit they have gleaned. That can enhance the sisterhood, the circle, so much more now. With their exuberance, resilience and outgoing natures, they can enhance your powers and help and assist their mothers and aunts. Then

I will go with pernicious intent to see off these, what mortals call, awlad at haram,[5] who defy any religious or moral code.

"That is what we hoped you would do. We would all love to come and see the ceremony with Victoria, Abgani and Nafisa."

After a long day of testing their knowledge, skills and patience, they all come out hand in hand, laughing, joking and joyous. Then seeing their father waiting, they stand before him and all together tell him:

"Papa, it has been a good day. We were very successful. We know we should be contrite, humble and demure. But we cannot, we excelled our own expectations, so we celebrate and are happy."

He hugs and kisses all three of his daughters. His eyes glint and sparkle, full of pride. He opens the door for all three of them. Taking them to the exemplary Nigerian eatery called Nutmeg, in Dulwich, south-east London. There they whiled the night away, he and his three daughters celebrating their coming of age. They ate, enjoying the varied menu, talking and reminiscing, partaking of the palm wine, red wine and an ale or two. They discussed their goals, lives and ideas and how they should spend their time without getting bored. All under the shadowy light of a full, beautiful hunter's moon.

They all giggled, then laughed aloud in unison when their father told them:

"I have spoken to the orishas, the sisterhood, the full circle. They all want to come and see you. They all want to be impressed by their daughters and nieces. So they are all

---

[5] Sons of bitches

coming, in their full regalia. All in a different colour. All prepared by Deola and Teni Sagoe, the artisans of Nigerian cloth and clothing."

"That will be beautiful. A spectacle to behold," Victoria says with tears in her big, bold brown eyes.

"The royal rainbow will be with us, for everyone to see," Nafisa retorts, as she clings to her older sister further as Rayowa comes into her mind. Then she adds to the conversation

"Does that include my mother as well?"

As all three break down together in a sisterly show of true affection. But then it has always been this way, with all the goddesses and their daughters.

"Of course it includes Rayowa. She will be there. Dressed as an orisha. Sharing all the delights of the sisterhood. Did you think she would be treated any less, my dearest daughter?"

"We both know she is not a goddess. Only my mother and your adopted wife."

"But not my adopted wife. I have known your mother carnally, more than once. She is with child, yet she does not know it yet. You will have a sister soon, Abgani. What do you say to that? But regardless, you are all the same in our hearts. Just as you are my daughter, my daughters are your sisters. We are all the same family, not because we say so. But because we are bequeathed to one another. We shall never be pulled asunder. Do you not feel part of us? Have I failed you and your mother somewhere?"

"No, my beautiful Papa. You have not failed me, nor Rayowa. I thank you from the bottom of my heart, for my sister. I will be eternally grateful to you. From the very first

254

time you called me your daughter, my heart and my soul sang. For the first time I had someone I could call Father, my father. Someone I could turn to for advice, help and inspiration."

"Abgani, your mother, my eternal wife, is up on the plateau with her sisters. She has been there for a while. She can hear us, as we speak. She is just as happy as you. Will be for an infinity. Listen!"

"Abgani, we are wife and daughter to the wise one. I did not know I was with child, that is a bonus, something to cherish, with you at my side. We will always be part of this family, so do not worry. You will never lose your father, nor your sisters, nor your aunts. We all love you beyond our comprehension. I send my love, and the love of the circle goes out to you all. We will see you all soon."

"Ahhhh, my Papa. I understand now. I will never question you again, about my mum, myself belonging ever again."

"Abgani, never be shy of asking me anything. I can feel it in your heart when you have a question for me. Even if you do not question me. If you need reassurance about anything, just ask anytime."

Abgani feels overcome as she sits on her father's lap, kissing him long with affection. He wraps his arms around her, cuddling, cradling. As he hears her sniffles, feels her warm tears on his cheeks. Feels her heart pound, skip a beat. He lays his hand on the middle of her chest, calming Abgani. As he breathes deeply so does his daughter. Slowly bringing her heartbeat down, so it beats in time with his. With this connection, Abgani see inside him. His love, pride, sincerity and passion for his earthly daughter. She whispers softly in his ear, with such empathy:

"Thank you so much, my dearest, darling Papa."

Then she resumes her own seat, to the upbeat chatter of her two devoted sisters, who she never wants to lose. Having settled the bill, father takes them all back to number 44 so they can all rest, recover and recuperate from a very memorable day. As he sits alone in the car, he calls upon the sisterhood. They all praise him for comforting the sweet, young Abgani.

Unabashed, the remaining orishas and all their daughters overwhelm the 'lioness of Africa', as Deola Sagoe likes to be known. So she calls for her three daughters, Teni, Tiwa and Abba, who quite happily come to the Mambilla Plateau, to give her all the assistance she requires. The deities to the one, relish the idea of wearing bright illusive and passionate colours for their abayas, geles and high-heels. All to go with their various hairstyles. All would be fulfilled in time, for their daughters' appreciation. So, instilling peace and calm for the night, he physically checks dark corners, nooks and crannies. He is looking for any insurgents, thieves or drug lords hoping to find the three NGOZI with a chance to harm, disable, maim or slaughter, or disrupt any of his darling daughters. Nothing is discovered, all is safe. As he sinks in, disappears and becomes with his shape-shifting abilities part of their front door. Thus he exists until they awake and finally appear at the front door, a father so elusive, reshapes into the parent, they all know and love.

"I have been told that everyone will be attending your awards ceremony, tomorrow. They have all had new outfits ordered; they go today to pick them up.

CHAPTER TWENTY-SIX

The whole circle, Yemeyah, Oshun, Oya and Sashante, Ochumare and Kayefi, Oba and Uyai, Amirini and Halimat, Ala and Chichima, Njoku and Marziya, Aje and Lenu, Oduduwa and Biebele, Rayowa had all been enjoying the personal attentions of Deola, Teni, Aba and Tiwa Sagoe. All the outfits are a perfect fit—the contemporary for the youngsters, and the old style for the orishas. Everything coordinates to the absolute delight of the magnificent orishas and their beloved daughters. A joy of colour, the fabulous material makes them all look stupendous.

A Ahon Ina waits as he directs all his loves to where the daughters await their arrival. He escorts all his family into the large, imposing auditorium. Unobtrusively, he sits at the back, to enjoy their glorious finery. The three daughters arrive, one after the other, to receive their hard-earned degrees. The Mother Goddess rose as a single fraternity, in awe of what their spectacular daughters had achieved in this mortal world. A loud standing ovation from all of their younger sisters, also acknowledging everyone else with a wild and untamed flash of colour, admired by everyone. Such a happy event. He the father and husband taking his complete family, the sisterhood to dinner. Taking over the large Enish Nigerian restaurant, it was a subdued atmosphere. But with the arrival of the whole circle, it soon livened up. Everyone joined in the dancing, enjoying the food. Partaking of the drink, which rarely happens. But once will not hurt, nor do any harm.

"Enjoy the moment, sisters, mothers, wives, aunts."

So they all did. Getting everyone to enjoy the sheer luxury of an imposing, awe-inspiring vision of colour, love, companionship and sisterly love was no problem at all. Then they enjoyed a sleep to end all sleeps—restful, peaceful, relaxing. They were lost in a world of over-luxurious glamour and ambience. Once again seated for breakfast. He being the only male, in the party announces, "If you wish to linger longer, to walk, indulge your senses, your love of culture, kindness, drama, clothes. The freedom of London is all yours to behold, to enjoy, to explore for as long as you wish, ladies. Myself I need to visit the Sambesi Forest, to get acquainted with some vicious mortals that need taking in hand. Show yourselves in all your splendour. Show them what true freedom is, an independent woman, a self-reliant woman. Not to be hounded by men, nor shut away, speak out for yourselves and revel in your new-found freedom. For it is yours for always, your right to express yourself in any form you choose, just as the freedom is bestowed upon our mortals. I will see you all soon. Enjoy all that you desire, my beautiful wives and daughters."

"*Ban kwana, ijeoma, o digba,*" was the loud retort. Followed by the chant of, "*Sai anjima, ka ahu oge n 'adighi anya, Ka ahu oge n 'adighi.*"

Asserting his inner power, force and direction, he vanishes from the hotel in the matter of a nanosecond. He stands amongst all the rebels within the stronghold that is the sacred forest. That they all think is their forest. Carnage and misprize their only achievement until now. Misuse of the forest and further abuses against the young females that were captives, these were a continuing source of scurrility and asperity. A Ahon Ina arrives like a sceptre, glowing and abounding in an aura. He stands amongst the unholy rebels as he casts his changeling element across the whole forest. He restricts the movement of the whole network, by encasing them within a central glade, so he has their complete and undivided attention. First with a wave of his hand, all the vehicles and weapons are returned to their constituent of ores, metals and by-products, that go to make up the plastics, fibres and other materials.

Then up in front, eyeballing the abhorrent individuals. Standing twice as high as Ikiki and Eshu, making everyone else cower. Making them look small, insubstantial, like rats and vermin. Glaring into the very eyes of a man, who cares for nothing or no one. Full of hate. Not a religious war, or jihad. Just a personal vendetta using a religion as a cover-up, for his real purpose. To steal the wealth of others.

"You Ikiki, Eshu do not revere any one thing or person. You show a pretence at reverence, when it suits your needs. When you live by the sword, you will surely die by the sword. Your time has come. I know. I tell you now you and your army will no longer be a problem, come the end of this day. Also we are told by some other religious book, that the meek shall inherit the earth. But I know, by the time the meek do inherit the earth, there will be nothing left to inherit due to the likes of you. The dark life is allowed to prosper, fester and survive, because no one will intervene to put a stop to it. I am here to act as that catalyst. It is within my power to save the impoverished from animals that dare to call themselves mortals. While you degrade all around you, I will not let you prosper, infest the world with your own personal immorality. So before I do it, I am going to tell you what I am going to do to you. Seeing as you like the forest so much, you will be kept here. Unseen, unheard by everyone that passes through here. You will be like the phoenix. You will burn to a pile of ashes, but you will feel pain as you burn. then you will be re-born. Then you will burn again, feeling the same pain again, so on and so on. You will be able to see, hear the people live their lives, in peace and tranquillity. You will see them eat, smile and talk, without renegades like you disrupting everything. You will see, but not be able to move. You will occupy a dimension in space that does not interfere with ours. You will know it as GEHENNA. But perhaps as kuffars, you may never have heard of it? Smile all you want. It will be your last!"

A Ahon Ina went into a starburst, supernova at the same time. The soldiers of Islam disappeared, still held within the mighty forest. To endure the longevity and constant pain, that would be all they could expect to gain from their exploits. To spend an eternity in pain and torture with no respite, no help, forever to burn and to have the rasping fever of a furnace instilled into their very soul.

So gathering himself together, reassuming his form as the wise one. Back in the now, all at once. He ascends slowly to the heights of the mighty Mambilla Plateau.

At peace with himself, he smiles. The smile makes him look charming, debonair and equitable, so very approachable.

All the daughters rushed to him, wanting his touch, his hug, his kiss and his caress of approval and his words of endearment. Which he gave them willingly, to each and every one, surrounded and unable to move, yet happy to be surrounded by his darling daughters. He would rather be nowhere else right at this minute, this hour, this day, this forever. Finally they allow him to sit. He spends all the time they want to be with him, his wayward, loving and charming strong daughters.

The orishas look towards him, big bold pure brown eyes, like glowing embers, glinting and sparkling. Calling him, telling him, it has been far too long since he had touched them, kissed them, fondled them and played with any one of them, satisfied them.

"*Anyi huru gi, A nife re, Mu son ka.*"

"I love you all too. My stunning, gorgeous, erotic goddesses. I am now all yours. I will spend more time with you all. I will be in your company constantly. I will take you to our chambers at any time you wish. Or you take me to your chambers whenever it suits you. Just take me when the fancy takes you. We are now inseparable, me and the sisterhood. Our daughters now make us stronger, invincible. So we have the time for each other. So we will make the most of it, enjoy it all with each other.

CHAPTER TWENTY-SEVEN

Victoria shouts out
for the salvation of
all women
in her own tongue
IGBO

"Nwa nwanyi nke iwo IGBO
a ga-ekwu ulo
na ebube jiri
ihunanya bughi
echiche mgbe."

TRANSLATION

"The daughter of an
Igbo Goddess
should be crowned and adorned
with love
not
feckless degradation."

"My father, my very dear papa has allowed me to have the final few words of our story. My sisters have given me the honour of representing all of them in this soliloquy. I am one of the Blessed, the NGOZI. I am the eldest, Victoria Ngozi. I am enthralled, enchanted and charmed by my mother, Yemeyah, as well as by my aunts, my amazing band of sisters. Our circle is invincible. My father keeps to the back, now he has endowed us with all his powers. Having bequeathed the Mambilla Plateau to the circle of the sisterhood. We want you with us, to take us forward, make us stronger. Please come out from the dark, come from the shadows, exit those voids that men make you hide within.

Come from beneath the boot of the slave master, show him you are not his chattel. Cast him to the darkness, if he does not relent or release you from his indiscriminate grip. Women need to be in the light, not hidden in the shadows nor kept as slaves. We hunger for education, learning and knowledge. Give this to us as our right or we will take it by force. You are not subservient to any one man, or group of men. You are a woman of great strength, knowledge and fortitude. No man can keep you in chains or enslaved, unless you want him to.

Fill our lungs with air, clear the despair. Shout at the top of our voice:

I want to learn.
    I desire to know more.
    I want to be a font of knowledge.
    I want to be able to read.
    I desire to understand, all that I learn.

I am a woman who wants her freedom.

I am a woman, I no longer want to live in the dark age of repression.

I am not property.

I am not a captive.

I am not a slave.

I stand by the Mother Goddess, she gave me my soul.

M ada site na chi nwanyi a o nyere m mkpuru obi m.

It was she who told me, to walk tall, open my eyes, to become part of her, part of her world. To learn to distinguish between truth and lies, between freedom and captivity. To live in the beauty of the cherry blossom, or to live in the squalor, damp of the dungeon of darkness. To learn truth, to be able to pick the cherry blossom, or just admire it from afar. Let the wonders of this beautiful earth fill our mind. Let them overwhelm it with the luxury of knowledge, learning.

Do not at any time be blighted, succoured, demoralised, depressed, stressed, by the lies of men. Throw away the shackles of the tyrant, despot, dictator and enforcer. Shut them down in the dungeon of darkness, for debilitating the growth of womankind.

Reach up to the Awon Iya Orisa, shout her name whenever you get the chance. Allow the light in, throw open the doors and greet the sun with a smile as she gives you her warmth and her soft, gentle care.

I am Victoria Ngozi, daughter of Yemeyah and A Ahon Ina. Hold onto these three ideals:

The sanctity of Womanhood

The strength of Sisterhood

The love and passion of Motherhood.

Compare yourselves not to man but to the eternal, most gracious Mother Orisa. The indestructibility of the circle, that is the one and only Mother Goddess. We love you all. I cry for freedom. I seek your love and your devotion. Give it freely to the sisterhood. Share it very sparingly with man. We must not turn this into a war of attrition, nor create a coven of misandrists[6]. Just use it wisely, then man will never be your better.

We cast our love upon you mortals. This is not goodbye, but to let you know we are here for you ladies, girls and women of whatever age. Whenever you crave our attention, just whisper or shout as loud as you can, feel the freedom, feel the anxiety cast aside, "Mother Goddess or Awon Iya Orisa." In an instant we are at your side.

All I can do now is thank you for your time. Know we are here for you alone. Victoria and Yemeyah are always beholden to you and believe in the strength of the circle and the sisterhood.

---

[6] Man hater. The opposite of misogynist.

Glossary

Main Characters

Orisas	Goddess
Aha Njoku (IBO)	Goddess of the Harvest and Yams
Ahon Ina (Yoruba)	Tongue of Fire (the creator)
Aja (Yoruba)	Goddess of the Forest
Aje (Yoruba)	Goddess of Wealth
Ala (Yoruba)	Goddess of Fertility, the Underwold, Earth
Amirini	Goddess of Light
Awon la Orisa (Yoruba)	the Mother Goddess
Egungun-Oya	Goddess of Diviniation
Oba	Goddess of the Santeria River
Ochumare	Goddess of the Rainbow
Odudua	Goddess of Unity Devotion Love
Oshun (Oso-Igbo)	Goddess of Love Sensuality Also Goddess of the Osun River
Oya	Warrior Goddess of the Wind and Chaos

Yemayah	Great Goddess of Nigeria
	Her name is explained thus: "Yey omo eja"
	Mother whose children are fish

Musical Instruments

Balafon	Ancient Xylophone
Bata	Double-headed hour-glass shaped drum
Calabash	A Water Drum
Dundun	West African Drum
Ekwe	Igbo Drum
Gbedu	Big drum. Ceremonial drum used by the Yoruba
Gangan	The Talking Drum
Igbin	Yoruba Footed Upright Cylindrical Drum
Ikoko	Yoruba Cermonial Drum
Ilu	Yoruba Brazilian Wooden Folk Drum
Ipesi	Yoruba Drum
Ivory Horn	Musical horn made from Drum
Ogene	Igbo large metal Bell
Sanza	Thumb Piano
Udu	Igbo Drum

Nigearian and Tribal Words

Abaya (hausa clothing)	Full length female wrap
Adesuwe (benin female name)	Queen, Crown of Beauty
Agbani (female name)	Sensitive, Creative
Ahun (type of tree)	Alstonia

Akok (Yoruba type of tree)	Tree of Life
Akuko (igbo)	She Tree
Alawefon (Yoruba type of tree)	African Tragacanth
Aroko (Yoruba)	Entangled
Ayan (Nigerian type of tree)	African Satinwood
Bankwana (hausa)	Farewell
Biebele (female name)	To be Overjoyed
Bredi	African form of meat and vegetable stew
Buba (female/ male clothing)	A loose-fitting top
Caitiff	A cowardly villain
Caliph	Islamic chief priest
Cassava	A tuberous edible plant
Chebe (Igbo)	Keep Safe
Chichima (female name)	Sweet and Precious Girl
Chi Nwanyi (Igbo)	Goddess
Empyrean	Purest heaven
Erin Mado (Yoruba type of tree)	African Nut Tree
Fiddausi (Hausa female name)	Paradise
Garri	Powdery food stuff
Gehenna	Place of torment
Gele	Traditional female headdress
Gaufa	Guava
Halimat (female name)	Gentle Generous
Ife (Yoruba)	Love
Ijeoma (Igbo)	Farewell

Imam	Islamic preacher
Iro (female clothing)	Long wrap-around full-length skirt
Jini Jini (Hausa)	Dragon blood tree
Kauna (Hausa female name)	Love
Kayefi (female name)	Wonder
Kiyaye Lafiya (Hausa)	Keep Safe
Kuffars	Non-believers
Kulawa (Hausa)	Take Care
Kwakwar (Nierian type of tree)	Oil Palm
Ledo Onwegi (Igbo)	Take Care
Lenu (female name)	Precious Things
Lewa (Yoruba)	Beautiful
Mangoo (Yoruba)	Mango
Marziya (Kazak female name)	Joyful Happy
Mujahid	One who fights a holy war
Neem (type of tree)	Indian Lilac
Ngozi (Igbo)	Blessedness
Nna (Igbo)	Father
Nupoid	Language from the Volta-Niger area
N 'jer (Tamazight)	River
O dabo (Yoruba)	Take Care
O digba (Yoruba)	Farewell
Odure	Unpleasent odour
Ogogoro (Nigerian)	Palm Wine
Oha Ojii	Nigerian fruit
Okpu Eze Agwa (Igbo a flower)	Crown of Thorns

Olid	Smelling extremely unpleasant
Orisa	Goddess
Oruwa (Nigerian type of tree)	Brimestone Tree
Ovia Osese	Celebration of Girls Transforming from puberty into a women
Pa Ailewu (Yoruba)	Keep Safe
Papa (Igbo)	Dad
Paynims	Infidel
Pele O (Yoruba)	Hello
Purdah	Screening women from the sight of male strangers
Rayowa (female name)	Life
Sabaya	Sex slave
Sapo (Nigerian type of tree)	Cabbage Tree
Soursop	Fruit of an evergreen tree
Ukutu Tree	Mammae Apple Tree
Utazi	Nigerian herb and medicinal Leaf
Uyai (female name)	Beauty